SECRET
OF THE
SHADOW
BEASTS

DIANE MAGRAS

DIAL BOOKS FOR YOUNG READERS

DIAL BOOKS FOR YOUNG READERS
An imprint of Penguin Random House LLC, New York

First published in the United States of America by Dial Books for Young Readers,
an imprint of Penguin Random House LLC, 2022

Text copyright © 2022 by Diane Magras
Map copyright © 2022 by Travis Hasenour

Dial & colophon are registered trademarks of Penguin Random House LLC.

Visit us online at penguinrandomhouse.com.

Library of Congress Cataloging-in-Publication Data is available.

Book manufactured in Canada
ISBN 9780735229327
1 3 5 7 9 10 8 6 4 2

FRI

Design by Sylvia Bi
Text set in Apollo MT Pro

To Benjamin and Michael

CONTENTS

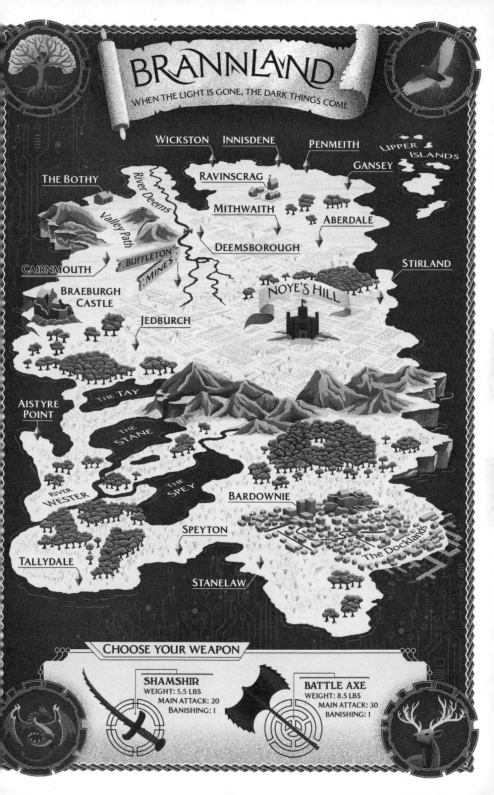

GLOAMING

When the light is gone, the dark things come:
creeping from shadows, their cruel minds afire.

When the light is gone, tell your dad and your mum
that it's safest inside 'til the sun grows higher . . .

—excerpt, traditional Brannland nursery rhyme

A dark woolly shape flashed by the window.

"Jacky?" Nora looked up from the table. The sun was a sliver behind the trees, its light almost gone. *It's not gloaming yet . . . I think.*

She dropped her pencil. All she wanted was to finish her homework before the weekend started and eat a roasted potato dripping with butter by the warmth of the fire. But if Jacky the sheep was out that close to the gloaming, there'd be no dinner until she was in.

Nora crept to the kitchen. Her mother, Deena Kemp, was washing dish towels in the sink.

"Mum?" Nora cleared her throat. "I think Jacky's out."

"How'd she get out of the barn?" Deena swept a strand of gray-blonde hair from her tired face. "Didn't you bother to close the door?"

Nora nodded—though in truth, as she'd done her outdoor chores, she'd been planning a detailed takedown of bog mobs in Warriors of the Frozen Bog, the video game she played with her friend Wilfred. She remembered crushing an army of undead with her own undead, but not if she'd actually shoved shut that crooked door. "I *think* I did."

Her mouth tight, Deena marched into the big room to the window.

"Jacky's gone clever, then, and figured out the barn door."

Nora's face burned. "Shall I fetch her?"

"And be out alone so close to the gloaming?" Deena grabbed her farm coat from its peg. "We can fetch her quick together."

Nora slipped on her father's heavy boots and scampered gratefully after.

Ever since Nora's father had died, Deena had changed: sometimes vulnerable, often strong, but never angry the way she used to be. The Deena from three years ago would have shouted at Nora for not closing the barn door—and Owen Kemp would have gently taken her hands and murmured her into stillness. It was as if the old Deena had died with Owen and the new Deena carried his warmth. Nora saw that in the look Deena shot over her shoulder.

"You've run out like a scarecrow without your coat."

A gust of wind tore over the field, blowing snow from the fence posts. Nora hurried after her mother down the snow-covered grass to the rickety stile—the steps on either side of the sheep fence—and climbed over. Ice flecked her cheeks. The bitter cold cut into her fuzzy blue sweater.

In the distance, a little brown sheep with stubby horns watched them from beside the river—a whole field away.

"Jacky!" Deena hadn't fastened her coat and the sides flapped as she sprinted. "Look at that: Risking her life for a drink of fresh water. I'd have that sheep's head on a platter if she weren't our only sheep. I *still* might."

Nora stumbled after. The sun had sunk beyond the trees. The cold was more intense and the woods menacing, shielding what hid in the dark.

"Mum? I think it's just about gloaming."

Gloaming: the line between day and night, safety and terror. Everyone knew of the unseen beasts that lurked outside between gloaming and dawn. Everyone heard them scratching at doors and windows, kept off only by the special iron on the thresholds. Whenever Nora heard them, she'd burrow deep into the warmth of Deena's arms in the bed they'd shared since Owen Kemp had died.

Dad was going out to mend the fence at the gloaming when a beast got him. The thought snapped into Nora's mind like a wet cloth. She'd never seen a shadow beast—no one she knew had—but everyone knew what they could do: kill with one bite. *We shouldn't be outside now. This is* really *bad.*

"Mum?"

Deena was ahead, crunching over the snow.

"Mum, it's gloaming! We need to go in."

"I know, but we have a minute. And look: Jacky's coming." Deena held out her hand. "Here, sweet."

The ewe stared at them—then broke into a gallop toward the river.

"You piece of mutton! You want to be eaten by the beasts?" Deena chased a few feet, but stopped, breathing hard. "Our last sheep."

Nora slipped her hand in her mother's. "Please, Mum. I'm scared out here."

Deena's hand tightened.

Together, they jogged up toward the little farmhouse. It waited at the top of the hill, lit by the oil lamp in the window. That shack was home: safe and warm. And the potatoes in the pot on the fire would be roasted and the house would be full of their smell.

"You first." Deena pointed at the stile.

Nora climbed the two wobbly steps. "I'm sorry for leaving the barn open."

"We all make mistakes." The second step creaked as Deena followed. "And it's not your fault that Jacky's being a pain. She's lonely—"

A rattle from behind the house broke into her words.

A clatter. A rustle. A sound like a huge bundle of sticks rolling down a hill.

No, not rolling, Nora thought. *Crawling—fast.*

It was a wrong sound. A bad sound. A horrible, familiar sound she'd heard many times on the other side of the window at night.

Then Nora saw it, lit by the windows, stark against the snow between her and Deena and the house: a huge, hairy, sand-brown spider—big as a hay bale—with blood-red mandibles and six gleaming black eyes.

SHADOW BEASTS

Aranea Umbrae:
Habitat: meadows, fields, gardens, beaches
Appearance: spiderlike, covered with fine hairs
Size: 3.5 feet (round)
Venom: bite (primary), saliva and hairs

—Bulletin, National Council for the Research
and Destruction of the Umbrae

"Run," Deena breathed. She scrambled back over the stile, into the field again.

Nora launched after her mother.

The snow-covered grass stretched ahead, gray in the darkness, the river now black.

Clattering—against the wood, over the fence—

Nora grabbed Deena's arm and dodged.

The clattering rushed past them. The beast flew down the hill in a shower of snow—then slid to a halt and pivoted.

Nora tugged her mother back toward the fence.

"What are you supposed to do if you get caught outside after gloaming?" Deena panted. "Do you remember?"

"*You're* supposed to be *inside* at the gloaming, Mum! If a beast bites you, you'll die! I won't because I'm immune, right, but you—"

A rush of snow, and a second giant spider clattered between them and the fence. It paused.

Nora dodged the second beast's lunge, hauling her mother with her. They were almost at the stile.

"Go first, Mum!"

A hard claw closed on Nora's ankle—and tore her back.

Just as Deena clambered over the fence.

Just as the second spider crawled after her.

Blood-red mandibles flashed before Nora's eyes, then a ring of shiny, sharp teeth. She dove to one side, then the next, and wriggled free. The claw seized her boot.

Nora pulled her foot out and stumbled to her feet. In one boot and her sock, she ran—just as the second beast seized Deena's foot and jerked it out from under her.

"Mum!" Nora reached the stile and pounded up the steps and over.

The second beast was on top of Deena, lowering its mandibles toward her face.

"No!" Nora crashed against the soft, furry body, dislodging it, and thumped to the ground between the beast and her mother.

Both spiders crouched in front of Nora. And paused.

"Run, Mum!"

Nora dodged the claws as they lashed out at her. She slammed against the second beast, then the first as it darted for Deena—

Who was at the front steps, the threshold, the door . . .

Both spiders flew up the snow, fast as a blink—

Just as Deena bolted inside, leaving Nora alone.

The shadow beasts turned back, then rushed for her.

And paused.

With a sudden flood of mindless terror, Nora scrambled over them. She raced up the patch of yard, onto the steps, and through the open doorway.

They can't come in. We have special iron on the threshold, so they can't come in.

The beasts clattered up the steps.

But they didn't reach the threshold: Deena slammed the door first.

NORA'S CHOICE

Nora and Deena backed away from the closed door.

"What did we just see?" Deena panted.

Nora grabbed the most recent Council bulletin from the kindling bucket and tore it open. "I don't know. I don't remember what they're called."

She was trying to sound normal. But her voice cracked. Before she could stop it, a sob bubbled up.

Deena wrapped Nora in a tight, tight hug. And started to cry.

Nora slumped against her. Deena smelled like soil and sweat. Like fear.

"Mum, please don't cry. It freaks me out."

"*That* freaks you out?" Deena sniffed. "Not being in the dark with a pair of huge spiders bearing down on you? To think: I've always freed spiders."

"They weren't spiders." Still in her mother's hug, Nora

fumbled with the bulletin. She found the sketch on the inside page, a distinctly spidery scribble. "See? *Aranea umbrae.*"

Deena grabbed the bulletin. "Why, here's our little friend. Goodbye." She thrust the paper into the fire. "I wish I could burn *all* those horrible beasts. Are they still out there, do you think?"

Nora straightened. "They are *definitely* out there. And I am *not* letting you go back out for Jacky—"

"Oh no, we've lost Jacky. She chose her own fate tonight. It's a miracle we got away." Deena wiped her eyes. "Was that rugby you were doing with the spiders?"

Nora thought. "No, it was like Slip the Bite, that game I used to play with Dad and Terry, remember?" She'd grown up dodging their sheepdog in the games Owen had invented. She hadn't realized what she'd just done outside, but all of it had been that rough play.

Nora closed her eyes. *We just escaped two giant shadow beasts. I bet they were the kind that got Dad.*

"Will you check the tatties, love?" Deena asked softly.

With a shaking hand, Nora took a cloth and carefully lifted the lid from the pot on the fire. Four potatoes, their jackets brown and crisp, were waiting.

Deena and Nora curled up in the cushioned chairs by the hearth—not in their usual spots at the table by the window that overlooked the field—and ate their potatoes with butter.

Deena talked as if it were a normal Friday night. About

homework. (Had Nora finished?) About prying parsnips from the ground for soup. (Would Nora have time for that in the morning before Wilfred's dad picked her up for their Saturday gaming?) About school on Monday. (Could she ask Wilfred's dad to stop at the grocer's on the way home so Nora could fetch a pint of milk?)

She doesn't want to go outside again, Nora thought, and shivered. *Can't blame her.*

And yet somehow, something else was in her mind: a tingling thrill, and the smallest breath of triumph.

I saw two shadow beasts. And I got away.

That night, Nora couldn't sleep. She waited until Deena was breathing softly, then slipped out from under the thick blanket and padded into the big room.

The fire was only embers now.

They can't come down the flue. Nora took a poker and scraped the red-hot chunks. *There's that special iron at the top of the chimney.*

MacAskill Iron—on every window, doorway, and fireplace flue to keep away the shadow beasts. MacAskill Iron made you safe—and so did childhood. But for some children more than others.

Nora closed her eyes.

Five years ago, she'd been in the clinic in town and had

her vaccinations—plus one more shot. All seven-year-olds got that one to see if their bodies could fight the beasts' venom.

She remembered the man who'd come into the doctor's office for that last shot: willowy and pale, fair-haired, with moon-like glasses. He'd laid out two syringes: one with the shot that mimicked a beast's venom, one with the antidote.

The venom shot had been more of a punch than a pinch. Nora had begun to cry, but the pain quickly faded. The man with the moon-like glasses didn't pick up the second syringe. Instead, smiling, he'd held out his hand.

"Congratulations, Nora. You have the immunity. We haven't seen it in a child in the Shires for years." He beamed at Owen and Deena. "Congratulations, Mr. and Mrs. Kemp: Nora will soon become a knight. This *is* an honor. I'll notify our headquarters of her test results, and in two days we'll take her away to start training—"

"You're not taking my daughter *anywhere*." Owen Kemp's voice had snapped like a branch in a storm. "And this isn't an honor; it's the worst luck in the world."

The man with the moon glasses had stared. Then, quiet but firm, he'd tried to persuade her father. He talked of the importance of the work and what it meant for the country; then the protected life and secure job that Nora would have when she grew up. And money—the monthly payment her parents would receive.

"You think we're going to sell our Nora so you can send her out at gloaming with kids who'd rather watch her die than help?"

"What are you talking about? Knights protect each other. And Mr. Kemp—I'm sure you know that no one but immune children can defeat the Umbrae. We realize the sacrifice, but it's the only way."

Nothing could convince Owen Kemp. He and Deena had taken Nora's hands and marched outside.

All the drive home, Deena had been strangely quiet while Owen had raged.

"They know what they're asking. Give up everything— for what? To go out in the dark and get bit and know you're going to die—"

"Calm down, love. No one's going to make our Nora fight the beasts."

Nora had stared out the window at the golden wheat fields.

Immune children learned to fight like storybook heroes. She'd learned that in school, that only immune children and their special weapons could destroy the beasts, and nothing else: not adults or soldiers; not explosives, fire, or even industrial poison. Beasts were venomous and could transform into a shadow so quickly that no one could touch them, then transform back again into a solid creature that could bite.

But before children, beasts did not take their shadow form and faltered, as if they didn't want to hurt the young. That made an immune child who carried the one weapon that could destroy them the most powerful creature on earth.

That weapon was MacAskill Iron. One blow, and the beasts would waft into mist—forever. The children who fought were heroes.

Heroes who started training at seven and became knights of the MacAskill Orders at twelve. Knights who carried their own MacAskill Iron sword.

In school, she'd sung songs about the brave young knights. She'd drawn pictures and written stories of the extraordinary children who lived in a castle and were treated like royalty.

And she'd always known about the need for them, even at age seven. Solar-powered sensors dotted the countryside all over Brannland, recording the number of shadow beasts. The National Council published two rates every week: sightings of the beasts, and the deaths of the people who went out at night.

In the car, Nora had leaned forward toward her father. "Why can't I be a knight? The man said I'm special. I want to be a knight and live in a castle and save Brannland."

"You save Brannland by saving yourself and staying inside after gloaming. And Nora—you're the most special girl in the world just as you are. You don't want to be a knight. You're not that kind of person."

Nora had gazed out the window and imagined the pictures at school of all the knights in Brannland. Young people with serious faces. Their photographs covered a wall. "I want to be that kind of person."

Owen had pulled over by the opening in a hedgerow and twisted around in his seat. "Well, you're *not*. And it's not your choice. So get it out of your mind, you hear? And don't you tell *anyone* about that test." He returned to the wheel. "I'd better take you away before they do."

They'd gone home, packed, and Nora and her father had moved to the Upper Islands for a month. They'd stayed in basement flats, cottages, once a bothy in the middle of nowhere. They'd read books, played their fiddles, and gone to concerts in inns and pubs. Owen knew all the haunts.

A whole month, and then they went home and life returned to normal. Nora went back to school. The first time she'd passed the photos of the MacAskill Orders again, her stomach had hurt. After that, she'd always walked by with her head down.

I can't be one of them.

That pang had faded over the years, though it had come back a month ago when she'd turned twelve: the age that immune children finished training and became knights.

Now it's too late.

Nora shoved an ember with the poker, scraping it over the charred remains of the bulletin. She wished she'd looked closer at it, especially the page of the beasts. She'd read about them and watched the documentaries, but nothing had prepared her for the rush of terror as they'd darted toward her, their horrible rattle filling her ears.

But I got away. I didn't think you could get away.

A creak. Deena hobbled out of the bedroom, her face shadowed in the dark. "Do you know where the antidotes are?" she asked hoarsely. "I think its breath got me."

Nora lit the oil lamp.

Red pinpricks covered Deena's face and neck like speckled blood against her stone-white skin.

"Oh, Mum! Does it hurt?"

"Like my face is on fire." Deena shook her head. "I should have taken that antidote as soon as we came in."

They weren't in the medicine box under the bathroom sink, nor in any of the cupboards. Deena stood in the kitchen, coughing as she drank a glass of water, while Nora hunted through the kitchen drawers.

"On the bookshelf?" Nora ran into the bedroom.

She found them not on the bookshelf with Deena's pills but under the bed: a box of gray canisters, packed in a row. The first was stamped with an expiration date from the year before. All the rest were older.

Nora returned to her mother, who was now slumped on the kitchen floor, her back against the cupboard.

"Find it?" Deena's voice was weak.

"Yes."

Deena flopped out an arm.

"It says—I need to stick your thigh. As hard as I can."

"Lord." Deena closed her eyes.

Nora twisted off the top. "I'm sorry, Mum."

"Just do it."

Nora took a breath, and pounded the silver point against her mother's thigh.

Deena gasped. "I can feel it. It's coming all cold through me. It's freezing, it . . . ah, that feels *nice*. I was just burning up."

"Why didn't you tell me before it got this bad?" Nora tossed the canister in the sink and huddled on the floor beside her mother.

"I was hoping it would go away." A bitter laugh. "Help me to bed, will you? And play me some fiddle. My heart's pounding like it wants to jump out."

They hobbled to the bedroom. Nora tucked her mother in and fetched her fiddle from its case by the door.

One of Owen's games had been to play musical messages on his fiddle: a jig for "Feed the sheep" or a march for "Clean your room." Nora had delighted in playing them back at him. She hadn't done it since he'd died, but one musical message came to mind now: "Go to sleep," a gentle air that wove back into itself, over and over.

When Nora finished the tenth repeat, Deena was asleep. Nora packed up her fiddle and returned to the kitchen to wash the glass, then slid onto the chair by the table near the window. Her homework waited, unfinished.

Nora reached for her pencil, but stopped. A thin red line stood out on the back of her hand: dried blood against her light skin.

Its claw must have got me. But no rash. I really am *immune.*

Impulsively, she pulled aside the curtain.

The field stretched white and empty. There was no sign of the beasts except for scratches in the snow—their tracks.

Nora hugged herself. Every year, all her life, she'd seen those tracks after the first snowfall. They'd always come right up to the door.

For five minutes, Nora sat still, arms crossed, head bowed.

Then, abruptly, she stood.

She found the bookmark she wanted—a piece of an old bulletin—in her book of Brannlandian myths, and carried it into the kitchen. On the back was the number of the local Council office.

Nora lifted the old phone from the wall. She'd ring them quick and leave a message before she could change her mind. She dialed.

One ring—then a click.

"National Council for the Research and Destruction of the Umbrae, Jedburch line," said a man's smooth voice. "This is Daniel Fenton. Can I help?"

THE CALL

"I—um—we saw a pair of shadow beasts tonight."

"Ah, Nora Kemp. Good to hear from you. Has your mum been exposed to their hair or breath? I can walk you through giving an antidote. Or are you reporting a bite?"

How does he know about Mum? Wait. He knows my name.

"No, we're okay. We just saw them." Nora paused. "Who is this?"

"Daniel Fenton." The voice was warm. "I'm Director of Testing for the National Council. I conducted your immunity test five years ago. You may recall that you passed, though there was reluctance to allow you to take the appropriate path. Has that changed?"

"I—"

"You lost your father, I know, to the Umbrae—by the way, *that* is what we call them, not beasts. May I ask which kind you saw?"

19

"A pair of—I forget. The spiders."

"A pair of *Aranea umbrae*. Did they approach you?"

"They chased my mum and me. But we got away."

"How did you do that?"

Nora curled up on the floor and told him everything: how the beasts had attacked and how she'd dodged and somehow escaped.

The voice was silent until she got to the end.

"You saved your mother's life tonight." Daniel cleared his throat. "What you've described, Nora, is the kind of quick thinking and swift action we need in the knights of the MacAskill Orders. And that need—it's even greater than it was five years ago."

Daniel Fenton spoke of the same things he'd mentioned years before: of honor and the noble fight, service and purpose. This time, however, his words felt real.

It was a battle that only immune children could fight.

It was a battle that only immune children could win.

A war that would save Brannland.

A war that she, Nora Kemp, could be part of.

When Daniel Fenton finished, they were both quiet.

They still want me. Nora's face warmed. *I could be a knight! Everyone would see my photo up on that wall. And I'd stop the beasts with a sword, just like the Paladin in Warriors of the Frozen Bog—*

She swallowed.

Dad would be so angry if he knew what I'm doing.

"I didn't call to be a knight," Nora said at last. "I just needed to tell someone what happened."

"I know why you called," Daniel said softly. "You understand the threat as never before. And you wish to act. You can't go back to your old life having seen and done what you saw and did tonight."

Nora's hand shook so much, she could barely hold the phone.

I could be one of them.

Then Owen's words came back to her: *You're not that kind of person.*

"I—have to stay and help my mum," Nora mumbled. "Is there something else I can do?"

"There's no greater way for you to make a difference than to join the MacAskill Orders—as you were always meant to. Join, and *we'll* be there for your mother. She'll have a caseworker visit every week to help her adjust, and a monthly payment into her bank account. We take care of our knights' families."

Nora glanced at the darkened bedroom door. "I—I'd love to go. I really would. But I don't think I could be a knight. I'm not that kind of person."

A smile was in Daniel's next words. "I think you are, Nora Kemp. You wouldn't have rung me if you weren't."

WARRIORS
OF THE
FROZEN BOG

sheepGrl9—Grand Necromancer

ACTIVE SPELLS
Bone Shot (AOE)
Raise Dead
Summon Shadows
Summon Phoenix

ACTIVE GEMS/SPELLS
Moonstone/Turn Undead
Opal/Petrify
Ruby/Stun
Amethyst/Poison
Emerald/Heal

ARMOR
Cape of Night (Ghostly Form X)
Hel's Crown (Hood)
Robe of Fortification (set, ultimate)
Leggings of Fortification (set, ultimate)
Shadow Killer's Boots (Stealth X)

WEAPONS
Ebony Staff (Equipped Spell:
Spectral Hammer)
Icy Steel Dagger (Piercing IX)

—Player Stats

SATURDAY

A little burgundy car rattled down the dirt driveway. Behind it, the snow-covered field shone gold in the rising sun.

Nora was waiting on the path with her overnight bag and fiddle case. She'd just finished putting Jacky, whom she'd found huddled on the front step that morning, in the barn—and had taken care to latch the door.

"Good morning, Nora!" Dr. Ogundimu leaned out from his open window, his breath steaming in the cold. He was a university professor and looked like a teacher from a story with his heavy black glasses, sleek locs, and colorful sweaters and ties. His gentle voice radiated warmth: one of the most soothing sounds of Nora's childhood.

From the back seat, Wilfred waved both hands.

"Hiya, Dr. Ogundimu! Hiya, Wilfred!" Nora climbed in next to Wilfred and put her bag and fiddle case on the floor.

"Hear me out," said Wilfred before the car started moving.

"We do Loki's Cave, get ten Evil Ice, and then do the altar at the West Barrows so we can start the River Quest from the East Entrance and not deal with Loki's Phoenix."

Nora had been thinking of her call with Daniel Fenton and wondering how she'd tell Wilfred, but her mind instantly switched to Warriors of the Frozen Bog.

"If we fight Loki's Phoenix, you'll get its drops—"

"Don't need them. And it always kills me."

"Be your Paladin, Wilfred. I'll be my Grand Necromancer and my undead will protect you."

"No."

"But you'll get a Phoenix feather, which will give your broadsword Melting Five—"

"My broadsword doesn't *need* Melting Five." Wilfred ran his hand through his tight, short hair. "It doesn't need Melting One."

"If it has Melting Five, we can do Frozen Depths—"

"Frozen Depths? Do you know how often that quest kills me?"

"—and you can melt Solreig's floor and she'll be stuck while you fight her from the other side—"

"No!"

"—and I'll take down her undead and keep you safe." Nora took a breath. "Wilfred, I *really* want to do Frozen Depths. Solreig's my favorite boss. I was thinking about that quest all yesterday. And I won't let you die. Or I'll resurrect you if you do."

They argued all the way to Wilfred's house—and on the sidewalk, up the stairs, and in the hall as Dr. Ogundimu, smiling, unlocked the flat. They didn't stop talking until Wilfred and Nora were on their beanbags with their controls and the monitor had flickered into the introduction to Warriors of the Frozen Bog.

"I'm off to lecture about Viking invasions. I'll be back an hour before gloaming." Dr. Ogundimu poked his head into the room. "There's money in the drawer for pizza and drinks. Have fun, kids."

"Get out, Dad," said Wilfred, his eyes on the opening animation.

"Good luck with your lecture, Dr. Ogundimu," said Nora. "And thanks for the pizza!"

Wilfred's eyes flicked to Nora as the front door closed. "You're making me look bad."

"Your own fault. You have the *best* dad."

They settled into the game, barely speaking. They didn't need to talk. They'd played Warriors of the Frozen Bog for eight hours every Saturday for years.

It had begun the Saturday after Owen had died.

That had been the worst week of Nora's life. She'd been utterly silent at school. At lunchtime, she'd sat in the corner, meeting no one's eye—until the third day, when someone sat down on the other side of her table: Wilfred Ogundimu, a boy she'd never spoken to. He was a grade higher, did competitive gaming, and had friends at other schools.

And he was going to make fun of her.

But Wilfred didn't make fun. Softly, he told her he'd heard about her dad. He knew what it was like: He'd lost his mother the same way. He invited Nora to come home with him after school to play a new RPG that had just come out.

He was doing it for kindness points, Nora thought, but she'd gone to his flat; she felt lost in a horrible dream at the farm without Owen. And she'd liked the name of the video game: Warriors of the Frozen Bog. When she saw the opening animation—a lifelike, icy landscape with a necromancer confidently circling a crowd of frozen zombies—she'd been hooked.

Nora had never played a video game. It took her ten minutes with Wilfred's patient help to figure out the controls. But once she had, she'd gone up fifteen levels in an hour.

"What is this?" Wilfred had demanded. "You've played Warriors before."

Owen had always said she had good reflexes and timing. Her fingers flew over the controls as they did over fiddle strings. She felt powerful—and, for the first time all week, distanced from the grief that had dragged her into its depths.

They'd played the whole day. Dr. Ogundimu had come home minutes before gloaming to discover them on the beanbags in the gaming room, their eyes on the screen. He rang Deena and introduced himself. Nora stayed for dinner, did more gaming, then spent the night on a bed that Dr. Ogundimu made up on Wilfred's floor.

From that day on, Wilfred Ogundimu had sat at Nora's table for lunch. They spoke the elite language of gamers. And she was the only one at their school good enough to play with him.

For Nora, there was nothing else in her world, not even the fiddle, that took away the ache from her mind and heart like Warriors of the Frozen Bog.

From that day on, she was no longer the strange, quiet kid from the sheep farm out of town: She was Wilfred Ogundimu's friend.

And Nora knew, as she chose her Grand Necromancer and started the game on the last Saturday she'd ever play it, that she needed to tell Wilfred Ogundimu that she was leaving to join the MacAskill Orders. On Monday.

An hour of gaming passed, and another. With barely a grunt, they began a five-part quest that would take them through lunch. Another hour. Then more. Nora played with her mind caught up entirely in the game.

At a checkpoint, Wilfred hit pause to stretch.

Nora lowered her controls. This room had become her safe space with its furry black beanbags, the crimson rug on the wooden floor, and Wilfred's school awards looking down from their frames on the wall.

This is probably my last time here.

Her lip trembled.

"Nora?" Wilfred had been reaching up toward the ceiling but quickly lowered his arms. "What's wrong?"

"I'm sorry. I just——" Her voice broke. "I'm sorry."

He dropped to a crouch. "Are you on your period? We still have my mum's stuff in the bin by the toilet——"

"No, I haven't started yet. I just—Wilfred, I saw some of the shadow beasts last night."

Wilfred settled on the floor. "From the window? You're not supposed to look out. It's really bad for your mental health. Didn't they tell you that in grief counseling?"

"I was outside. With Mum."

He flinched. "Did you get bitten?"

"No. I had to give the antidote thing to Mum because she got its stuff on her face. But she's all right." Quickly, Nora told him what had happened.

Wilfred's eyes never left hers. At the end, as she wiped her nose, he leaned forward. "Can I hug you?"

"Of course."

Wilfred's arms closed tightly around her. "Never, *never* go out after gloaming. Will you promise me that?"

"I will never go out after gloaming with Mum."

He sat back. "Can you promise *never* to go out after gloaming?"

"No." Nora took a deep breath. "Wilfred, I'm—I'm going to be in the MacAskill Orders."

He stared, then snorted. "Oh my god, Nora, you just gave me a heart attack. *Don't* do that."

"What?"

"What you just said." He swallowed his laugh. "Sorry.

28

Um, Nora, it's totally normal for kids like us to want to go out and kill all the monsters—did you even *read* your grief pamphlet?—but we can't just join the MacAskill Orders."

"Wilfred—"

"You know they only let in super-special kids, right? So they're not going to take you, no matter how much you want to kill the monsters."

Nora crawled off the beanbag to her knees. "Wilfred, *I'm* one of those kids. I'm immune to the shadow beasts. I should have been taken away when I was seven. But Dad wouldn't let me go, and he told me not to tell anyone. Then last night—" She clenched her hands. "I rang the National Council. And they want me."

Wilfred's smile faded. "You're making this up."

They stared at each other. Behind them on the pause screen, bog mobs flitted past the motionless Grand Necromancer and Paladin.

"I'm sorry," Nora said. "It happened so quickly."

Wilfred pulled his knees up to his chin. "You should have told me you're immune a long time ago. And *this*—you should have told me *this* as soon as you got in the car."

"I wanted to. I couldn't. I was thinking of sending you a note—"

"You were going to go away forever, possibly *die*— because that's what happens to some of those MacAskill kids—and not tell me? I don't know what to say to you."

They sat for ten minutes without speaking, the creepy music from the game the only sound.

Then Wilfred asked if he could give her another hug.

They spent the rest of the day on the private National Council website; Daniel had given Nora the URL and password. The site had all the training guides with information about knights' exercises, Umbrae bites, weapons, and more, including a diagram of something called a bait-post, which had a sinister web of roots under the ground. There were also podcasts—internal interviews—of the MacAskill Orders, and photos of all the knights and the Legendaries who served as each group's adult leader.

Wilfred's commentary was nonstop:

"Check out that Legendary dude: He looks like your Grand Necromancer!"

And:

"That sword is *incredible*. Nora, this is *so* right for you."

By the end, she was feeling better.

She hadn't yet told Deena—"You're hopeless, Nora."—and so they didn't tell Dr. Ogundimu when he came home. Over dinner, Dr. Ogundimu talked about his lecture, then joined Wilfred on the sofa as Nora practiced her fiddle. Close to midnight, after a final round of Warriors, Dr. Ogundimu prepared Nora's sleeping bag and mat on the floor of Wilfred's room and wished them both good night.

"I can't believe this is the last time we're going to do this." Wilfred turned over. He'd just put his remote Warriors of the Frozen Bog player, the one he used when he went on trips, in Nora's fiddle case.

"Don't talk about it," whispered Nora, on the floor next to his bed.

"Why? Dad's not going to hear."

"No, I mean let's talk about happy things."

Wilfred peered over. "Are you not happy?"

"I'm scared."

He was quiet. "What you're doing is important, though. The knights of the MacAskill Orders—Nora, it's *so* cool you're going to be a knight—they're doing this super-critical thing for our country. I mean, they're the *only* ones who can do it. Talk about an elite force. Yeah, it's a risk, but it's a good risk. And you'll be okay."

"Are you sure?"

"I know you, Nora. You're going to be okay."

For many hours after they stopped talking, she couldn't sleep. She listened to the creak of the floor downstairs, the gurgle of the heater, and Wilfred's gentle breathing.

I might never be here again. I might die out there in the dark with the shadow beasts—

But Wilfred said I'm going to be okay. He read all that stuff too and saw how scary it is. And he thinks I can do it.

But . . . that one page said if you don't train well, you'll die. What happens if you don't train at all?

DEENA'S GOODBYE

"How many people did you tell before you told me?" Deena was at the table, a mug of black tea in her hands.

"Just Wilfred."

It was Monday morning. Nora had given Deena the news at dinner the night before. At the time, Deena had been strangely quiet, as if, having seen the Umbrae for herself, she understood Nora's decision.

But this morning was different.

"What does Wilfred think of this? Is *he* glad to see you go off to your death?"

"*Mum*." Nora plopped into the opposite chair. For the first time that morning, she met her mother's eyes.

They were red and speckled—like Deena's face.

That's what venom does to adults. Even if they get the antidote.

"You don't need to do this, Nora."

"I'm doing it, Mum. I *have* to."

"Who told you that? All I'm saying is that if you have doubts and it's not sitting well with you—it's not sitting well with *me*—then don't go. I know they say they need you. I know bites are up; the news *never* stops talking about it. But adults should be doing this, not kids. Just because I was a numpty on Friday—"

"Mum! Adults *can't* do this! If I hadn't distracted the shadow beasts and got them to pause, they'd have bitten you and you'd be dead!"

"That's not true. I was getting away just fine."

Deena went on. Nora closed her eyes.

She'd packed her bag. Daniel Fenton had told her to bring a change of clothes but nothing more; the National Council would provide the rest. So it was just her schoolbag and her fiddle—which had once been Owen's—and Wilfred's game player.

I'm going away. Dad never wanted me to. Mum doesn't want me to. And I'm leaving Wilfred, maybe forever. But I have to do this.

Nora opened her eyes.

Deena was staring out the window. In the morning light, the rash was vivid on her chin and throat.

"Right before he died, Dad told me he thought it should be your choice. Going or not. Being trained."

"*What?* He never told me that."

"He didn't have the chance. We were arguing about it the

33

night he went out." Deena rubbed her eyes. "He was probably trying to calm down and went out without thinking."

"Why didn't you tell me?"

"I couldn't believe he meant it. He was so angry at the Council all those years. I couldn't see how he'd change his mind." Deena shook her head. "And I disagreed. I didn't want to give up my girl."

"Mum, I shouldn't have stayed home when other people were sending their kids. That's not fair. And I wanted to go. I'd be *so* much better off now if I'd gone." Nora leaned back and hugged herself. "So Dad *wanted* me to go—"

"He did *not*. He only said we'd consider it if *you* wanted to go, back when you were nine. And you didn't mention it, so I wasn't going to mention it, and now—it's too late. You're too old."

"The National Council doesn't think so."

Deena's jaw tightened. "You *really* want to throw away the rest of your childhood? You don't get any more, Nora. You're trading what's left—growing up, having your first love, figuring out what you want to do with your life—for a castle and a sword. You're not going to have a *real* childhood where you're going."

An hour later, an elegant black car pulled up in front of the house. A willowy man in a suit and tie with fair hair and moon-shaped glasses came to the door.

34

Nora opened it before he knocked.

"Nora Kemp." His smile and hand were warm. "I'm Daniel Fenton."

He shook Deena's hand warmly despite her frigid expression, and presented her with a paper with a fancy silver seal. She read it, her mouth tight, and signed. Then he set down a teal folder emblazoned with *The National Council for the Research and Destruction of the Umbrae* in silver script.

"This has our contact information, details of your monthly payments, and phone numbers you might need. You'll receive calls today to arrange various matters, including someone who will come to counsel you—"

"Keep watch of me, you mean," grumbled Deena.

"That's right," said Daniel smoothly. "Your own caseworker. We do that for all the MacAskill families because we understand how *very* hard this is." He set a small paper bag on the table. "Here's an antidote gel and healing eye drops—a dose each morning and night for the next seven days should clear up that rash. Now, Nora and I have a long drive. I suggest we say goodbye quickly." He started toward the door.

"Wait. I've one more thing I need to say to you." In two steps, Deena was in front of him. "Keep my daughter safe. If I learn you haven't, I will find you and rip out your heart."

Daniel clasped his hands. "Please don't worry, Mrs. Kemp. We take *exceptional* care of our knights. They are this nation's most valuable assets."

Nora gave her mother a quick kiss, grabbed her bag and fiddle, and hurried outside after Daniel to the car.

The winter air was fresh and clean, wafting away the tension of the house.

Daniel opened the back door for her, then settled behind the wheel. "Were you wearing that top on the night you met the *Aranea umbrae*?"

Nora fingered her fuzzy blue sweater. "Yes. You said I should wear comfy clothes. This is my favorite sweater."

"It must have bits of *Aranea umbrae* in it. We need to get going, but I'll stop once we're out on the road so you can put it in the trunk."

"Am I not allowed to wear it?"

"It's just that my eyes are stinging. You're wearing, shall we say, a potent weapon. That you *can* wear it without breaking into a rash proves your immunity." Daniel started to put his arm around the back of the passenger seat, then thought better of it and kept it by his side as he reversed the car out of the driveway.

NOYE'S HILL

They drove toward the shortcut that led to downtown Jedburch—and passed it.

"Where are we going?" Nora looked over her shoulder as the side road disappeared around a snowy bend.

"Noye's Hill: where the National Council trains the MacAskill Orders."

Her stomach tightened. "Is it in Bardownie?"

Daniel's eyes flicked to her in the rearview mirror, then back to the road. "We wouldn't put it in the capital. Too obvious. It's in an undisclosed location."

"Is the castle there?"

"Oh, yes. You'll live in our castle. But Noye's Hill is more than *just* a castle. It's the National Council's headquarters and chief training ground. Your arrival there is eagerly anticipated." Daniel glanced at her in the mirror again. "The

Legendaries of our top Orders—Hawk and Oak—are especially keen to meet you."

Nora and Wilfred had read about the MacAskill Orders: Boar, Fox, Hawk, Oak, Stag, and Wyvern. And their Legendaries—adults who had once been knights—who led the five knights in each Order: the immune children who'd been training since they were seven, the only ones sent to battle the Umbrae.

"When will I be a knight?" Nora asked.

"I would be astonished if you were not made a knight before the day is through."

"Don't I need to be trained?"

"It'll be impossible to give you full training at this point, but I expect you have enough natural ability to make this work—you *did* just escape from two *Aranea umbrae* without a weapon and without getting bit." Daniel added quickly, "Don't be afraid: No one's going to send you out until we're sure you're ready."

I'm going to get bitten. Nora clenched her hands in her lap and thought about what she'd read on the website. *I won't know what I'm doing out there, and I'll get bitten four times right away. And after four bites, you're done and not a knight anymore because your immunity is mostly gone, and then* all *gone after the fifth.*

"Nora? I understand you're nervous. But remember: You'll be serving your country as you were always meant to. And you're doing it when we need you most."

Daniel slowed the car at a roundabout and twisted to face her.

"We have a serious shortage of immune children. It's been that way for years. We've had to drop Orders, which means fewer bands of knights. Thanks to that, we've seen Umbrae rates increase more in the last month than all last year. That's why it took me only two days to get your paperwork through and arrange for you to come. That's why your call in the middle of the night was routed to my phone. Because we *need* you, Nora. There's no time—"

The car behind them honked. Daniel waved and drove on.

"Why didn't you just take me when I was seven?" Nora blurted.

"We don't 'just take' children from their parents." Daniel raised his chin. "I know we ask families to make a mighty sacrifice. And I'll tell you this: What you'll do is not easy. You'll devote your life to battle. And when you're eighteen and your immunity fades and the Umbrae see you as an adult, you leave that world forever. That's even harder. But in the end, it's worth it. Because Brannland's citizens— people like your mother, your friends, their parents—are facing certain death. You knights are the only ones who can save them. No one will take your sacrifice lightly."

They drove on past familiar landmarks: woods, fields, a camper ground, roads to ruined abbeys.

Then Daniel turned onto a road that led to a train station and drew into the car park.

"One moment. There's someone I need to pick up."

He strode across the asphalt and through the little gate to the platform. In two minutes, he reappeared with a small boy Nora's age in rust-orange running gear—a stretchy top and leggings—and matching glasses.

The boy strode like a cat: smooth and fast. When they reached the car, though, he hesitated. He carried nothing, not even a schoolbag.

"Go on." Daniel opened the back door. "She's not an Umbra."

The boy slid silently into the seat beside Nora's.

"Nora, this is Shaun Ku. He's Level Three from Region Four. He'll be joining us. Shaun, this is Nora Kemp."

Shaun's gaze sank to the armrest between them.

Level Three, Region Four. What does that even mean? Then she remembered: Level Three was one level lower than a knight.

"What Order are you?" Nora asked. The words felt funny in her mouth.

Shaun stiffened.

"Shaun is currently between Orders," Daniel said. "He's coming to Noye's Hill, like you, to be assigned."

"Are you new at this? Is this your first time?"

"No," said Daniel patiently, "he's Level Three. He's been training since he was seven. Shaun just turned twelve yesterday. It's time for him to take his test and see if he's ready to be a knight. That's all."

"I'm new," Nora said. "This is my first time dealing with any of this. I don't know what Order I'm going to be in. Or what level."

"Actually, Nora," said Daniel gently, "we *do* know: You're going to be a knight."

The boy raised his head. His look was of pure hatred.

They drove for over an hour. Daniel turned onto a smaller road, then another, and another, until nothing was familiar. They passed miles of hedgerows and tiny villages with medieval churches. The land grew rocky, the road signs scarce.

Another hour. Nora tried to sleep, but her mind went in circles. She thought of Deena's harsh words and Wilfred's tight hug when they'd parted Sunday morning, then of Deena's new bank account and caseworker, and of the shadow beast—the *Aranea umbra*—that had pinned her mother down. And of her own purpose now.

The car stopped. Cold air gusted in. Nora opened her eyes.

"I realize there's no time—the mother took longer than usual—but could I have an hour? She's not eaten since we left." Daniel was leaning on his open window, talking to a woman in beige camouflage and a teal beret.

"I'm sorry, sir, but they've called down twice now."

"Ten minutes? I expect she could use a cup of tea."

"I'm sorry, sir. I had to tell them you'd come."

Daniel sighed. "Thank you for warning me."

The soldier saluted and Daniel rolled up his window. "No time, as you can see."

Nora yawned. "So I can't have a cuppa?"

"I will give you as many cuppas as you like when they're done with you." Daniel drove through the open gates.

Nora sat up. The gates were massive and black with glimmering dark metal filaments lacing the bars. The bars themselves extended into a wall of bars wrapped in wire.

"What makes the wire sparkle?" Nora asked.

"That's MacAskill Iron stripped to its core, a powerful Umbrae repellent."

"Is this Noye's Hill?" Nora craned her neck. "I don't see the castle."

"You will soon."

The car drove over the flat, paved road through an empty meadow. Nora twisted around and looked back at the gates.

Thump.

They'd driven over a bridge—and the ground fell away around them. The road circled up, past huge hewn sides of glittering stone. Beyond it, snowy fields extended in all directions toward the distant wall.

"Here's our hill," Daniel said. "It was blasted out during Sir Colm MacAskill's time and filled with a core of MacAskill Iron."

Another turn led onto a straight drive—which ended in a fortress.

A huge block of gleaming black Iron loomed over them. Towers reached up from its five corners and the center, their points like spines. From the highest snapped a bright teal flag, the only color.

That is the coolest and creepiest castle I have ever seen! But where are the windows?

"Noye's Hill was a traditional castle more than five hundred years ago," Daniel was saying. "It was updated to this more functional style as Sir Colm MacAskill's offices when he created his Iron and the Orders eighty years back. Noye's Hill has always been the center for our research and training. Thanks to its life as a top-secret laboratory during the MacAskill era, it's utterly secure. No one who doesn't belong has ever got in, and those who belong don't ever get out. Except for duty, of course. Which means you'll live here in perfect safety for the next six years . . . or even, like some of us, the rest of your lives."

Wait—the rest of our lives?

Daniel parked the car and twisted around in his seat to beam at Nora. "Welcome home."

LEGENDARIES

Nora's bag, her fiddle, her sweater, and the car all had to be cleaned, so they left everything behind. A soldier in beige camouflage and a teal beret waved them inside.

Daniel led Nora and Shaun through a series of doors, pausing each time for a retinal scan, and ended in a large room with a black pedestal table and black paneled walls. A map of Brannland and its islands, rippling with colored lines and hundreds of yellow dots, covered an entire wall.

Daniel walked to the center of the room. "This is the first stop for everyone at Noye's Hill."

A panel opened—a hidden door—and a thin woman with a pixie cut of gold-tipped black hair stepped out. She wore a white lab coat, black trousers, and a shimmering gold blouse that was unbuttoned enough to reveal an intricate black tattoo of a two-legged dragon near her collarbone.

Two legs—that's a wyvern. Wait—there's an Order of the

Wyvern here! Is she one of the knights? Oh! Do we get tattoos?

"They're waiting. And not very patiently." The woman slipped on a pair of surgical gloves and picked up a glowing red bar from the pedestal table. "So who do we have here?"

Daniel beamed. "Dr. Liu, this is Nora Kemp and Shaun Ku." Then, to Nora: "A necessary formality." He held out his arms.

Wordlessly, Shaun did the same.

Dr. Liu ran the cylindrical, glowing bar down Daniel—his arms and legs, torso, back, and head—in less than a minute. She did Shaun next. His eyes never left the floor.

"Your turn, Nora." Daniel nodded encouragingly.

Nora held out her bare arms. She was wearing just the T-shirt she'd put on before her sweater at home. The room was very cold.

The glowing bar was also cold—and flashed bright red almost as soon as Dr. Liu touched her arm.

"Whoa, what have *you* been messing with?" Dr. Liu lowered the bar. "Did you just come back from duty or something?"

"What?" said Nora.

"She had an encounter with *Aranea umbrae* a few days ago," Daniel said. "There may still be fragments from her sweater."

"Looks like you hugged them *without* your sweater." Dr. Liu swept the bar over Nora's arm. This time, mist covered her skin—as cold as ice.

"That's the antidote," Daniel said. "It'll destroy whatever fragments you're carrying."

"Here, give me your boots." Dr. Liu slipped on a mask. "Those need to go in the wash."

"Oh! I'm sorry." Nora stumbled out of her father's boots.

"No worries." Without missing a beat, Dr. Liu picked them up. "Daniel, I don't know how you breathed with these in the car. You must have great air circulation. And you, PK, your immunity must be off the charts to have stood up to all these *Aranea umbrae* hairs."

"Are their hairs that bad?"

"A single *Aranea umbra* hair could poison any adult in this building," Daniel said. "That's why we destroy all contagions before we leave this room."

Nora held very still as Dr. Liu continued to disinfect.

"All done." Dr. Liu lowered the glowing bar. "PKs and Daniel: You're clear."

Daniel marched toward the door, Shaun at his heels.

"PKs?" Nora asked. *In Warriors, that means "player kills." I don't think she means that.*

"It's what I call knights before they're assigned to their Orders: pre-knights." Dr. Liu grinned. "Good luck, PK."

Nora padded after Daniel and Shaun into a long, empty hall lit by electric torches. Dark gray panels lined the walls, divided by colored panes: blue, green, purple, red, orange, and gold. The purple and red panes were glowing. Nora stopped at the first purple one. A string of numbers ran down a screen behind it.

"The lit panes show the Orders that are in the field just

now," Daniel said. "The numbers show how each Order is doing."

"Doing?" Nora echoed. "Do you mean, like, if they're safe?"

"I mean how many Umbrae they've destroyed." Daniel clasped his hands behind his back as if waiting.

Seconds later, a door in the hallway opened and a tall man in a close-fitting black uniform stepped out, followed by a much shorter woman dressed the same way. They were younger than Deena, close to Daniel's age, and were wiry like athletes and moved with a stride that seemed to own the floor. The man had a mass of wavy dark hair down to his chin and a royal-blue badge on his front pocket, the woman a braid of ice-blonde hair wrapped around her head and a jade-green badge. They looked familiar.

Wait—those are Legendaries! I saw their photos on that webpage. Wilfred was right: That man does look like my Grand Necromancer.

"Nora Kemp," said Daniel, "meet Murdo Patel and Sophie Moncrief."

Nora waved. "Hiya! Thanks for letting me come even though I wasn't trained."

The two Legendaries exchanged a look. Then Sophie Moncrief's eyes flicked to Nora.

"Tired?" Her voice was not sympathetic.

"No, I slept in the car," Nora said. "Thanks for asking."

"Eager to show what you can do?" Murdo Patel's eyebrows lifted.

"Oh, yes, and I hope to do a lot." Nora glanced at Daniel. "Is that right?"

A snort, then Murdo nodded at Shaun. "Who's he?"

Shaun's gaze dropped. His jaw trembled as if he was about to cry.

"That's Shaun Ku," Nora blurted. "He's Level Three, Region Four. You're lucky to have him too, you know."

Shaun reddened.

"*What* did I just hear?" Sophie's eyes narrowed.

"An untrained child: full of nonsense—with filthy socks. Didn't you know they're all like this?" Murdo winked at Sophie. "Yours."

"No, yours: I insist."

Murdo pivoted on his heel and marched back up the hall.

Sophie followed and said over her shoulder, "Come along, Shaun. It's not as bad as you think." A curt glance at Nora. "You too."

Nora waited until Shaun fell into line behind Sophie and Murdo, then padded damply after them.

Daniel drew up beside her. "Don't mind them."

"I said something stupid, didn't I," Nora whispered.

"You did just fine."

"My socks *are* filthy."

"So take them off before your test." Daniel patted her shoulder and increased his pace, his shoes clicking, to catch up with Murdo.

THE TEST

"I didn't have the best attitude when I came to Noye's Hill. I was all, 'I'm a knight and I'm not going to take *anything* from anyone.' Then I met Amar. He's my senior knight. He's . . ." [pause] "If Amar told me to jump off a cliff, I'd do it. Because I'd know he'd have a good reason. And he'd be right there with me."

—Eve Adeyemi, Order of the Hawk
The Noye's Hill Interviews (internal)

Halfway up the hall, Murdo opened a door on the left. He waited as everyone walked through.

Nora, who'd had to jog to keep up, ran through—straight into a lean, athletic girl close to her age with one large braid of micro braids. The girl's skin was the same dark bronze shade as Wilfred's.

"Watch it!" the girl snapped.

49

"Sorry." Nora backed up.

Kids filled the narrow hallway: four on one side, including the girl, in royal-blue stretchy tops, leggings, and boots; four on the other side dressed the same but in jade green. The kids in both groups all looked like athletes: graceful and intense.

All at once, Nora realized who they were: the knights.

I don't remember the pictures of these kids. Or do they just look different in real life?

Shaun, Daniel, and Sophie stood between the groups. Murdo closed the door and strode past Nora.

"This is Shaun, Region Four," Sophie said, her hand on Shaun's shoulder. "He's going to test. And *that*"—her eyes flicked to Nora—"is Daniel's project. I'm not hopeful."

Nora's face grew hot. *Do they know there's a shortage of knights?* She tried to catch Daniel's eye, but he'd followed Murdo. Face burning, she trailed after the group in blue.

A pasty-pale, bone-thin boy with a mop of black hair and blue-framed glasses was at the end of that group. He glanced at Nora, then nudged the tall, older white girl with the intricate ginger braid ahead of him. "Something smells like rubbish. I swear I'm going to throw up."

The tall girl touched a tiny silver earpiece in her left ear. "You don't need to throw up, Cyril."

The girl with the micro braids snorted.

The serious-looking boy at the head of the line sighed. He was older than the rest but still a teen, with thick dark hair combed neatly and warm brown skin. His eyes met Nora's, then flicked away.

I wish Wilfred were here, thought Nora, a lump in her throat.

The line snaked down the hall and parted in front of a door between two huge windows. The knights in jade green went ahead with Sophie and Shaun to the farther window while the ones in blue stayed in their line with Murdo, Nora at the very end.

"Nora?" Daniel was between the groups. "Come here."

Only the girl with the intricate ginger braid stepped aside. Nora had to slip past all the other knights, even the boy with the serious face at the front, who stared at her coldly.

But Daniel smiled when she reached him. "Nora, this is the simulation room. It'll give you the experience of battle in perfect safety and allow us to see what you can do. Don't worry: You're brand-new, so we'll just see what comes naturally."

"Have Shaun go first." Sophie opened the door. "You've done a target room? This is similar in principle."

Shaun nodded, eyes down.

"Do you know which weapon you'll pick?"

A nod.

"Come."

Shaun followed her into the room.

An older girl in jade green with a tall bun of box braids

gestured to Nora. "Come watch with us. We'll tell you what's happening."

Nora gratefully padded over to them. "Thanks."

"I'm Averill. That's Bronwyn, Isaac, and Kazu."

The younger girl and the two older boys behind her waved.

Averill leaned on the window. "Look: He picked the sword."

"Why do they *always* pick the sword?" Isaac rolled his eyes.

Averill grinned. "It's true. Every one of us in this hall picked the sword during our test."

"Is that what you use when you're fighting?"

"Bronwyn tried the axe once, but it didn't work for her."

"Too heavy." Bronwyn twisted the tip of her thin auburn braid. "It was cool, though. I wish I'd trained with it."

Sophie shut the door. "What shall we give him?"

"Everything." Murdo reached over her shoulder and typed a code into the panel. "Give them both everything."

Sophie sniffed. "Good luck to the untrained child."

Nora leaned against the glass.

Shaun was a tiny figure in the huge white room as he walked away from the door.

"He's going to see the Umbrae any minute," Averill said. "They're not real—it's a simulation—but they'll look and sound and *feel* real—and they'll pause before they strike. He's got to fight . . . and there he goes."

52

A foggy shape appeared—and rushed at Shaun. He dodged and swung his sword. A neon-blue stain spread on his ankle.

"A bite already." Kazu clicked his tongue. "That's an abysmal start, poor kid."

Nora cringed.

More foggy shapes. Some were long and low to the ground. Others were higher—the size of hay bales. They darted in toward Shaun, circling him, but paused. At each pause, he slashed, then dodged.

"There, that's good," breathed Isaac. "He's doing it."

"Not quite." Kazu shook his head as a second blue stain spread over Shaun's back.

"Ouch." Bronwyn winced. "That must have hurt."

Shaun lashed out and ran.

"That's what you do if you're tired or get bitten." Averill's eyes didn't leave the small figure in the white room. "Give yourself space. He's trained well."

Nora rubbed her palm. "I'm not going to remember *any* of this."

"Don't worry. Just watch and see what you learn. It's not fair, you going in without training—"

"How's it not fair?" called Sophie sharply. "She has to show us what she knows."

Averill's mouth tightened.

The foggy shapes backed Shaun into a corner. He lashed wildly and pushed through.

"No, no, no," moaned Bronwyn.

"What was *that?*" called the bone-thin boy with the knights in blue. "He wields that sword like it's a dead fish."

Shaun spun, slashed, ducked, and ran. Over and over. Another blue stain, then another. Nora watched, holding her breath.

I can't do that. Why didn't Daniel tell me I was going to have to do that?

Suddenly, the foggy shapes disappeared.

Sophie opened the door. "Let's see how many hits and bites, Shaun."

He staggered through.

Colors—neon orange, neon blue, red, and yellow—spattered Shaun's clothing. He was panting hard. Sophie took a glowing green bar from the door and ran it over him. When she was done, she studied it.

"Not bad. Ten hits and only seven bites. That's decent, considering we gave you everything." She held out her hand. "Well done. I hope you'll be assigned to Oak."

Shaun stared at his boots.

Sophie smiled, then turned to Nora. Her smile dropped. "Right. Let's pick your weapon." She marched into the room.

"Good luck." Averill patted her back. The others in green did the same.

"I don't think all the luck in the world could help *her,*" said the girl with the braid of micro braids.

"Are you coming or not?" snapped Sophie.

Daniel squeezed Nora's arm as she passed. "Remember what I said."

"Do your best," Murdo murmured.

Nora padded into the white room.

It was dark, as if it were minutes before the gloaming. Trees towered over her. A small clearing lay ahead. It looked real. It smelled like the woods at home. And it was cold.

"Pick your weapon." Sophie was barely visible in the gloom. She held out a black tray with a curved sword and a double-sided axe.

I have no idea how to use a sword. I'd probably cut myself. But that axe . . . it looks a bit like my axe at home.

She thought of all the firewood she'd chopped over the years and the brush she'd cut through that autumn to make a path for Jacky.

Right. I can handle an axe.

Nora's fingers closed around the axe's shaft—

The tray and Sophie disappeared.

Nora jolted back, heart thumping.

It's a simulation. She's still there. She's probably walking to the door right now. And they're all watching me, and—what did Daniel say? I'm supposed to remember it. Oh! My socks.

She set down the axe, pulled off a wet sock, hopped, then the other. The ground—soil, not tiles—was cold against her bare feet. Quickly, she picked up the axe.

Okay, this feels like a normal axe. It's a double-headed

axe with big curved blades, but other than that, it's perfectly normal—

The words shriveled up in her mind.

Something was moving in the trees.

Something as tall as a sheep but long—eight feet or more, and wet, black, and slimy.

It was slithering straight for her.

10

THE SIMULATION ROOM

"It's incredibly scary the first time you see them."

—Lucy Ahn, Order of the Hawk
The Noye's Hill Interviews (internal)

All feeling left Nora's body—and returned in a rush of panic. She sprinted across the clearing, away from the trees.

It's not real. It's a simulation.

But that *sound*—slick and slimy—was real behind her.

Suddenly, it was in front of her too, a second slimy beast oozing through the grass.

Nora yelped and stumbled aside.

The two beasts narrowly missed each other, then whipped around to face her.

They paused.

And lunged.

Nora dove out of their way, almost dropping her axe. Then she remembered what it was for, and swung.

The blade sank into one of the beasts. With a puff, the whole creature disappeared into mist.

The second beast circled her, and paused.

They pause before they strike. Isn't that what Averill said?

Nora swung as the beast whipped toward her.

Puff—it was gone in a cloud.

Calm down. They're fake. They can't hurt you. They're just like sheep: big, slimy, snake-like sheep—ugh, that's disgusting.

A growl. Another slick black shape raced toward her from the trees.

What would you do if a ram was going for you? It kind of ducks its head like a ram—

Nora dodged and swung.

Puff.

She panted and looked around.

Everything was strangely silent.

Was that it?

Something shimmered silver deep in the woods, and howled: a high, eerie sound.

A ghostly silver wolf with shining red eyes burst from the trees, faster than the first beasts.

They pause before they bite. Don't run away; that thing is much faster than you—

Closer. Closer. It was almost upon her, its red eyes gleaming—

It paused.

Nora swung.

Puff.

Another silver wolf came, then two more. Nora held still and watched them approach. Half of her mind screamed at her to flee, while the other half remembered Terry, the nimble, frantic sheepdog who'd died the year before Owen, and the dodging games she'd grown up playing with him and her dad.

They're like Terry, only they want to hurt *me, not* herd *me . . .*

She watched them draw near and held back her urge to swing wildly. She kept her eyes on the beasts and waited for their pauses.

Then swung.

Puff. Puff. Puff.

More black slimy beasts. More silver wolves. The sight and sound of each shot a bolt of fear down her spine—yet they moved like animals she knew. And they always paused.

Soon Nora was dodging beasts through clouds of mist. Soon her hand on the axe shaft grew sweaty.

And soon they were gone and all was quiet.

Am I done? Nora took a deep breath.

A rattling, clacking rustling came from the meadow behind.

Her chest tightened.

Nora whirled around—and bolted to the side, but the spidery beast was on her heels.

A claw caught her ankle and tripped her. A second leg pinned down her shoulder. A furry maw under the blood-red mandibles opened over her face—and paused.

Moaning, Nora swung up her axe.

Puff.

She was on her knees when the next one appeared.

And then on her feet and running, the clacking and clattering filling her ears.

Dad. These are the beasts that murdered my dad.

Nora pivoted and swung her axe in time to catch the spidery beast that had just grabbed her ankle.

"I *hate* you!" She swung at another, sinking her axe deep in its body, which fragmented into mist.

Clacking from all around.

Spidery beasts scuttled toward her from every direction.

But Nora was ready.

A beast caught her ankle. She struck it from below and rolled, then struck the next, and the next. She didn't wait for their pauses now but rushed toward them: shouting, roaring, slashing. She aimed each time for their soft furry bodies and those hideous eyes. Each time she caught one, she whirled around to catch another, rage feeding her on.

Until they were gone and she stood panting in a circle of mist.

Click.

The forest and meadow disappeared. The room was white and bare.

Nora's breath thudded painfully in her chest. She collapsed to her knees and buried her head in her arms. A sob burst from her throat, then another.

"Nora?" A quiet voice—Daniel's. "Come here, please."

Somehow, she dragged herself to her feet and plodded to the open door. Everything was blurry through her tears.

Someone pried the axe from her hand. Someone ran the glowing green bar over her.

"Nora." Daniel's eyes were wet, but he was grinning. "Take a look at your shirt, my friend."

Neon-orange, red, and yellow splotches covered her shirt, arms, jeans, and bare feet—every inch of her.

"The *Cochlea umbrae*—the slimy black Umbrae—are the orange hits," Murdo said softly. "The *Lupus umbrae*—the wolf-like ones—are red. *Aranea umbrae*—the spiders—are yellow."

"Thirty orange," said Sophie breathlessly. "Thirty red. Thirty yellow. Every. Single. One. With no bites." She lowered the green bar. "Excuse me, but where did you train?"

Shivers ran up and down Nora's body. She could barely breathe. "Home. My dad's farm. And I'm going back."

Nora shoved past the knights in blue and sprinted to the door and into the long black hall.

"Wait." Murdo was at her heels. "You can't go. We can't lose you." And then he was in front of her, blocking her way. "That wasn't fair, what we just did. But *you* did what you had inside of you. I promise, Nora, it won't ever be like that again. You'll never fight alone."

She stood there and cried great hacking sobs that hurt her chest, but Murdo did not leave. He waited silently until she was done.

Nora wiped her nose on her shirt. "Am I getting this on my face?" she croaked.

"The dyes? They'll wash off."

For a few seconds, they stood there, staring at each other.

He's trying to be nice, but I don't think he is nice. He's not like Dr. Ogundimu. He's like . . . my Grand Necromancer.

"Are you ready to come back to the hall?" Murdo asked gently.

"What's going to happen next?" Nora's voice shook.

"You'll wait, maybe for an hour. Dr. Ursula Chong, our director, is looking at your results. She'll think about what she wants from each Order and then assign you. You'll either go to mine—Hawk—or to Sophie's, which is Oak. Come back, and we can all wait together."

"May I use the toilet first?"

Murdo pointed to the door across the hall.

Nora sat on the toilet seat for ten minutes and cried a little more, then washed her hands and face in the warm water at the sink. When she was done, she looked in the mirror. Her face—blotchy, with reddened eyes, her brown ponytail spilling out of its elastic—looked like the face she'd always known. The face she was. The face she loved.

A face that didn't belong at Noye's Hill.

11

URSULA'S CHOICE

Daniel was alone in the hall when Nora finally emerged. He promised her a cup of tea, fresh clothes, and a shower.

She chose the shower first. For thirty minutes, she stood beneath the driving hot water until her body was like jelly. Her schoolbag was waiting outside the stall. Nora dressed in the change of clothes she'd brought—and her fuzzy blue sweater, which was now clean and smelled like spring.

"Feeling better?" Daniel asked.

She was curled up in a cushy chair, halfway through her second cup of tea, in a cozy wood-paneled room with soft lights on the ceiling.

"I apologize for putting you through that with no warning. It's supposed to be a test, so . . . we tested you." Daniel grinned. "And *you*, Nora Kemp, did better than any knight ever tested at Noye's Hill, even Murdo Patel. By the way, they're arguing. Murdo rang Ursula to put in a formal request for you, then Sophie did the same. She says he gave you up in the first hall and has no right. He says *you* should decide."

"*Can* I decide? Can I have Murdo with Sophie's knights?"

Daniel's eyes sparkled. "Why do you say that?"

"They like me."

"Whoever you're put with will more than 'like' you soon enough. It's magnificent how Orders bond: Your fellow knights will be there for you in ways you could never imagine. And don't worry; you'll be put where you belong. Ursula's quite strategic in that." Daniel leaned forward. "This is *so* exciting. I don't usually get to see the simulation room tests *or* the results. I'm only involved with the immunity tests at the very beginning."

Nora sipped her tea. "Can I ring my mum and tell her how I did?"

"No ringing anyone. Sorry."

"Can I write to her? And my friend Wilfred. I promised—"

"No. No writing, either. Or seeing them. I explained this on the phone with you, remember? It was also in the paper your mother signed, so she'll expect it."

Nora set down her cup. "You mean I don't ever get to see my mum or my best friend until I'm out of here?"

Daniel took a deep breath. "You have *one* purpose now: to fight the Umbrae and survive. To do that, you need to bond with your Order alone. Sir Colm MacAskill was very clear about that when he made the Orders. Remember, Nora, this isn't a school: It's a government-sanctioned military base."

Is this what Mum meant about my sacrificing everything?

For an instant, Nora wished she were home.

But then she thought of Wilfred and how proud he'd been.

It's a big deal that I'm a knight. And I really am *good at this.* Nora held in her sigh. *I wish I could tell Wilfred.*

Then she sat up.

There's chat in Warriors of the Frozen Bog.

"Is there wireless?" Nora asked innocently. "I brought a video game."

"I saw. You also brought a violin. Knights aren't allowed personal possessions. I'm afraid those will have to go—"

"What? No! I need my fiddle. That was my dad's before he died." Her eyes suddenly filled. "Did you get rid of my dad's fiddle while I was in the shower?"

"No, no, we just disinfected it. And the video game." Daniel gestured to the corner of the room where her fiddle case waited. "I was going to ask you where they should go. Back to your mum?"

Nora's heart began to pound. "They should go with *me*. I need my fiddle. It's part of who I am. And my video game—I need that too. If you take them away from me, I won't be able to fight."

Daniel's mouth tightened. "I asked you *not* to bring anything but a change of clothes."

"I *know*, but I need my fiddle and my game." Nora's lip wobbled. "I will not fight unless you give them back."

They glared at each other. Then Daniel sighed. "It'll be up to your Legendary. But I'll tell them—I'll say I allowed your fiddle because of your father."

Nora let out her breath. "Thank you."

"The video game, though . . . I'm sorry, but they don't allow knights to play any games except ones that prepare them for the Umbrae—"

"It *does* prepare me for the Umbrae! It's why I did so well out there. I fight tons of mobs just like Umbrae in that game. It's been my training. And it relaxes me. Please, Daniel?"

Daniel sighed again. "If anyone finds out, both you and I will be in serious trouble."

"I'll hide it in my fiddle case under my neck-cloth and only play it when I know I'll be alone." Nora hesitated. "Is there wireless? I need it to play."

Daniel scribbled on a scrap of paper and handed it to Nora. "My personal wireless code."

"I'll hide it with my game." Nora tucked the scrap into her pocket. "Thank you."

Daniel's smile was thin. "I guess this is why they don't let me be involved so late in the process. I'm soft."

"You're *wonderful*," Nora told him. "And you've made me feel like I belong. You should tell my mum all the nice things you've done for me."

"I don't think I'll be talking with your mum anytime—" He stopped, listening. "Do you hear? Footsteps. That's going to be your fellow knights. *And* the ones who *won't* be your fellow knights."

Seconds later, a line of people poured into the room: Sophie Moncrief and the knights in green and Murdo Patel and the knights in blue. And Shaun, at the end.

Bronwyn darted to Nora's chair ahead of everyone. "Nora Kemp, you're *amazing*! You didn't stay long enough for me to tell you when you came out."

Isaac knelt at her feet. "If Ursula puts you with us, I will serenade you with a glorious song every morning. Or not: Your choice."

Averill gestured at her knights. "The Order of the Oak stands for wisdom and mastery—and great fun. I *really* hope you're put with us."

So do I, Nora thought, but said nothing. She was jumpy and nervous.

Her gaze drifted—to the knight with the serious face in Murdo's group. He was standing with the others in blue, all of them quiet, their eyes intense upon her.

"What does the Order of the Hawk stand for?" Nora asked.

The serious knight raised his chin. "Precision and excellence." His words were distinct and cold. "I had one bite in my test. Eve?" He didn't look back.

"One," said the girl with the braid of micro braids.

"Tove?"

"Just one," said the very tall girl in a warm, low voice.

"Cyril?"

"One, but it wasn't fair because I had a stone in my boot and someone put it there to mess me up, so it shouldn't have counted," said the bone-thin boy.

The serious knight stepped forward. Scowling, the Order of the Oak parted. "I'm Amar, Hawk's senior knight. We don't get hurt. If you're one of us, *you* won't get hurt. Hawk is the best Order the Council has ever had." He held out his hand.

Nora hesitated, then took it. He shook her hand firmly.

"Hawk has the best numbers." Averill leaned on the back of Nora's chair. "But all of you were just the *worst* to her. I hope Ursula heard about *that*."

"They're excellent in the field." Kazu crossed his arms. "But do you actually want to *be* with them in the field? Or be with them *here?* Because you live with your Order, you know. If you were to live with us, you'd hear Isaac's dulcet tones each morning."

"Do you want to laugh," Amar said, "or do you want to live? It's as simple as that."

"We are not very nice," Eve called. "But we're *very* loyal."

Tove looked around. "That's not true. We're nice as well as loyal. We take care of each other. We're a good team."

"Only shabby knights say being 'nice' is important," said Cyril.

"What *is* important?" Nora asked.

Cyril blinked. "What do you think? Being good at chopping Umbrae."

Wilfred would say he has no social skills. Kind of like me.

Behind the knights, the two Legendaries stood apart, watching everything, but glancing often at Daniel.

Shaun stayed by the door, his eyes on Nora.

"Any moment." Daniel took his phone out of his pocket and propped it on the table. "And no, Ursula hasn't rung yet."

"I hate waiting." Averill bounced on her toes. "Just call, please, and let Nora go where she belongs."

"Agreed," said Amar.

Nora stood up. She was getting even more jumpy. "Do you mind if I play my fiddle?"

"You're not allowed to have instruments here," snapped Sophie. "Who told you you could bring that?"

"I did," Daniel said. "It was a special circumstance—"

"No. All knights in an Order are equal, and that means no personal possessions. Have you been out of it for so long that you've forgotten, Daniel?"

Murdo smiled. "I don't think *we'd* mind if Nora had a fiddle."

"I'd love it," breathed Tove. "I haven't heard anyone play fiddle since that time we were in the Upper Islands."

Amar's eyes glinted. "I don't think it'd be fair for Oak to have a knight who sings *and* a knight who plays fiddle."

"I don't *really* sing," said Isaac. "I know only 'This Gracious Land' and 'Biddy, the Pirate Queen.'"

But the knights of Oak shifted nervously.

"Go on and play your fiddle, Nora," said Murdo.

Nora walked gingerly across the room to her case. Quickly, she tuned her fiddle and put it to her chin.

She played a brisk, traditional reel. It felt good to play, to run her fingers up and down the fingerboard, to feel the instrument humming under her chin.

Everyone watched.

Suddenly, Daniel grabbed his phone and held it to his ear. "This is Daniel."

Nora lowered her fiddle.

"Yes, of course," said Daniel. A pause. "Yes, they're all here. Would you like to speak—" He broke off, was silent. "I'll tell them. . . . Yes. . . . Oh, yes, I think you're absolutely right. Thank you."

Daniel set down the phone. "Ursula asked me to relay her choices and her reasoning. Oak, she wants you to focus on preparing your new knight for the field—"

Sophie's eyes flashed triumphantly.

"—so she's assigned you Shaun. Hawk, she wants you to focus on excellence in battle. She's assigned you Nora."

With a smile that transformed his face from stern to almost sweet, Amar strode to Nora and shook her hand again. "Welcome. The Order of the Hawk is *delighted* to have you."

"Yes, welcome!" In three big steps, Tove was at her side. She grabbed Nora's hand from Amar and shook it, beaming.

"She wants Hawk to focus on excellence, so we get the

best." Eve sauntered over. She did not reach for Nora's hand.

Cyril squeezed past Eve. "This is the happiest day of my life. Well, second-happiest day. Here are my personal rules: No hugs, no annoying laughter, no snoring—"

"It doesn't matter if she snores," said Eve. "She's not going to sleep in *your* room."

"You don't know that," said Tove. "And Nora might be 'they' or 'he,' not 'she.' People called me the wrong pronouns when I first went to training, and that hurts, you know. Don't make assumptions."

"Good point. Pronouns." Cyril pointed to himself. "He, him."

"She, her," said Tove.

Amar smiled. "He, him."

Eve did not smile. "She, her."

"He, him," said Murdo. "Do you feel comfortable sharing, Nora?"

"I—she, her."

Behind them, the Order of the Oak was filing out of the room: Sophie, then Averill, Kazu, Isaac, Bronwyn, and Shaun. Bronwyn shot Nora a little pout. Shaun didn't look up from the floor. But his jaw was tight and shaking.

He gave up his childhood and trained all his life and they just made him feel like nothing.

Murdo approached Nora. The Order of the Hawk stepped aside, suddenly quiet.

"Welcome, Nora. You're finally where you belong."

71

WARRIORS
OF THE
FROZEN BOG

PLAYERS LOGGED IN:

TechnoLad—Paladin (103 minutes)

sheepGrl9—Grand Necromancer < (1 minutes)

sheepGrl9: wilfred? i'm at our base

. . .

TechnoLad: sorry was fighting but i'm safe on tree. nora!!!!!!!!!!!!!!!!!!!!! are u at macaskill castle?

sheepGrl9: yes!!!!!!!!!!!!!!

TechnoLad: are u a knight?

sheepGrl9: yes!!!!!!!!!!!!!! i did really well @ this fighting test. better than everyone else here??!!

TechnoLad: POG!!!! not surprised

sheepGrl9: they want me!!!!!!!!!!!!!!!

TechnoLad: totally as they should

sheepGrl9: it's weird though. tons of rules. i'm not allowed to play this.

TechnoLad: lol lol but you are! want to do sea of horrors?

sheepGrl9: i cant. i need to go soon. i just had to tell you that you were right & i'm good at this!!!!!!

TechnoLad: u abandoning me?

sheepGrl9: no! i have to eat dinner w/my legendary (he=the 1=grand necromancer!!!!) & tell him anything i need here but i wanted 2 talk to u first

TechnoLad: i was joking. u *already* abandoned me. jk

sheepGrl9: . . .

sheepGrl9: are u mad at me for coming here?

TechnoLad: yes jk

sheepGrl9: i thought u were happy for me

TechnoLad: u are not my friend jk

sheepGrl9: no i am x100 please don't hate me wilfred i'm sorry

TechnoLad: nora? i'm not serious. i'm joking. jk=just kidding. u knew that y/n?

sheepGrl9: . . .

TechnoLad: nora?

sheepGrl9: . . .

TechnoLad: nora are u ok?

sheepGrl9: sorry they don't have tissues here.

TechnoLad: want a hug?

sheepGrl9: yes! do u want a hug?

TechnoLad: yes. here's yours: hug x1000000

sheepGrl9: ...

sheepGrl9: ...

sheepGrl9: got to go someone's coming byeeeeeee!!!!!!

SHEEPGRL9 LOGGED OFF.

TechnoLad: ...

TechnoLad: i'm really proud of u nora so cool that knight=*my* friend

TechnoLad: ...

TechnoLad: proud x 1000000000000000000000000000

TechnoLad: ...

TechnoLad: ...

TechnoLad: i miss u. lunch=weird today. weird 2 be alone.

TECHNOLAD LOGGED OFF.

THE TROUBLE WITH RUNNING

An electronic buzz in the common room woke Nora. She curled up in her tiny bed. Her stomach hurt, just as it had the night before during her dinner with Murdo.

Someone knocked. The bedroom door opened a crack and Amar peered in.

"Time to get up. The alarm says you have five minutes. If everyone doesn't get up, the lights start flashing. It's really annoying, so . . . please get up."

Nora scrambled out of bed. "What do I do?"

"Get dressed. Then come run with us. We eat breakfast after we run. So we run quickly."

She dressed in the uniform Murdo had given her—a stretchy royal-blue exercise top and matching leggings with boots that felt like sneakers—and joined her Order in their common room, a brightly lit space with three azure-blue sofas where the five bedrooms opened up. Amar, Tove, Cyril, and Eve were waiting, dressed in royal blue like Nora. Only Amar met her eyes. The euphoria of the day before was gone.

It's okay. They're probably tired because it's super early.

Nora followed them to a well-lit track on the floor below the bedrooms. She watched the others stretch and did the same.

They were the only ones running.

At first, Nora ran with her Order. It felt good. Her leggings were snug and kept her thighs from rubbing—a relief; girls had always made fun of her for her bunched-up shorts in gym. And it just felt good to move, to stretch her legs and feel the air rush past.

Until the third lap.

A sharp pain tugged at her side. Her chest began to burn. Nora slowed.

"Don't tell me you can't keep up." Eve pounded on with the others.

But Tove slowed until she was running beside Nora. "Can't you run?"

"I *can* run, but I *don't* run," Nora panted. "Not if I don't have to."

Tove burst out laughing. "I'm sorry. But that's the funniest thing I've ever heard. And if you knew—everyone's saying there's this girl from the Shires who'd been training in secret—then we meet you and you have a giant sheep on your shirt *and* you don't run—"

Nora sped up to a sprint. "I'm *trying*. I'm not good at this. Maybe I should switch with Shaun and get trained—"

"No!" shouted Amar from across the track. "You stay where Ursula puts you!"

"It's okay." Tove kept pace with her. "You're not what we expected. But you know what? That's fine. It's good to have you with us."

Then she took off and in ten seconds was with the others.

Nora dropped to a walk and caught her breath.

After a minute, the group came up behind her and passed one by one. This time, Cyril slowed.

"So do you hate running, or waking up to the alarm, or did Murdo feed you spikes and slime last night and your stomach hurts?"

"I'm not good at running; I get tired. You don't have to run when you deal with the Umbrae, do you?"

Cyril shrugged. "Not if you don't mind getting bit." He rejoined the other knights as they passed.

Amar stayed behind. "Running and endurance are pretty important for what we do in the field. So . . . please *try* to run?"

If I don't try, I'll look like I don't care about being a knight. Why wasn't there anything about running on the website?

She broke into another sprint.

"Thank you," said Amar. For a few seconds, he ran beside her. "Can you go any faster?"

"What? Look, I'm going as fast as I can! How often will I be doing laps with a beast coming down on me?"

The others jogged past them again.

"More often than you might think." Jaw tight, Amar sprinted ahead.

As soon as the others were across the track, Nora slowed, gasping. She sped up, though, as they neared again from behind.

This time, Eve stopped a few yards away.

Nora stopped as well. Something warned her not to get too close to the other girl.

"Who do you think you are, marching in like you make the rules?" Eve's voice was like a whip. "Your senior knight tells you to run. You run. Got it?"

"I'm doing my best," Nora mumbled.

"No, you're slacking. Do you know what happens to slackers in the field? They *die*." Eve's eyes narrowed. "But you wouldn't know, would you. *You* didn't want to be trained."

Nora's face was hot. "I would have been trained if my dad had let me."

"Oh, so it's all about your *dad*. Is he evil or stupid or both?"

Nora flinched. "My dad died—"

"Sorry: *Was* he evil or stupid or both?"

Now Nora was shaking—a snarl and sob vying in her throat.

The snarl won.

"My dad told Daniel I wasn't for sale. He loved me. He

wanted me to have a *real* childhood and grow up with him. I guess *your* dad wanted to get rid of you!"

Eve's eyes flashed. Her hands curled into fists. "*What* did you just say?"

Nora retreated a step.

"Get out of here." Eve pointed at the door. "We don't need *scum* like you around with your sheep and your fiddle and your *stink*."

The sob now winning, Nora ran toward the door.

Footsteps thumped. Tove came up beside her.

"Wait!" She grabbed Nora's arm. "She can't talk to you like that. But you can't talk to her like that either. You both need to apologize."

Tears dribbled down Nora's cheeks. "I'm sorry, I just . . . I'm sorry."

Tove bent until her face was even with Nora's. "You're a good person. I can tell. You were just reacting. And Eve—I know. She's having a bad morning. It's not you. It's just that this was the first morning someone who wasn't Lucy walked out of Lucy's room."

Nora wiped her eyes. "Who's Lucy?"

"The knight you're replacing."

"Why am I replacing her? I shouldn't be here—"

"Lucy fell in our last duty. Six bites."

Nora froze. *Six bites . . . that means she's dead.*

Tove's jaw was tight. "Eve blames herself because they'd argued before the battle and Lucy stopped fighting and started to cry. You can't cry in the field. The Umbrae will notice, and they'll swarm you. And if we're not ready for it, no one can protect you." Tove looked out at the track.

"I thought Amar said you didn't get hurt."

"We don't. Unless something like that happens."

For a minute, they stood without speaking.

"I'm sorry," Nora said at last. "Poor Lucy. And all of you. I know what that's like. My dad died from a bite. It's horrible."

"It is. And it's hard to go on, isn't it?" Tove crossed her arms. "But we *need* to. And we need to be able to trust each other and work together, each one of us playing our part. If we can do that, we won't get hurt. What do you think? Can you do it with us?"

Nora nodded. "Yes."

"Then come back with me and finish your laps. And tell Eve you didn't mean it. And don't be angry; Lucy was her best friend through training, and she was just thinking you're not Lucy. But you know what? You're *you*. And we're glad you're here."

Slowly, Nora jogged with Tove back toward Eve.

Eve stood with her head lowered, arms crossed. Cyril jogged in place a few feet away. Amar was speaking softly to them. As Nora neared, Eve's arms tightened.

"Eve? I'm sorry. I didn't mean it." Nora spoke quickly, before she lost courage. "Of course your dad loved you. My dad—he didn't understand—and he was scared."

Eve raised her eyes. "*You* should be scared. You're going to meet the Umbrae in real life soon."

"I *have* met them in real life. And I *am* scared. But I'm more angry: They tried to get my mum, so I want to mash them all into little bits."

"Mash them?" Cyril wrinkled his nose. "You don't mash them. You chop them. Or slash them. Or cut them—"

"It's okay, Cyril," Tove said gently. "It's a different way of speaking."

"Is this resolved?" Amar glanced between Eve and Nora. "We have five more laps before breakfast. Nora, let's try two as intervals: Run hard until I catch up with you, then walk until I catch up with you, and repeat. I'm sorry I didn't think of that before. Ready, knights?"

"I'm ready. I'm starving." Tove winked at Nora and sprinted off.

Cyril followed.

"Eve, make sure you say something to Nora before you start." Amar launched after them.

Eve didn't move. Her eyes hadn't left Nora. "So you *want* to mash them into little bits. The question is: *Can* you actually do it? There. I said something."

And then she was gone, leaving Nora to run alone.

BREATHE

After the track, Nora followed the others down the hall into a long, narrow room. Large screens hung on the walls over rectangular tables. Each screen had a logo, a number in the Order's color, and a map of Brannland flecked with yellow dots.

Amar circled back to Nora. "The screens show the MacAskill Orders. Wyvern and Fox don't have enough knights, so they're not going out on duty. They get this room last. Boar and Stag are on duty now. Oak's on the track. We're going out on duty next, so we get everything first."

"The Orders don't do things together?"

"Too many of us make the Umbrae go wild—even with six, they see us as prey and don't pause—and too few of us is too vulnerable. MacAskill figured all that out."

"No, I mean eat together. Or run together."

Amar stared. "Why would we do that?"

At a table at the end of the room, they picked up their breakfast: a metal canister, a bottle of water, and two small flat breads wrapped in a cloth napkin.

Nora peered around.

"What are you looking for?" Cyril asked. "If it's a knife to stab someone, use the one on the table."

"Is there butter for the bread?"

"You don't need butter for this bread," said Amar.

They sat beneath the screen for the Order of the Hawk—a hawk in flight above the number 30 in electric blue.

A screen with an oak, close to the door, was 53. Boar was 73 and Stag was 80. Wyvern and Fox were both 20.

"The numbers are the percentage of Umbrae we took out on our last duty compared to the numbers detected—the Umbrae we *could* have destroyed." Amar unwrapped his bread.

"Is thirty percent good?" Nora tore off a piece of bread and took a tentative bite. It was pure wheat—but soft and tender.

"No." Amar grimaced. "Hawk's never done this badly. But we had to come back after the second night, and it counts for the whole two weeks." He cleared his throat. "Our number will go back up to a hundred fifty or so. We always get way, way more than the sensors pick up."

"I *hope* we get back to a hundred fifty next time," said Eve softly. "We're missing one of our best knights."

Amar met her eyes. "I know."

Everyone was quiet.

Nora opened her canister to an earthy-scented black soup. "Oh. I thought this was tea." She dipped a piece of bread into her canister and popped it in her mouth—and spit it into her napkin.

"Too hot?" Tove asked.

"No, it's awful!"

"What? It's a protein shake, and this one's the best." Cyril pushed up his glasses. "Black urad dal, chiles, turmeric, and garam masala. Do you have taste buds?"

Nora put down her canister. "Is that what yours has? You're lucky. Mine's sour and horrible."

"We all have the same thing." Amar's voice had dropped ten degrees. "I'm guessing you've never had black urad dal or garam masala."

Nora lowered her eyes, her face burning. "I . . . don't even know what those things are." She swallowed. "I'm sorry. I'll eat it."

"You don't have to eat it." Eve shrugged. "In fact, *don't* eat. Ever. Then you'll starve."

"She's apologized, okay?" Amar lifted his canister. "Now let's have a toast: Here's to our new Order. We're going to push that number higher than it's ever been."

They all raised their canisters and drank.

Nora was gulping the last of her protein shake, followed by water, when the door to the dining room opened and the Order of the Oak came through.

She straightened. As she'd run, she'd wondered what it

would have been like to be with the Order of the Oak. Seeing them now sent a pang to her stomach.

Averill marched past, her gaze straight ahead. Kazu, Bronwyn, and Isaac also didn't meet her eyes.

Only Shaun glanced at her. And scowled.

"Ten hits," said Cyril. "And he struggled for every one. How many hits did *our* knight get?"

Shaun looked away.

"Ninety hits," said Amar. "*Every* one."

Cyril leaned over the table and put his hand next to Nora's. "You've a brain like a piece of MacAskill Iron and you look more like a chicken than a knight, but you're *really* good at this."

Was that a compliment?

"You're fantastic at this." Tove set her hand on Nora's.

Eve crossed her arms. "Do we know that? We haven't seen her in the field."

"We *know* that." Amar added his hand to Tove's.

After a few seconds, Eve touched her pinkie to his hand. Then she crossed her arms again.

"Thanks," Nora whispered.

A minute later, the Order of the Oak neared Hawk's table on the way to their own table with their breakfast.

"Good morning, Hawks," Averill said lightly, eyes straight ahead.

"Sorry we're taking so long." Amar's voice could have frozen the protein shakes. "We're just about to leave."

"Take your time."

As Isaac passed, he shot Nora a faint smile.

That smile—it was the first smile she'd seen all morning.

Nora struggled out of her chair. "Hiya, Oaks! I just want to say thanks for being so friendly yesterday. It was super nice to meet you. And Isaac—do you want to play sometime? I know a folk version of 'This Gracious Land' that's strange but wonderful and it'd be fun to riff together."

Isaac's face lit up. "I'd *love* to. Maybe during library this afternoon?"

Eve bolted to her feet and to Nora's side. "*Don't* talk to other knights. Whose Order do you think you're in?"

Amar was on his feet. "Eve."

Tove grabbed Nora's hand and dragged her past the Oaks, between the tables, to the doors, and through.

Nora caught her breath. "What just happened?"

"Nora, you don't talk to other Orders. It's a *big* deal here. Didn't anyone tell you?"

She shook her head. "Why can't you talk to other Orders?"

"Because it makes it look like you don't want to be with us. Isaac shouldn't have said anything either."

Nora's mouth opened, then closed. "Is this a friendship thing?"

"No, it's a MacAskill Rule. He wanted all the Orders separate and completely devoted to *their* Order alone. That's the way we're trained—*in* our Order, *for* our Order, our whole lives."

"But why?"

Footsteps, then Eve marched past the doors. "Where is she?"

Tove planted herself in front of Nora. "Leave her alone. She didn't understand."

"I think she needs to learn the hard way what you do and what you *don't* do around here. Get out of my way, Tove."

Cyril, who had just stepped through, was suddenly at Tove's side. "I'm usually all for violence but I think this could have a negative effect on our ability to bond—"

"Just shut up for once in your life, Cyril!"

"Eve." Amar closed the doors and marched in front of her. "Take a deep breath."

"Did you hear what she said? Are *you* going to do anything?"

"Eve, listen: We're in this together. We need each other. Every one of us. And we *all* need to calm down. Now *breathe*. In for one, two, three . . . out for one, two, three, four, five, six. Again . . ."

Nora breathed to Amar's count. So did Tove and Cyril.

And so did Eve, her eyes clenched shut.

When Amar finished four rounds later, Eve's face was strangely calm.

"Sorry, everyone." Without meeting anyone's eyes, she slipped into the hall.

THE ARMORY

The Axe

Blade: double (2), hooked, light serration

Blade Lengths: 7 inches (average)

Weight: 8 ½ pounds (average)

Features: MacAskill Iron core and coating, MacAskillSharpV®, and a comfortable grip

—Level Three, Chapter 49: "Your Weaponry"
Becoming a Knight (National Council training text)

To Nora's relief, the Order of the Hawk parted: Eve, Tove, and Cyril to the Order's library, and Amar and Nora to the Armory to fit Nora for her axe. He walked her to a spiral staircase across the fortress and led her up.

"That was just a test axe you used in the simulation,"

Amar said as they climbed. "It was heavier than the one you'll get, and more awkward— Are you all right?"

"I'm fine," gasped Nora. She was five steps behind him. "I've never seen so many stairs."

"Catch your breath, then." He leaned against the railing. "You're going to *love* your weapon. They make it fit you perfectly. And they adjust and improve it to your fighting style as you grow up. I've had three now."

"How old are you?"

Amar smiled sadly. "I just turned fifteen. I've only got three years left. Which stinks, because I'm *finally* getting good at this."

"How many times have you been bit?"

"Twice."

Nora winced. "I'm sorry."

"Don't be; if I can keep it at two, I'll become a Legendary. Poor Eve's had three. One more and she's gone—"

"Is she *always* like that?" Nora blurted.

Amar's face hardened. "Yes. And she's our friend. So we don't talk about her behind her back." He continued up the steps.

Cringing, Nora grabbed the railing and followed.

"You mentioned you were out with your mother when you saw the Umbrae," Amar said over his shoulder a few seconds later. "Did either of you get bit?"

"No." Nora thought back to that night. "They paused for me and I dodged. I distracted them so Mum could get inside."

"You had an adult around—which usually means the Umbrae won't pause—and no MacAskill Iron weapon, and you *still* didn't get bit. By dodging." Amar gave a short laugh. "Nora, you're incredible."

As they went on, he spoke of the facilities at Noye's Hill: training rooms, a huge library for each Order, and the laboratory downstairs.

"We have *so* much medicine. There's a whole floor where they're doing experiments to create a permanent antidote: a vaccine for the venom."

And he told her about the laundry floor, and the kitchen, where knights could request anything they wished.

"Everyone who works here is a former knight." Amar ran his finger down the railing. "They do a lot of little things to take care of us, make us feel special. They know what it's like."

The Armory was at the top of the tower behind a black door with a single teal button.

"They know we're coming, but this is the standard procedure." Amar pushed the button. "Order of the Hawk," he said loudly, "fitting for an axe."

The door clicked open.

A short woman with silver hair and round black glasses was waiting behind a desk.

"Ah, our newest Hawk." She rose and looked Nora up and down.

Amar blinked. "Wow. Ursula. I didn't expect to see you

here. Nora, this is Dr. Ursula Chong, our director. Ursula, this is Nora Kemp."

"Oh! *You* put me in Hawk." Nora blushed. "Thank you for thinking I'm excellent."

"You *are* excellent: I saw your numbers. I wanted to meet you and personally fit you for your axe."

"Thanks," said Nora, blushing more.

"You picked my favorite weapon." Ursula pushed a button on her desk. A tray with a thick blue cushion slid out directly above it. "Roll up your sleeve and put your whole arm here."

Nora obeyed. The cushion was cool against her skin—and immediately molded to the shape of her arm and wrist.

"Good." Ursula rose and walked to the other side of the room. "Now come over here. Amar, turn your back."

Amar pivoted to face the door. Ursula pressed a button in the wall.

A panel slid out, covered by a blue cushion like the one on the tray.

"I need to get an accurate measurement of your muscles and how your body will move, so take off everything but your underwear and stand on that step. It's going to be cold. Hold your breath before you lean in."

"I hate cold." Nora sat on the floor and struggled off her boots.

"So do I. Which is why I'm giving you a cup of hot tea when you're done. Black, green, or herbal?"

"Oh! Black tea with milk, please." Nora slid off her leggings, tore off her stretchy top, and, holding her breath, climbed onto the step.

"Reach out your arms. Ready?"

The pale blue cushion molded over her body—as cold as slush.

"Ooo. Ooo." Nora clenched her teeth.

"That's it. Hold still. A few seconds more . . . and . . . step down."

Ursula threw a warm cotton robe over Nora's shoulders. "Go sit in that chair and I'll have your tea in a snap. Amar, want a cuppa?"

"I'd *love* a cuppa. Black tea with milk for me as well, please."

Five minutes later, Nora was curled up in her robe in a wooden chair against the wall, a tall, hot mug between her hands. Amar was in the opposite chair with his own mug, sipping slowly, eyes closed. The tea was rich and malty with just a splash of milk. With that and the soft lighting, Nora could almost imagine that she was home.

"Amar? What kind of weapon do you have?"

"A sword. We all have swords. They're based on a shamshir from sixteenth-century Iran. You're the only one at Noye's Hill with an axe."

"That's a good thing," called Ursula from behind a monitor on the other side of the room. " 'In weapons, as in life, our differences make us strong.' Remember?"

"That's a line from training," Amar whispered.

Nora sipped her tea. She had another question, a possibly stupid question, but she felt relaxed enough to ask. "Where do the Umbrae come from?"

Amar shrugged. "Everywhere. They've always been in Brannland. About twenty-five years ago, researchers found fossils of them in Marlow Sands that dated from the early Holocene Epoch. Apparently they weren't violent then, just for the past two hundred years."

"Why did they become violent?"

"People destroyed their habitats. The early scientists thought they originated from underground, and historic environmental degradation—mining, pipelines, pollution—set them off. It's a good thing Sir Colm MacAskill was around to invent his Iron and create his Orders. If it weren't for him, the whole country would be overrun."

"Isn't it overrun now? I mean, I saw two of them outside my house—"

"It's only overrun if we don't destroy them. Any Umbrae you don't destroy one night produces spores at dawn, so there's more than twice of them in that area on the next night." Amar leaned forward. "But don't worry. We can control it. The Order of the Hawk always gets way more than the sensors detect. It's kind of like we have our own bait-post. We truly clean up every place we go."

"Is it . . . really dangerous?" Nora faltered.

"Well, *yes*. That's what we're here for, though."

"Is she worried?" called Ursula from behind the monitor. "Her simulation room score couldn't have been better *and* she has an amazing arm. Nora, didn't you learn all about the Umbrae at training?"

"I didn't go to training."

Ursula's face appeared. "What's this, Amar?"

"She . . . missed training. Daniel Fenton was keeping an eye on her."

"*She's* the one who wasn't trained?" Ursula rose. "Nora, what do you know about fighting the Umbrae?"

Nora straightened. "I know we need to fight them. It's crucial. And I'll fight them with my axe, the way I did in the simulation."

"Why do we fight them?"

"Because they're beasts and they're horrible and—*I'm* fighting them because they murdered my dad and two of them tried to get my mum—"

Ursula winced. "Amar, tell Murdo he'll need to talk to me. I might need to shift people."

"No." Amar twisted around in his chair. "You saw her test results."

"Did Daniel touch the panel?"

"Murdo set it. And nothing changed between Nora and Shaun—he's the one from Region Four—and he went first."

"I don't take any knight's life for granted. If she's not grown up with this, she's not ready. And if she's not ready, she's not going on duty with you in three days."

"She's ready," Amar said firmly. "Look, Murdo wouldn't take her if he didn't think so. And *I* wouldn't take her; I wouldn't risk the rest of my Order."

Ursula let out a long breath through her nose. "Nora: Do you know what you're getting into?"

"Yes."

"Do you understand the danger you will face?"

"Yes."

Ursula held her gaze for a whole minute. "You have three days to tell me if you change your mind. Amar, I expect a report from you before you go on duty." She returned to the monitor.

"Thank you," mouthed Amar.

Ten minutes later, Ursula handed Nora a small, neat battle-axe. It was very different from what she'd used in the simulation room. Two glimmering black metal blades curved out on either side of the shaft, each with a claw at the top and bottom. Tiny claws ran all the way down each blade, covered by hardened wax.

"Wow." Nora rotated the axe in her hand. "Thank you."

"You're welcome. Use it wisely and well."

Yet as soon as she was heading down the stairs with Amar, Nora's heart sank.

I guess it fits me . . . but it doesn't feel anything like my axe at home.

WARRIORS
OF THE
FROZEN BOG

PLAYERS LOGGED IN:

TechnoLad—Paladin (96 minutes)

sheepGrl9—Grand Necromancer (1 minutes)

sheepGrl9: wilfred? where are u?

. . .

TechnoLad: where are u? i'm in ravine

sheepGrl9: boghouse coords 2459X, 735Z

TechnoLad: k. 2 min. coming 2 u

. . .

TechnoLad: nora! how are u?

sheepGrl9: i want to come home

TechnoLad: what happened?

sheepGrl9: i'm horrible at this

TechnoLad: are they mean 2 u?

sheepGrl9: mean x100 & it's scary here. did u know umbrae come from people making a muck of natural world???

TechnoLad: i thought they came from nuclear disasters=did school paper on that.

sheepGrl9: i'm risking my life 4 mess other people made. not fair!!!!!

TechnoLad: yeah. it's kinda important u do it, though

sheepGrl9: . . .

TechnoLad: . . .

sheepGrl9: what quest are u doing?

TechnoLad: i'm just bagging loot

sheepGrl9: . . .

TechnoLad: . . .

TechnoLad: i met your mums caseworker. name=horace. nice x 100000

sheepGrl9: really? he's nice?

TechnoLad: he gave your mum a pressie: a book o' poems

sheepGrl9: awww sweet. how did you know?

TechnoLad: dad said we should check on yr mum so we go after school

sheepGrl9: is she reading poems now?

TechnoLad: she put poems in fire. dad took it out be4 it burned much

sheepGrl9: *gasp* . . . that's actually a wee bit funny

TechnoLad: she's a wee bit mad at you 4 going

sheepGrl9: . . .

TechnoLad: she asked dad to find out where u are so she can come & get u

sheepGrl9: tell her to stop it. i'm fine.

TechnoLad: can i tell dad abt yr brilliant fight?

sheepGrl9: if he promises not to tell anyone. supposed to be secret stuff

TechnoLad: should i tell yr mum?

sheepGrl9: no!!!!!!!!!!!!!!!!!!!!!!!!!

TechnoLad: ok

sheepGrl9: . . .

TechnoLad: . . .

sheepGrl9: guess what i had 4 lunch: pizza!!!! weird crispy pizza but *shrug*

TechnoLad: weird crispy pizza=pizza=triumph

sheepGrl9: & i got my weapon

TechnoLad: omg yr sword!!!!!!!!!!!!!!!!!!!!!!!!! what does it look like?

sheepGrl9: i have axe & so cool & looks=axe of orm when u fight orm's daughter remember?

TechnoLad: omg u are so lucky

sheepGrl9: wish i could take pic

TechnoLad: what abt pic of u? when's it going on wall @ school?

sheepGrl9: ? no one said anything abt it

TechnoLad: tell them to take pic. I want signed copy please

sheepGrl9: lol *blush*

TechnoLad: i'm talking to a knight *blush* *blush* *blush*

sheepGrl9: lol stop it

TechnoLad: can u play warriors saturday?

sheepGrl9: . . .

TechnoLad: dumb question. sorry

sheepGrl9: no i want to but i'm going to be out

TechnoLad: out=training?

sheepGrl9: out=fighting

TechnoLad: *hyperventilates*

sheepGrl9: wilfred? want 2 play now?

TechnoLad: do u have time?

sheepGrl9: everyone else=asleep

TechnoLad: YES!!!!!!

THE COMING DUTY

The knights of the Order of the Hawk were waiting in the common room when Nora emerged red-eyed in the fresh uniform she'd found at the foot of her bed with a handwritten note:

> Welcome to the MacAskill Orders, Nora! We're so glad to have you. Please let us know if you need anything. Have a great day!
>
> —Staff, Order of the Hawk, Noye's Hill

"Are you having trouble sleeping?" Amar frowned. "We're going out on duty in two days and you need to get a full night's rest."

"I stayed up thinking; that's all." Nora rubbed her sore eyes.

"Or stayed up bawling." Eve rose. "Are we going to run?"

Amar ran his laps, but afterward kept with Nora as she hobbled around the track for her intervals. His manner had changed: He was gentler, more patient.

After breakfast, they went to the library. Nora wandered among the stacks, then to the front again.

"What are you looking for?" Amar was in one of the cushy chairs by the wall, a massive book in his lap.

"Do you have books on history?"

"Don't get Amar started on history." Eve rolled her eyes.

"If you're keen on history, *absolutely* get me started." Amar grinned. "I'll show you the *best* part of this library."

He took her to the very back. History books covered the entire wall, stretching eight shelves high: new, old, leather-bound, and paperback; separated by era and then by region. Dr. Ogundimu had once taken Nora and Wilfred to his university's library, but even *its* history section had been nothing like this.

"Sir Colm MacAskill was into history and rare books. The Council kept up his collection after he died and added to it. What do you like to read? I promise we have it."

Ancient Brannland! Castles! Medieval weaponry! Viking invasion techniques, like what Dr. Ogundimu studies! I bet they have his book.

But then she straightened. "Is there anything about the history of the Umbrae?"

"That entire case behind you. Take your time." Amar

plucked a book from the bottom of the case and began to read.

Nora climbed the ladder slowly, scanning titles as she went.

The "Peculiar" Countryside: A Geographical History of the Umbrae

A History of Brannland: Industry & Umbrae

Origin Stories: Volume 1, Umbrae

She chose a tall, faded volume in the corner of the bookcase—*The Umbrae: Our Strange, Spectacular, Uniquely Brannlandian Beasts!*—and brought it down to show Amar.

"I haven't seen this one before." Amar ran his finger down the spine. "Its pages are falling out."

"It was squashed."

"I bet someone read the title and did that on purpose."

They walked back to the chairs to find Murdo with the other knights around a polished wooden table.

"Sorry to interrupt your library time. Ursula suggested that I talk you through a duty for Nora's sake."

"Good idea." Amar slid into one of the empty chairs and patted the one beside it for Nora. "Where's Ursula sending us?"

"North or west, our choice. Any preference, knights?"

Amar glanced around. "Let Nora pick, okay? Nora, north or west?"

Nora dropped into the chair, her face flaming. "For what?"

"Do you know what a duty is?" Tove asked. "Murdo, I don't think she knows."

"Daniel didn't tell you?" Murdo pointed at Cyril. "Tell her what a duty is."

Cyril fixed Nora with a fierce stare. "A duty is a fortnight—fourteen nights straight—of endless battle. The Umbrae rush at you in waves, twice as bad as your worst nightmare. Are you scared? Yes. Do you want to run screaming? Yes. *Do* you run screaming? No. You stand and slash, over and over. When you're done, you want to throw up and you feel like you could never take another step—but you take another step. And you don't throw up. Again. And again. For fourteen nights."

Nora let out the breath she'd been holding.

"It's pretty intense," Amar admitted. "We travel to a region and hunt Umbrae. We fight at night and sleep during the day. But it's not always nonstop fighting."

"Sometimes you spend a whole night, and it's just five or six." Eve's voice was soft. "Sometimes there's swarm after swarm. You never know what's coming."

"But at dawn, it's *all* done," said Tove. "And we go back to our house or bothy, get scanned and disinfected, and rest."

"What happens if I get bit?"

"You get an antidote straightaway," said Amar. "And there are Council clinics in just about every town."

"Anyone else?" Murdo looked around. "Nora, a duty is fourteen full nights of action with days of driving in between. There can be downtime, though not often for *this* Order. When you're in the field, you move. Don't expect to relax." He sat back. "So pick our battleground: north or west. North is more driving. West will be wet and cold."

"North," whispered Nora.

Murdo pushed a button under the table. A huge hologram appeared: a colorful topographical map of Brannland.

They would be going from town to town, Murdo told them, to villages tucked between mountains, and busy city streets: anywhere National Council sensors had detected Umbrae.

"Are there more Umbrae in towns?" Nora asked.

"Often," Murdo said. "It's as if they plan a raid: They hold back for a few weeks until citizens feel safe to go out past the gloaming. Then they strike."

He touched a yellow-filled section on the hologram, which zoomed in to a main street with a church at one end.

"This one's going to be the worst: Ravinscrag. No Umbrae seen for a month, yet our sensors are picking up close to a hundred in the surrounding countryside."

A hundred? How are five kids going to fight a hundred Umbrae? Nora's mouth was dry.

"A hundred's not too much for this Order," Murdo said, as if he'd heard her thought, "but we'll need to be ready for them. *And* for citizens. Listen carefully, Nora: Stay away from citizens in the field. If you're stopped, grabbed, or spoken to, ignore them. If you respond, you'll risk your life and the lives of everyone in this room."

THE CASTLE IN THE SKY

Once Murdo had left the library, the knights settled back to read. Nora reread the same page over and over. She'd known that each outing would last two weeks and they'd fight shadow beasts, but it hadn't felt so real before.

After an hour, Amar put down his book.

"Who wants to go for a swim?" He added to Nora, "There's a pool downstairs."

Three hands shot up: Tove's, Eve's, and Cyril's.

I need to talk to Wilfred. He might be home from school now.

"Could I go back to my room?" Nora asked.

"We're supposed to always be together before a duty and bond," said Cyril, "like five melted, mashed-up gummies."

Amar gave her a faint smile. "Try swimming with us?"

Nora's face burned. "I don't know how to swim."

"Bring your fiddle and play while the rest of us swim," Tove suggested. "Then we can stay together."

Nora's heart lifted. "Is that all right? I'd *love* to. I haven't played in days."

The pool was underground behind an unlocked bright teal door. Beside it stood a black door with a round retinal scanner.

"That's the laboratory entrance." Amar gestured at the black door as they passed by.

The pool was an otherworldly expanse of water, lit from below with lines of blue lights. Above, dim bulbs shone down like moonlight. The air was warm and humid.

"Why isn't anyone else swimming?" Nora walked carefully down the ghost-white tiles beside the water. They were warm through her boots.

"Orders don't mix, remember?" Amar said over his shoulder. He and the others were heading into changing rooms. "Even if they did, Oak's giving us space since we're leaving for duty in two days. Nothing's supposed to distract us. That's a rule in the books."

"Can you show me the books?" Nora called after him. "I should study them."

Eve burst out laughing. She disappeared behind one of two doors after Tove.

Cyril ducked behind the other, giggling.

"I didn't mean real books." Amar paused outside that door. "That was just an expression." He followed Cyril inside.

Her face hot, Nora walked to the far end of the pool. A white metal chair was bolted to the tiles. She took a long time tuning her fiddle and was still at it when Cyril ran out in royal-blue swim trunks and blue-rimmed goggles. He dove cleanly into the water.

A minute later, Eve strode out, then Tove, both in royal-blue swimsuits. Like Cyril, their dives were clean and graceful.

Amar was last. He walked to the edge of the pool and met Nora's eyes.

"Don't worry too much about the things you don't understand right now. You'll get it all soon enough. And keep on with the questions. Seriously. I don't mind."

He dove in, and the four began to swim laps.

Nora set her fiddle to her chin. *He must have been thinking about how I was feeling while he was in there. That's sweet.*

She almost started a random jig, but a memory of the last piece Owen had played for her made her stop.

He'd called it "The Castle in the Sky," and it was different from Owen's other pieces. It was a set of classic fiddle tunes—reel, jig, march, and air—that were modernized, and challenging. Owen had taught her the tunes one at a time, yet had never told her they were parts of a bigger piece, not until the night before he died.

No one could have known that this was his last night. Nora just knew that her father was doing something special. By the fire, just the two of them, he'd played all the pieces straight through: as "The Castle in the Sky."

She'd never heard anything like it. She'd practiced each

tune and knew them well, but somehow, together in the order Owen had chosen, they formed an entirely new blast of emotion. She'd caught her breath.

When Owen lowered his fiddle, he was panting, his forehead slick with sweat.

"That's a message," he'd murmured, "like 'Feed the sheep.' But this set means something else. It means: 'I belong here.'"

"Why does it mean that? Is it a sad piece, Dad?"

"It's . . . There's sadness in it, sure, but it's more a call to claim your life, to say that you *will* be who you want to be. Nora, this is your piece now. When you know you belong, no matter who says otherwise, that's when you play it. When you play the whole thing like this, you'll be playing the message for yourself."

After Owen's death, Nora had continued to practice each tune, but separately. She'd never played the full set: It had never seemed like the right moment.

I'm about to go on duty and do something I've never done, and it's dangerous and scary and . . . I need to tell myself this. I'm a knight. I belong.

Nora fixed her eyes on the tiles and launched into the three-note drop that began "The Castle in the Sky."

It felt good to play. Her fingers and bow were eager. They shaped the swift opening reel, rushed into the drawn-out jig, pounded through the march, and finally let loose with the sorrowful air. Then the opening reel came back—fast and blissful. The end was three fierce sweeps—"Play as hard as you can," Owen had said, "because that's your shout of joy."

When Nora finished, her hands were trembling and she was out of breath.

Her fellow knights were leaning against the poolside, arms folded and watching, as if they understood.

"Wow," Eve murmured.

"Beautiful." Tove applauded softly.

"I don't know how you made your fingers move that fast." Cyril held up his hands. "I think you've got twenty fingers, not ten."

"Thanks for playing, Nora," Amar said. "That was incredible."

As the knights got out of the pool and changed back into their uniforms, Nora packed up her fiddle. She was about to latch her case when the door to the hall opened. A tall woman with wire-rimmed glasses, a smooth black bun, and a white lab coat stepped through.

There was something tender in the way the woman was looking at her that made Nora think of her dad, and Wilfred.

"I've heard one of those tunes before," said the woman in a soft, low voice.

"Really? My dad wrote that piece. I didn't think he'd played it for anyone but me. His name was Owen Kemp."

"I thought *I* was the only one who'd heard that reel." A

faint smile. "I knew he had a daughter, but I didn't know you were a knight."

"I just became one." Nora's heart lifted. "You knew my dad?"

"A long time ago." The woman's eyes flicked to the changing rooms. "Is the rest of your Order in there? Didn't they let you swim?"

"I can't swim, so they asked me to play my fiddle instead since we're supposed to be together the two days before duty. When did you meet my dad—"

"You're about to leave for duty?"

"Yes. My first."

The woman stiffened. "I'm so sorry. I shouldn't be here." She retreated toward the door.

"Wait!" Nora stood up. "What's your name? I'm Nora Kemp. I'm in the Order of the Hawk."

The woman paused. "I'm Nadia Bakari. I was Nadia of the Wyverns twenty years ago." She reached for the door.

"How did you know my dad?"

"I'll tell you when you come back from duty. You need to stay focused now." Nadia Bakari opened the door. "Good luck."

And then she was gone.

Thirty seconds later, the rest of the Order of the Hawk rushed out of the changing rooms.

"Hot chocolate in the library, knights," Amar said.

"Whipped cream for everyone but Eve? Cyril, ancho chiles again for you?"

"And black pepper, cinnamon sticks, and star anise."

"Got it. Nora, what do you like in your hot chocolate?"

I just met someone who knew my dad! A former knight. I wonder how she knew him.

"Nora?"

"I just met—" She broke off. *I'm not supposed to talk with people outside my Order.*

"A fly? A water droplet? A song you couldn't say no to?" Cyril suggested.

"Sorry. My mind's wandering. I'd like whipped cream in mine, please." Nora latched her fiddle case without another word.

DEPARTURE

> "As a senior knight, I'm responsible for their lives. Yes, I care about our numbers. And it's cool that we have the potential to make history. But in the end, none of it matters if someone gets hurt. When I'm out there, I want them to be safe. Nothing's more important than that."
>
> —Amar Bukhari-Masood, Order of the Hawk
> *The Noye's Hill Interviews* (internal)

Running, weightlifting, and reading filled the final two days before duty. Each night, Nora chatted briefly with Wilfred. She felt guilty keeping it a secret from her Order, but she needed her friend.

Then the final days were over and a buzz in the common room jolted Nora awake. She stumbled out of bed and tripped over a small leather case.

Inside were tidy stacks of clothes: ice-blue leggings, tops, underwear, and socks. Her axe was there too, wrapped in a piece of ice-blue silk.

No fresh royal-blue top and leggings waited as usual, so Nora dressed in the ones she'd worn the day before. Amar was the only one in the common room, clad in ice blue, his black hair damp.

"Grab an on-duty uniform from your suitcase and then shower time, Nora. Enjoy it: You won't have reliable hot water for a fortnight."

Nora scrubbed herself carefully. She dressed in the ice-blue top and leggings, tied her hair back in its usual floppy ponytail, and returned to the common room.

Now all the knights were there, in ice-blue uniforms like hers.

"Do something with your hair," said Eve. She was sitting alone on one of the sofas, her leg bouncing. "Ponytails come undone in battle."

Tove patted the sofa cushion beside her. "Come. I'll give you a Dutch braid."

Nora sat and felt Tove's fingers separate her hair into sections. In two minutes, she was done.

"It looks cute on you." Tove examined her work. "That's going to make the Umbrae pause and go 'Aww.'"

Nora ran her fingers down the braid. "Why do they pause for children?"

On the adjacent sofa, Amar raised his head. "There are a ton of theories: Umbrae treasure their young, or don't see us as a threat, or a child once did them a kindness and as a species they've never forgotten."

"One of my teachers says it's because we're cute. I think that's rubbish. Not all of us are cute." Cyril huddled down in his sofa.

"*Maybe* they want us to fight other Umbrae for them. *Maybe* it's a fluke and one day they *won't* pause. *Maybe* there's no reason at all." Eve threw her hands up. "Could we stop with the theories?"

Silence.

"May I bring my fiddle?" Nora asked.

Amar nodded. "Put it with the cases."

Breakfast arrived outside their door. Nora was so nervous, she barely ate.

Then they waited.

Eve bounced both her legs, fists clenched. Tove and Cyril played rock, paper, explosion. Amar sat with his elbows on his knees, hands clasped. Nora sat beside Amar and hugged herself.

A tap came from the door.

Amar sighed. "I guess she's really going to do this." He stood. "Come in."

The door opened. It was Averill and Shaun.

"What are *they* doing here?" snapped Eve.

Amar scratched his nose. "Ursula wanted us to try a new tradition: Any knights going out on their first duties at the same time should shake hands. Oak's going out next week, so . . . here's Averill and Shaun."

"It's to spread courage or something," Averill said. "But I'm kind of glad we're doing this. And I just wanted to say good luck to you all."

Eve rolled her eyes. "Get on with it."

Nora jumped up and ran over to Shaun. "Are you staying with the sword? Do you like it? My axe looks like one from a video game and it's *so* cool."

His hostile expression shifted into a shy smile. "Yeah, I have the sword. It's—yeah, it's cool."

"I bet it'll feel like it's part of your arm when you're out there. Look, I have to ask: Does Isaac *really* sing for your Order?"

His smile widened. "Yeah. It's—weird. He sings two songs and combines them and they sound, like, really funny. He wakes us up with it."

"Oh, that's great! I should try—"

"Are you done?" Eve's voice cut into Nora's.

Nora and Shaun both stiffened.

Averill bit her lip. "So, maybe just say one more thing to each other, something about having courage out there?"

Nora held out her hand. "You *will* do well on this duty, Shaun. You're super, super good at this. Never forget it."

"You—you too." He touched her hand, then darted out.

"Thanks, Nora." Averill flashed a smile and followed.

Amar sat down again. "That was a waste of two minutes."

"At least she didn't *hug* him," muttered Eve.

"I'm sorry," said Nora, "but he looked scared."

Cyril raised his chin. "I think that's a fantastic tradition. I wish someone had come up and told *me* I was good at this before *my* first duty."

"Didn't you already know?" Amar looked surprised. "I mean, you don't become a knight unless you're *extremely* good at this."

Cyril slumped back. "No one's thinking that their first duty."

The door opened and Murdo stepped in.

"Ready, knights? Leave your cases."

A minute later, the Order of the Hawk marched down the center of the hall at the bottom of the fortress—Murdo, then Amar, Tove, Eve, Cyril, and Nora—in single file.

They turned the corner—and faced a crowd.

People packed the sides of the hall. There were adults in cleaning smocks, suits, or lab coats—Nora spotted both Daniel and Nadia Bakari—and knights: three kids in rust-orange uniforms, two in gold-colored uniforms, five in burgundy-red uniforms, and Averill and the Order of the Oak in jade green. Everyone waved vigorously.

At the end of the hall stood Ursula in a black tunic with four adults in black uniforms like Murdo's: Sophie with her jade-green patch, a bearded man with a burgundy patch and a matching turban, a tiny old lady with a gold wyvern pin above her gold patch, and a younger woman with a rust-orange hijab and matching patch.

The other Legendaries.

Back straight, arms crossed, Murdo stood with his knights. They fanned out around him.

Ursula's gaze flicked to each one of them. "Good luck, knights."

Then she walked in front of Amar.

"Fight with honor and courage, Amar of the Hawks. And bring them all home."

Amar did not take his eyes from hers. "I will."

Tove was next.

"Fight with honor and courage, Tove of the Hawks, and come home."

"I will."

Then Eve.

Then Cyril.

Then it was Nora's turn.

"Fight with honor and courage, Nora of the Hawks, and come home."

I'm a knight! I really am! This is amazing! I can't believe this is actually happening—

"Have you something to say, Nora of the Hawks?" Ursula waited, her eyes twinkling.

"Oh! Yes, I will. Fight with honor, I mean. And courage.

And I'll come home. I mean, *here,* not home. But yes, yes, I really will."

"*I* believe her." The Legendary in the burgundy turban flashed Nora a grin, as did the woman with the rust-orange hijab. The old lady's lips pressed sternly.

Sophie's bitter expression did not change.

Nora fled after Cyril down a narrow hall, through a door—

And outside to where a massive black off-road car waited.

It was daytime, overcast but bright. The crisp, cold air smelled of snow.

Murdo marched to the driver's seat. Eve climbed in next to him, Tove and Cyril in the middle seats. Amar slid in the back and held the door open for Nora.

"Is my fiddle—"

"In the trunk with our cases."

Murdo drove down the hill past the slabs of stone, down the winding road to the Iron gates, and through. When they were on the main road, he called back, "Grab your eye masks, drink your sleeping vials, and get some rest, knights. It's a four-hour drive and that dose will keep you under. And remember: The gloaming still comes early—it's less than a month past the solstice—so we'll have some long nights ahead."

Amar showed Nora the little black case in her door. It held an eye mask, a cloth square that unfolded into a blanket, and two foil-sealed vials.

"The silver vial's for now, the gold to wake you up when we get there."

In front of them, Tove and Cyril clinked vials and drank.

Amar helped Nora peel the top off her silver vial and watched her swallow. Then he tucked her blanket around her, set her seat to lean back, and drank his own vial.

"Amar?" Nora looked up at him from her blanket. "I know I'm good at this, but . . . I'm scared."

He found her hand. "I'm scared too—that never changes—but we'll be all right. Just remember: We're going to do this together."

BEFORE THE BATTLE

"Tonight we're on one of their paths. We'll set up on a hill. There'll be a moon and you'll see the Umbrae as they come out—Nora? Pay attention." Murdo's voice was sharp.

Nora tore her gaze from the window. The sun had just begun to set, breathing a rich orange glow over the hillside.

They were sitting on wooden chairs around a low table in a National Council bothy, a stone building the size of Nora's house with the same kind of rough walls. A small fire crackled in the stove. Like in Nora's house, the fire did little to dispel the cold.

Murdo touched the center of the holographic map he'd projected over the table. It zoomed in.

"Here's the path." His lips twitched. "The Umbrae have no idea what's coming."

Everyone exchanged smiles—except Nora, who sat with her chin in her hands.

"We're talking about *Cochlea umbrae,* of course, with this river nearby. Being on the hill means they'll find us easily."

Nora hesitated, then raised her hand. "Is it *good* if they find us?"

"Yes. Then they'll be out in the open, surging toward us up that hill. We'll use a schiltron formation, something Amar developed—"

"Murdo?" Amar interrupted. "Sorry, but I just remembered Nora chose an axe. I'm wondering about the schiltron formation with four swords and an axe. We should practice."

Murdo rose. "Do it now. I'll move the table."

Amar, Tove, Eve, and Cyril shoved back their chairs and raced to the wall where their cases were waiting.

Nora dragged behind. She was wide-awake, but a fog of unease filled her head.

Amar handed Nora her axe. In his other hand, he held a sword.

It was long and curved, the back edge honed and sharp to the tip, the front edge covered with jagged points. The metal gleamed dark and seemed almost to glow. A white wax coated both edges.

Murdo carried the table to the door. The four knights gathered in a tight circle facing out, elbows touching. Murdo examined them, his hand on his chin.

"Cyril and Eve, switch places. Amar, step forward two inches. Tove, let me see you swing. Now poke. Good. Let's see, where to put Nora—" He glanced at her. "Why didn't you choose a sword?"

"I don't know how to use a sword."

"You don't look as if you know how to use an axe. Hold it up."

Nora raised her weapon, shaking.

"This is not a game." Murdo's voice was dangerously soft. "Hold it up. Both hands."

Nora grabbed the axe with her other hand. It still shook.

"Who measured you? That axe is too big."

"Wait." Amar left the circle. "Nora, take my place but step forward half a foot."

She shuffled to that spot. Amar bounced on his feet in front of her.

"Okay, now I'm going to fight you. Block me. Hard as you can. Don't move your feet. Ready?"

He lunged.

"Stop!" Nora squeaked, and swung.

Their blades met with a clang. Amar pulled his sword back and thrust it forward.

Clang.

He feinted up and slashed down.

Clang.

Again and again he lunged, the firelight flickering over his dark blade as it circled and darted in: above, around, even toward Eve, who stood like stone at Nora's side.

Clang. Clang. Clang.

Finally, Amar lowered his sword. He grinned at Murdo. "That axe is just right."

But Murdo didn't smile. "Be sure you fight like that, Nora, when we're in the field. If you falter, someone's going to get bit."

Tove reached across and grabbed Nora's shoulder. "I want her next to me."

"You're not fast enough if she needs help. Amar and Eve: She'll be between you. If she falters, shove her back and close ranks. All right, everyone. Let's practice."

Gone was the charming Murdo Patel with his winning smile. He impatiently gestured to Cyril to right his position and sharply called out Tove to demonstrate a move. Nora froze often, swung clumsily, always too slow. Murdo stood in front of her and in that horrible soft voice told her to try again. And again. And again—until she began to cry.

"Nora." Murdo knelt and put his hands over hers on the axe. "The first battle is the worst. Remember your years of training—" He stopped. "Remember your *extraordinary* natural talent—and remember to breathe."

He rose. "Amar? What do you think?"

"I think we're good. Okay, knights, ten minutes." Amar stepped out of the formation. "Eve, help me move the table back. Then let's do a weapons check, toilet, and a team chant or whatever."

"Can we have a minute from Nora and her amazing fiddle?" said Tove.

"That sounds great. Are you okay with that, Nora?" Amar jogged over to the table and grabbed one end. "You get the toilet first. Then while we're prepping the weapons, go on and play."

Nora gave Tove her axe and scampered to the bathroom, a closet behind the hearth. The toilet seat was ice-cold, as was the water in the sink. Nora splashed some of it on her face and blew her nose.

When she came out, the table was back in the middle of the room. Murdo was behind it, holding a sword. He ran a purple-lit box down each waxy jagged edge, then set the sword—now bare—near Nora's axe on the table.

Nora stumbled toward the cases. She took out her fiddle and closed her eyes.

She launched into the jig from "The Castle in the Sky." She played it quickly, tapping her boot against the wooden floor.

A minute.

She ended with a flourish.

The four knights were by the door, swords in their hands, eyes fixed on her.

"Nice," Murdo said. "Now time to go."

Nora packed up her fiddle and ran to the door, where Murdo still waited. The others were already outside.

"Forget something?" He nodded at the room.

"No, I don't think—" Nora broke off.

She stumbled over to the table for her axe and rushed out into the setting sun.

THE UMBRAE

Eve sat in the front passenger seat, holding a black tablet—a Council-issued satellite navigation system—with directions to the spot Murdo had marked on their map.

"We should be able to get there before the Umbrae emerge. The gloaming's not for seven—no, five minutes." Murdo swore softly. "Hold on."

The car jolted as he drove off the road.

"Shortcut."

Nora watched the scenery fly past. They were in a grassy valley studded with rocks. Lights sparkled in the distance: a town. Everything else was almost dark.

How will we see the Umbrae? She glanced at Amar, but he was leaning back, eyes closed, shoulders limp.

Nora closed her eyes too and tried to relax.

Calm down. You're a knight now! You're part of the Order of the Hawk! And you're good. You're fast and—don't cry. No, don't. Stop it.

A tear trickled down her cheek.

Think of Amar. He showed everyone what you can do. Think of the fiddle. Fighting's just like playing the fiddle . . . okay, it's not, but—think of Wilfred. He believes in you. And what if someone in that town like Wilfred has to go out after dark and a beast comes upon him? You can stop it first on its path—wait, do they always take a path?

The car lurched to a stop.

"Everyone out. Quick." Murdo flung open his door and sprinted up the hill.

Nora grabbed her axe.

They were in the valley, the sun just a glimmer on the horizon. A fierce wind cut across the frozen grass and into Nora's stretchy ice-blue top—yet the fabric held off the chill.

Tove slammed the door in front of her. "Race you, Nora!" She sprinted away.

Murdo was already on the hill's summit with a case. He opened it and took out a long, stretchy black jacket, a black mask for his nose and mouth, and a pair of goggles.

"Will that protect him from their venom?" Nora asked Amar, who had waited for her halfway up.

He took her hand and pulled her along at his faster pace. "Yes, as long as they can't reach him. If they get to him, their venom will sink through everything he's wearing. That's why we're surrounding him."

"Why's he there? He should be in the car."

"He's the bait."

"But won't he die if they bite him?"

"He hasn't been bitten yet." Amar grinned. "It's great having him there; he attracts a ton. That's why our numbers are so good. Only bait-posts produce more, but those are way too dangerous. They've been outlawed since before we were born."

Murdo had on his gear, including a black hard hat with a light, and was pulling on a pair of long gloves when Nora, gasping, finally reached the top.

"Okay, knights," said Amar. "Take your places."

Amar and Eve stood side by side, elbows almost touching. Tove was by Eve, Cyril by Amar. The four formed a tight circle around Murdo.

"Make room for Nora," said Murdo from behind the mask.

Everyone stepped forward. Amar and Eve parted. Axe trembling, Nora took her place between them.

The hill was longer than it was steep, the car at least ten yards away. Down the opposite side, a frozen brook disappeared behind a cluster of spindly trees. To the west, a river stretched toward mountains. All was dark, silent, and cold.

Suddenly, a blinding light from Murdo's helmet flicked on, illuminating the hillside.

"Gloaming. Now the fun begins." Murdo's voice was tight. "You might as well relax. They're not going to be bursting from the seams quite yet. I'll tell you when—" He broke off. "I'll correct myself. Here's our first *Cochlea umbra*. It's coming for you, Eve."

Something moved in the darkness beyond the light: a long, low black shape. It wriggled and crunched over the icy grass as it neared.

Nora froze. This Umbra was far bigger than the ones in the simulation.

Eve bounced from foot to foot, her sword at the ready.

The Umbra slithered to the bottom of the hill and the brink of Murdo's light. It lifted its head: rounded like a snake's with a slug-like softness and two quivering black feelers. Its body rippled, slowly bunching: a massive slimy spring.

It released.

Up the hill—stretching out, eight feet, nine feet, more—toward Eve.

Then it jerked to the side, directly for Nora.

Don't move your feet.

Amar's words rang out in her head. She knew she should have waited for the pause, but the Umbra was almost upon her.

Nora swung down.

The massive shadow beast disappeared—in a puff of lavender mist.

Then the hillside was swarming.

She had no time to think. They rushed for her, for Amar and Eve, for every knight of the Order of the Hawk.

And for Murdo most of all.

One thumped against Nora and launched up above her head. Eve slashed it and the Umbra disintegrated. Nora stumbled, choking, and came face-to-face with another that tried to shove her out of the way. She whacked it with one axe blade, then whirled her weapon and whacked another with the other side.

They know I'm new. They can see I'm the smallest. They're coming for me!

"Keep your places!" shouted Murdo in his muffled voice. "They're trying to draw you toward Nora and open a space. Nora, stay *firm!*"

"Can I move my feet?" She shrieked as a beast dove for her ankles, its soft jaws open wide.

Amar's sword swept it into mist.

"No," said Murdo.

It was a nightmare. Umbra after Umbra slithered, sprang, and flung themselves against the knights.

But the knights didn't move—except their weapons.

129

Their swords and axe flashed, landing in *Cochlea umbrae* flesh with juicy thumps. The lavender mist grew thick.

And then it was quiet but for the knights' puffing. Wreaths of sparkling lavender mist lit by Murdo's helmet dissipated around them.

"Breathe," said Murdo. "Stretch. Is everyone all right? Did anyone get bit?"

"I'm fine," said Amar hoarsely.

"Same," wheezed Tove.

"Yes," said Eve.

"I could use a pee, a pipe, and a penny dreadful." Cyril pushed up his glasses. "No, I'm fine."

"Nora?"

Her knees were wobbling. Before she could stop herself, she thumped to the ground.

"Don't sit during battle." Murdo's voice was sharp. "Get up. Unless you're hurt. They'll be on me if they see a gap."

Amar crouched at Nora's side. "Were you bitten?"

"I don't think so."

"Up, then." He pulled her to her feet.

Nora wiped her face. "Why aren't they pausing for us?"

"They are," said Amar, "just not much because Murdo's here. But they're not switching into shadows right before they attack, which they do normally around adults. Again, because of us."

"Do they turn into that pretty mist because of us?" Nora asked.

Cyril snorted. "That's their venom. Venom's the last thing to die in an Umbra. When it's mist, it's poisonous like their slime or hair, so we don't feel it. When it's pure, it's the color of a rotten plum. You see a lot of *that* when they bite you because they slather it all over you. It's slimy and smells like sour milk—"

"Okay, Cyril," Amar cut in. "You've explained. Thanks."

Tove leaned forward. "You're doing really well, Nora."

Eve bounced on her feet. "Yeah, you are." She met Nora's eyes. "Thanks for getting that first one for me, Kemp."

Nora blinked. "Kemp?"

"That's your name, isn't it? And that's what it sounded like when you thwacked it. *Kemp*."

Nora cringed.

"Get ready, everyone," Amar murmured.

Another wave of *Cochlea umbrae* slithered from the shadows to the edge of the hill. They paused in the darkness, just outside the light, their number increasing, until a rippling, quivering mass stretched out.

They struck.

The knights fought wildly against the never-ending wave. One knocked over Cyril—but Tove pounded it before it could reach Murdo and dragged Cyril back to his feet. The gap between Amar and Eve widened as they helped the knights on their sides.

And suddenly Nora was alone, defending a space much bigger than she was.

A *Cochlea umbra* slithered up slowly, its black eyes fixed on her. Its massive tail vibrated, propelling it closer and closer over the icy grass.

"Go away, please," Nora said, a sob in her voice.

The Umbra froze.

Amar darted forward, slashed it, then returned to his spot.

The wave ended. One stray *Cochlea umbra* circled the hill, then seemed to think better of it and slithered through the grass toward the river.

Amar cleared his throat. "Murdo, I think we've had enough."

"Right. Everyone: To the car. *Now!*" Murdo raced down the hill, his long legs carrying him swiftly to the driver's door.

The knights sprinted after him. Tove, Cyril, and Eve reached the middle door and piled in.

"I'll open the back door for us," called Amar over his shoulder as he pounded ahead.

Nora lagged. In her mind, swarms of *Cochlea umbrae* were bearing down on her, jaws open, teeth shining—

At last, she was at the door.

It opened—and knocked her to the ground.

"Nora!" Amar hauled her in and slammed the door.

A huge black shape thumped against it. The car rocked.

"Hold on!" cried Murdo, his voice muffled behind his mask, and set the car in reverse.

It went up and over a *Cochlea umbra*. Another slammed the hood and slithered onto the windshield.

Murdo wrenched the wheel and the beast slid off.

The car plunged forward. For a minute, a swarm of *Cochlea umbrae* kept beside it. Finally, they fell back. The Order of the Hawk barreled alone over hillocks and icy grass, through the valley, until the car bumped onto the road.

Murdo screeched to a stop and tore off his goggles and mask. Slower now, he drove on, the road and meadows around them completely dark.

Nora was curled up in the corner on the floor, Amar's arms locked around her.

In front of them, Tove was crying.

It seemed a full hour before Murdo pulled up in front of the bothy.

"You can get out," he said gently. "Remember: Every Council bothy has a MacAskill Iron ring in the ground. We're inside that ring. Take your time, knights." He staggered out and flung open the front door.

Eve climbed out with Tove and walked her inside, while Amar carried Nora. He deposited her by the hearth near Tove, then went back with Cyril and Eve to collect the weapons.

As they left, Tove lifted her head. Her eyes were red and swollen.

"Sorry. I got frantic. I held it in until I was in the car. See, that bit about not crying in the field? That was for me too."

"Really?" Nora croaked. "You were wonderful out there."

"So were you. And so was Cyril. But . . . he almost got bit." Tove raked her sweaty hand over her face. "I try really hard to be there for all of you. I'm not the senior knight, but . . . Amar and me, I've always told him I'll keep an eye out. See if anyone needs a boost. I got frantic out there thinking of what happened to Lucy." She exhaled. "We're not little kids. But tonight—for five seconds, *I* was a little kid. And I almost lost Cyril."

It took Nora two attempts to speak. "But you didn't. He's fine."

"I know. I just . . . I felt so helpless." Tove breathed slowly, as if counting to three. "I haven't always felt like I could trust my body. These days my body and I get along fine, but when we were out there just now, I felt like I was carrying someone and I was about to drop them—which is a *big* problem, because when you're in the field, your body *has* to do its thing. They teach you in training how to get your mind in the right place. But in that battle . . . I couldn't."

The other knights came back before Nora could think of what to say.

"Good job, everyone." Amar knelt beside Tove and Nora. "How are you doing, Tove?"

She shook her head, eyes shut. "I almost lost Cyril. The way I lost Lucy."

"He's right behind me, Tove. You didn't lose him. And

you didn't lose Lucy." Amar put his hand on her shoulder and bowed his head to touch hers.

Eve and Cyril stood a few feet apart, heads bowed too.

The fire in the little hearth crackled.

A minute passed. Tove's tense shoulder relaxed under Amar's hand. She opened her eyes.

"Are you okay?" he asked gently.

"I'm okay now. Thanks, Amar."

They exchanged a nod, and then Amar stood and crossed the room. He hauled down a case and came back to the knights with a cylindrical red-glowing bar. His face was limp with exhaustion.

"Right, we need to check everyone."

He ran the bar over Eve first, who held out her arms, face stiff.

Nothing.

Cyril was next. He was trembling but held the necessary pose.

Tove hauled herself up and stood like a statue as Amar scanned her.

Nora tried to stand, but couldn't.

"I'll do you, Amar. Give Kemp a breather." Eve took the bar.

Amar held out his arms and closed his eyes, his face tight and tense.

The bar only hummed.

"Give her another minute." Murdo hauled himself to his feet and held out his arms.

Amar scanned Murdo, whose face did not change.

It's as if they're all expecting something horrible to happen.

When Amar came back to Nora, Eve helped her up.

"It doesn't hurt," she promised.

Amar scanned Nora's hair—and the bar flashed red.

"Hold your breath."

A spray of antidote soaked Nora's hair and face.

He brought the bar down her chest—

More flashing.

More antidote.

But the flashing didn't stop.

Murdo leaned away from the wall. "What's going on?"

Amar frowned. "I don't know."

But then, at the bottom of Nora's top, where she'd tucked it into her leggings, something moved against her skin.

Eve whipped up the hem—

A three-inch wriggling black shape plummeted to the floor—and shot toward Murdo.

Thump.

Cyril set a sword back on the table. A tiny plume of lavender mist rose from where he'd slashed.

"Give me the bar and everyone turn around." Eve seized it and pivoted to Nora. "Take off your uniform. Quick. In case it bit you." She tore off Nora's top, leggings, and boots, until Nora was standing in just her underwear.

"Hold still, Kemp." Eve carefully drew the bar over Nora's head again.

Her head, shoulders, legs, and feet were fine, but her stomach was covered with mucus—and soon with the antidote. Eve ran over to the cases to grab a towel, fresh top, and leggings. She wiped Nora down, then helped her dress.

When she was done, Nora dropped to the floor and buried her head in her arms. She could not stop shaking.

"No bites or wounds?" Murdo's voice was very soft.

"None," said Eve. "Maybe *Cochlea umbrae* that small don't have teeth."

Tove crawled to Nora and wrapped her in a tight embrace.

Eve dropped to a crouch and hugged them both. Cyril leaned against her.

Amar knelt and put his hand on Nora's elbow, which was sticking out of the tangle of hugs.

"Not a single bite. Knights, we have our Order back again."

NATURAL TALENT

There wasn't any bath or shower in the bothy, but Murdo said everyone could wash in the sink. Nora scrubbed with cold water and hard soap until her skin was raw.

The first night had been bad. And they had to spend two more at the path in the valley before going on.

When Murdo told them that, he was handing out mugs of strong hot tea and buttered hearth-toasted scones.

"Last night was unusual; you destroyed close to seventy. The sensors haven't picked up more than a hundred on the whole path, so the other nights won't be that bad." Murdo leaned over the table and refilled Nora's mug. "And there's one more thing we can do to reduce the flow: I won't be out with you tonight."

Eve banged down her mug. "What? *Why?* You're excellent bait."

"I vote for you being there." Tove sat up, her face stormy. "Because I can't wear an earpiece to hear you. I have *two* earpieces already, remember? The transmitter's obvious, but I have a tiny receiver too. I can't give *either* of them up."

Murdo put his hand on hers. "We didn't forget, Tove. No one's going to ask you to compromise your hearing. Amar will give you my instructions. Would you be okay with that?"

"Oh." Tove sat back. "Yeah." She touched the silver earpiece.

"And Eve—I appreciate what you're saying, but Amar and I were thinking: They're taking advantage of Nora's inexperience. That was as bad as I've ever seen them."

"Was this *your* idea?" Eve leaned over and poked Amar's chest. "Stop it."

"My idea was to try it once. Tonight."

Eve shook her head. "That's the stupidest idea you've ever had."

Tove looked up. "You know what, though? It's not just the earpiece. I feel safer when you're out there with us, Murdo. No offense, Amar."

"I get it." Amar set down his mug. "But look, everyone, that's not fair to Nora. They kept going for her first."

"Oh, *come* on." Eve scowled. "Kemp can take it. She's got loads of endurance, right? Don't let her wreck our numbers."

Nora flinched.

"Eve." Amar's voice had dropped into a new tone: hard, cold, and furious.

Eve crossed her arms, mouth tight.

"Nora?" Tove leaned toward her. "Can you try it one more time with Murdo? The first night's always bad."

It was more than bad. Nora's hands dropped to her lap, nervously clutching.

"I nearly got bit five million times," announced Cyril. "*And* they almost broke my glasses. But they'll be gloomy and slow tonight because they failed."

Amar met her eyes. "We're going to do whatever you need us to, Nora. And we're going to be fine with whatever you decide."

Except . . . they all want Murdo there. He's what brings in their numbers.

"I can handle you being out there, Murdo," Nora said, her voice wavering.

"Are you sure?" Murdo frowned. "We had to carry you to your sleeping bag last night."

"My mum always said I'd feel better in the morning. I feel better now. And I'll feel *even* better . . ." She held out her cup.

Murdo refilled it.

"You're the one who's going to need a pee, a pipe, and a penny dreadful," said Cyril.

"I can hold it for eight hours when I'm playing a video game. I can hold it when we're fighting." Nora sipped. The tea was hot, rich, and dark with just the right amount of milk. And the buttered scone—she could still taste the butter.

She *almost* felt better.

There was an hour before they would go out for their second night.

Nora played the wide-open air from "The Castle in the Sky," then joined Tove and Cyril at rock, paper, explosion. She used the toilet three times, and on the third took the fluttery piece of ice-blue silk that had been wrapped around her axe and tied it on top of her hair—double French braids by Tove—in a bow.

"Is that what you're doing with your scarf? I made a headband with mine on my first duty." Tove bit her lip. "That's way cuter."

"Cute and deadly: A perfect combination." Murdo swept the purple bar down her axe blades. "Do you want the front seat this time?"

It was drizzling when they went out to the car. Amar and Cyril climbed in the middle, Tove and Eve in the back.

Nora slid into the front passenger seat and held her hands up to the hot vents.

"Don't worry about the satnav. Seriously, get warm; I know the way."

Everyone—even Eve—was more relaxed this time. They'd seen the worst and it wouldn't be so bad now. It was always like that after the first battle, Murdo told Nora, even when he'd been a knight.

As he drove, he shared stories about his time as a knight in the Order of the Hawk: his best battles, his worst, and the close calls he'd never forget—such as the battle in which his Legendary had accidentally locked the car doors just as the exhausted knights had reached them, a pack of *Lupus umbrae* at their heels.

He drove mostly on the road this time.

"I didn't think anyone was supposed to drive at night," Nora said as they turned onto the meadow. "Is this car special?"

"It's built entirely from plates of MacAskill Iron, so the Umbrae can't climb in—unless they're riding on someone, apparently."

"Maybe being inside my top protected it." Nora ran her finger down the door. "Do you know how MacAskill Iron was made? I'm reading this book about the Umbrae, but it doesn't say."

"Colm MacAskill invented his Iron with a bonded chemical alloy. You didn't learn that in school? Actually, they probably only share that in training. That's a Level Two science class."

"I wish I'd been trained."

"You fight as if you have. Where did you learn to use an axe like that?"

Nora shrugged. "On the farm. I also play this video game, Warriors of the Frozen Bog. A *lot*."

"That's some video game if it taught you to fight *this* brilliantly."

Nora's face warmed. *I've got to tell Wilfred he said that.*

They arrived with ten minutes before the gloaming. Murdo walked Nora up the hill.

"When people first learned how MacAskill Iron could keep back the Umbrae, they sprinkled it everywhere. I remember my mother dumping shavings on our front path when I was little. But that's not reliable; their shadow forms can avoid small pieces. And it doesn't help to shower the Umbrae with pellets. Everything misses them, even MacAskill Iron machine gun bullets, liquid Iron flamethrowers, and bombs."

"How do the Umbrae dodge everything?"

"They don't dodge; they switch from a solid creature with teeth to a literal shadow, and then back again—in a fraction of a second. When they're shadows, they're like air: Nothing can hurt them. But they don't switch around children. *Why* is a great mystery."

They'd reached the top. Murdo unlatched his case and pulled on the stretchy jacket and the mask, helmet, and goggles. Everyone arranged themselves as before, though Murdo switched their positions so that Nora was facing the car.

"Three, two, one, and . . ." His helmet light flicked on, illuminating the hill and the spattering rain. "Gloaming. Though you'd never know by looking."

Nora touched the bow in her hair. The rain had already flattened it.

But though the rain was chilly, every part of her beneath the stretchy fabric was dry and warm.

"Here comes our first adoring fan," Murdo murmured. "Ten points if it goes for Nora. How beloved we are in these parts."

The *Cochlea umbra* advanced as all the others had: It paused at the bottom of the hill, then shot up.

But the knights were ready, even when the beast rose on its tail and flew at Nora's head.

She slashed and ducked at the same time, then straightened through the lavender mist.

"Nice move, Nora," called Murdo. "Cyril, watch your feet."

There were fewer *Cochlea umbrae,* just as Murdo had predicted, and only one massive wave. Many hesitated at the bottom of the hill.

"Look at that," Murdo said. "They're waiting for us, blocking the way to the car. Slimy creeps. They think we can't handle being out in the rain all night. Well, let them wait. We'll watch them disintegrate when the sun rises."

But it's night, thought Nora. *And it's winter. And the sun isn't going to rise for a long, long time.*

A few beasts shot up the hill, but most stayed below. Nora soon understood why.

They weren't just waiting: They were trying to tire the knights and trick them into relaxing—then catch them.

But Murdo had seen that tactic. He told the knights to move, bounce on their feet, stretch their arms, and keep ready.

It was hard to stay awake. Nora understood Tove's words about the importance of Murdo being there.

They waited in the freezing, soaking rain for hours until at last the *Cochlea umbrae* lost patience and surged up, a wild onslaught from all directions like before.

Nora had been half asleep.

"Get away!" she shouted at one that slammed against her stomach, then drove her axe into its neck.

The next *Cochlea umbra* rose like a cobra.

"Stop it, please," Nora said, her eyes fixed on the beast. If it lunged from that height, it would easily reach over her to Murdo. And she couldn't run forward to slash it without leaving her place. "I'm asking you *please* not to do that."

It lurched, the whole length falling—

Nora threw herself down the hill, into the beast, axe-first.

It disappeared around her in a puff of lavender mist—

But then she was surrounded: Umbrae rushed at her from every side.

"Come back, Nora!" cried Amar.

She stumbled toward her Order—

And slipped on the icy grass.

Nora slid helplessly down the hill, past the *Cochlea umbrae,* and thumped at the bottom just inside the circle of light from Murdo's helmet.

A *Cochlea umbra* reared over her. Its shimmering maw opened—and faltered.

Nora brought the axe up into its head.

Puff.

Another. And then another. And more.

It was like the simulation: *Cochlea umbrae* all around, attacking, but faltering first.

Though she was tired, her muscles remembered the simulation room: being exhausted, needing to use the toilet, and fighting nonetheless. Nora used their faltering as she had in her test. She slashed again and again. The rush seemed as if it would never stop.

Then, suddenly, they were gone.

Nora looked around, panting. Heart pounding, she sprinted through the thick lavender mist, up the hill, and took her place again between Amar and Eve.

"Don't *ever* insult Nora again," Amar said softly.

"Who, me?" Eve shrugged. "I'm just standing in awe here."

"*Great* job, Nora," said Tove.

"I think you're lying about not having been trained," said Cyril. "I think you've been training since you were born."

A second later, the light on Murdo's helmet flicked off.

All over the field, the Umbrae disappeared into puffs of mist—pearl gray this time, not lavender.

"Dawn."

Everyone climbed into the car without talking, soaked. Amar kept by Nora's side and grinned as he opened the front passenger door for her.

"Well done, Nora." Murdo climbed into the driver's seat. "You may have three cups of tea anytime you like on duty."

Nora smiled and buckled her seat belt. "Why did they turn into gray mist when they died just then? Is that different from the lavender mist?"

"They weren't dying. Umbrae transform into spores at dawn; that's how they reproduce. Tonight, there'll be two or three Umbrae for every one we didn't destroy. But don't worry; we'll finish them off when we come back."

Nora swallowed. Outside her window, the gray mist spread like fog. She no longer felt like smiling.

RAVINSCRAG

At the next night's gloaming, the Order of the Hawk trudged to the top of the hill—and waited. It was sleeting. Within minutes, Nora's bow and hair were frozen.

"We should have caps," she said to Amar, whose black hair was flattened over his forehead.

"I have a cap." Cyril tapped his frozen curls. "Pure Greek wool."

"We don't look as young in caps. *You* could probably handle it with your dimples, Nora, but not the rest of us." Amar leaned over and propped up her bow. "There, let's freeze it standing."

"Ugly knit caps would make us look younger. The *Aranea umbrae* at home gave me lots of chances when I was wearing my ugly sweater." Nora paused. "I thought it was ugly-cute, but kids at school made fun of it."

"Someday bring me to your school and show me those kids," Eve said softly.

Murdo shifted behind them. "I don't think you would look young enough in knit caps, especially Amar. Even if it works for the rest of you, I don't want Amar to be the only one in the cold."

"That's okay." Amar winced under a new burst of sleet. "No reason for everyone to suffer."

"If I get chunky fuzzy yarn, I'll knit you a cap that makes you look eight years old," Nora told him. "I'm *really* good at knitting ugly-cute things."

An hour passed. Nothing. Another hour.

Amar and Murdo called the night off. They marched down the hill without seeing even one slimy ripple.

"I think all that talk about ugly caps scared them." Tove crawled into the middle seat after Nora. "Will you knit me one, though? Even if I can't wear it on duty."

"*We* scared them," said Amar from the front. "I wish I could say it was the wet and cold, but I'm pretty sure the weather doesn't bother them." He leaned over the vents.

"Whatever," called Eve from the back with Cyril. "It's good to have time to breathe."

"There won't be much of a breather," said Murdo. "We're going to tidy up the bothy, then head off to Ravinscrag. We'll do some late-night hunting there."

The drive to Ravinscrag took two hours down slick, icy

mountain passes and twisty roads. The snow let up as they reached the town's sign.

They drove by a farmhouse, a trailer, and an old stone church—with lights on in each one.

"Look at that," muttered Murdo. "The *church,* of all places, has people out tonight. I'm tempted to leave and let the Umbrae get the best of this place. But let's see our whole battleground."

He drove on: past the tightly packed row of dark shops with lit windows above, to the garage at the end of town, then to a tall stone building in the middle of a cobbled square.

"This is the clinic, launderette, café, and lodging house." Murdo gazed at it. "I'm not hopeful about their resources. Do me a favor, knights, and don't get bitten here."

"Is that a Council clinic?" Nora asked.

"No. But they should be decently stocked with our things. Unless they've let everything expire." Murdo twisted around in his seat. "Nora—I should have mentioned this before: I always carry two antidotes in my upper sleeve pockets. Do you know how to give them?"

"You pound it. Into their thigh." Nora winced. "I did it for my mum."

"This one's for knights and you pound it *twice,* quick as you can. There are two doses in each canister. The first freezes the venom to stop it from reaching the heart. The second follows the path set by the first and kills every trace. If I get bit, I need both canisters: four doses in my thigh, one after the other. It won't save my life on its own, but that dose and what's left of my immunity will give me a chance if you get me to a hospital quick."

Murdo opened his door.

"Well, knights, shall we stroll?"

Suited up in his mask, goggles, and helmet, Murdo looked sinister in the gloom. The knights arranged themselves around him: Amar at the front, Tove at the rear, with Cyril and Eve at the sides. Nora walked between Amar and Cyril, almost even with Murdo's gloved hand.

They marched down the street toward the dark garage. Murdo looked out at the hills.

"It's going to be either *Lupus umbrae* or *Aranea umbrae,* but I'd bet on *Lupus umbrae*. Who can tell me why?"

"*Aranea umbrae* like green farmland and lovely gardens," said Eve. "And this place is a dump."

"*Lupus umbrae* like stone buildings, and just about every building's stone," said Tove. "I think it's beautiful here."

Murdo nodded. "In a city, Nora, we get *Aranea umbrae* in the parks, *Lupus umbrae* on the streets, and *Cochlea umbrae* in streets near a river." He gestured toward the road with his chin. "Let's pay a visit to that church."

Music streamed from the stone church's front door: a string quartet, the tune sweet and merry.

Murdo stepped inside with Amar and Eve to talk to the citizens. Tove, Cyril, and Nora waited in the car park.

"I can't believe they're out like this." Tove shook her head. "They must not have seen Umbrae for a long, long time."

"They're boneheaded twits who should be flushed down their own toilets." Cyril polished his glasses on the hem of his top.

"I wonder if they don't think the Umbrae are real," mused Tove. "You know, people who've never seen an Umbra—"

A shrill howl sounded in the distance.

Cyril slid on his glasses. "Here comes the truth. I hope it sticks its slimy nose in their faces."

A DREAM DESTROYED

LUPUS UMBRAE

Habitat: forests, towns, drawn to stone edifices
Appearance: lupine, thick fur
Size: 42 inches tall, 200 lbs (estimated weight)
Venom: bite (primary), fur, and saliva

—Bulletin, National Council for the Research
and Destruction of the Umbrae

The music stopped. Murdo and the two knights rushed outside.

"They're scared now," said Amar. "That howl cut right through the music."

Eve's eyes narrowed. "I hope they get permanent neck aches from sleeping in those pews for the rest of the night."

"Get ready." Murdo looked around. "When you hear it like that, they're close. In fact . . . there, at the end of the drive."

In the light from Murdo's lamp, a deeper shadow in the darkness flickered into shape: a silver wolf, twice as big as the ones Nora had fought in her test. Its bright red eyes gleamed, darting over the children, then fixed on Murdo.

It howled: an eerie, triumphant sound.

"Let it come to us," said Murdo. "Then if it's just one, close on it like a pinch: Tove and Cyril. Ready?"

His voice was tight but comforting in its authority.

The *Lupus umbra* trotted up, keeping its distance. It drifted to the side, as if searching for an opening.

A second one materialized from the shadows, and a third. And more, until ten had plunged into the light.

"Get them!" shouted Murdo.

Are we not still protecting him? thought Nora as the knights around her launched forward.

Suddenly, she crashed to the ground, a *Lupus umbra* on her chest.

A blade cut it into lavender mist. Eve grabbed Nora's hand and yanked her to her feet.

"Pay attention, Kemp!"

They won't pause like in the test. They'll try to surprise me. What did Terry like to do?

Another *Lupus umbra* pounded against her, and she only just caught it with her axe before it reached Murdo.

Don't think. Just move!

She launched herself in front of the next one and slashed before it could hit her; then threw herself at another. Two *Lupus umbrae* dashed for her, and she caught them one by one.

Then she saw what they had done: drawn the knights far enough down the car park to leave Murdo alone.

A single *Lupus umbra,* as big as a small cow, bolted for him.

"*Bad* dog!" screamed Nora, rushing after it.

The *Lupus umbra* glanced over its shoulder, its red eyes meeting hers with a look like Terry's: defiant yet alarmed.

"No, you *stop,* you filthy thing!"

And then she was upon it and cut it into mist.

Nora planted herself in front of Murdo and waited.

The next *Lupus umbra* slunk between the cars and crept up from the side. Nora pointed her axe.

"You'd *better* not!"

Tove ran for it. The cringing Umbra disappeared under her sword in a cloud of lavender mist.

"Is that all?" Amar jogged back toward Murdo. "Do you see any more?"

"Not right here." Murdo stepped away from the church door and shone his light in a circle. "Nothing."

Cyril marched up to Nora. "That was *fabulous*! You're a banshee!"

Nora blushed. "I didn't even know I was doing that. I was thinking—"

"There's no time!" Murdo grabbed her shoulder and strode through the car park. "Where's the pub? If the Umbrae came for citizens here, they're going there too."

The knights gathered around Murdo once more.

"The minister said the pub's between the shops," shouted Eve from the head of their formation.

The streets were empty, though they heard laughter in the distance. Murdo's pace increased. Soon they broke into a run.

Nora trailed. There was a long stretch of empty road.

"Keep up," called Amar.

The laughter grew louder. At last they came to the row of stone buildings and the first alley between the shops.

The Cow's Head pub was at the end, its cheery yellow sign shining in Murdo's light.

"Ho! It's the cavalry!" laughed an old white man in a ratty tweed coat.

The younger white man at his side let out a hoot.

"Twits," muttered Cyril. "Do we *really* have to save them?"

"Go inside." Amar marched in front of the two men. "You'll be dead if you stay out any longer."

"But you'll protect me, lad, won't you?" The old man grabbed Amar with a guffaw.

Just as a *Lupus umbra* flashed past Nora, followed by three more.

Murdo backed up against a wall. Eve and Tove took positions in front of him, slashing all that came near. Cyril was a step away.

But Amar was on the ground where the old man had tripped in his drunken effort to retreat. Amar struggled to rise, but the old man was holding him as a shield.

The first *Lupus umbra* closed its jaws on the young man's ankle and flung him aside.

Another darted right up to Amar. Its mouth clamped onto the old man's shoulder and tore him away.

Both turned to Amar.

He'd dropped his sword but was reaching for it, on his knees.

Nora ran faster than she'd ever run, axe weaving, and slashed one beast as it lowered its mouth to Amar's leg, then the other just as its mouth closed on his arm.

Amar rolled through the lavender mist, bolted up with his sword, and stepped over the howling young man to plunge his blade through a *Lupus umbra* leaping at him.

Sweat streaked down Amar's face. Blood and a dark purple sap ran down his arm.

It bit him.

Nora cut a path back to Murdo.

"Give me the antidote! Amar got bit!"

Murdo ripped open the zipper of one of his sleeves and thrust the heavy canister into Nora's hand.

Nora cut her way back to where Amar was fighting four

Lupus umbrae and dropped to her knees beside him. "I have the antidote!"

"Cyril, go protect Amar and Nora!" roared Murdo.

Cyril lunged over and soon was in front, sword flashing.

Nora dropped her axe and wrenched off the top of the canister. Amar sank to the ground, breathing hard.

"Sorry. This will hurt." She put her hand against his thigh and plunged the antidote into him as hard as she could—then pulled it out and plunged again.

Amar groaned at each hit. Then he turned aside and threw up.

"Go inside, Murdo!" shouted Eve. "They'll pause if it's just us!"

Swearing, Murdo edged to the door and ducked in.

With a bellow, Eve attacked. A cloud of mist rose around her. Tove followed.

The two joined Cyril in front of Nora and Amar and kept the *Lupus umbrae* at bay.

Nora barely noticed. She'd left her axe near Amar's sword and had clasped her arms around him. Curled up on the ground, he was sobbing uncontrollably.

Three bites. Tears trickled down Nora's cheeks. *He'll never be a Legendary. And that's all he ever wanted.*

23

THE BOOKSHOP

"The book in training says the first bite gives you burning, nausea, and dizziness. Then the second's burning, nausea, dizziness, and your breath comes out fuzzy for a few minutes. The third makes your heart go wild—because your immunity's starting to go. The fourth makes your arms and legs stiff, so it's hard to move. The fifth makes you unconscious. And the sixth stops your heart." [pause] "I have it all memorized."

—Cyril Panagiotakopoulos, Order of the Hawk
The Noye's Hill Interviews (internal)

"One more." Murdo cut a fresh strip of gauze and wrapped it around Amar's forearm over the pad.

Amar's eyes—red and swollen—fixed on the floor.

"That could have been a lot worse, Amar. A wound from

a bad bite would be dripping pus right now. Your wound's clean."

"Good." Amar's voice was hollow.

"That means you don't have venom in your body. That's more than good."

"I know."

Eve marched over and held out her fist. "Welcome to the three-bite club."

Without looking up, he raised his fist. She bumped it, then hugged him.

They were in the lodging house at the top of the old stone building. The clinic below had fresh disinfectant, healing gel, and plenty of gauze and pads. It also had a young clinician, who waited just outside their doorway.

"I have offers from the entire town to fetch you anything you want." She faltered. "We're grateful for your sacrifice."

"Tell them to stay in after gloaming." Murdo shut the door, then stretched his arms above his head. "What a night."

People in the pub had seen what had happened. And when the flow of *Lupus umbrae* had paused, big bearded men had poured out and carried both Amar and Nora inside and wept over them.

And over the old man and the young man, whose hearts had already stopped.

Nora had heard the whispering, Murdo's terse answers, and the silence of the other knights.

Amar had sat at the end of the counter with his head in his arms, a white bandage from the pub tied around his wound, until it was dawn and safe to walk back to the lodging house. He'd barely spoken.

"Knights, I'm sorry," Amar said hoarsely. "I lost my focus. I stopped fighting. I put you all in danger."

Murdo lowered his arms. "Don't blame yourself for what happened. It was bad luck—especially to meet those citizens. You're an exceptional senior knight. Don't ever forget that."

Without meeting anyone's eyes, Amar plodded down to the bedrooms.

Tove started after him.

"Let him be by himself," Murdo said softly.

Tove didn't stop. "It's not good to be alone on duty."

The door of the boys' room closed behind her.

Cyril stifled a yawn. "Do you want me to sleep out here? Give me a blanket and a dry floor and I'm happy."

"Wait until Tove comes out. Then you can go in. Eve, Nora: Go to bed."

Eve marched down the hall.

But Nora didn't move. She was exhausted yet filled with nervous energy, seeing only one thing: the hopelessness stamped on Amar's face.

"I don't want to sleep," she blurted. "I want to feel better."

"What would make you feel better?" Murdo looked tired, but his voice was gentle.

"It's silly, but . . . I wish I could read my myths book from home." She bit her lip, tears welling. "Daniel said I wouldn't need it."

"Bookshop run?" Cyril nodded at the front door.

"Great idea, Cyril. Go for it."

Bookshop runs were an on-duty tradition for the Order of the Hawk—a brilliant tradition, Nora thought as she followed Cyril down the stairway.

"It's the nastiest feeling when someone gets bit," said Cyril. They'd just emerged into the sun. "Especially when it's someone like Amar. And the last one—that was with Lucy—we *all* got bit and he didn't get an antidote right away because he and Tove said Eve and I should take them. But this really stinks. Two bites in two duties in a row. That's the universe spitting on you."

Nora's throat was too swollen to speak.

Cyril stopped walking. "Oh. You're about to cry again. Sorry. Um. We're getting books, right? As many as you like. I love books. I *really* like graphic novels. I even like the quiet ones."

"Have you read *The Goblin's Wish*? That's my favorite." Nora's voice shook, but she forced out the words: It felt good to be in the sun and talk about books. "It's creepy, but the goblin's adorable."

"I *love* that book! It was my best friend in Level Three.

My favorite part's when the goblin rips up the athletes who bully him and eats their fingers one by one."

They went on past two side streets to the bookshop Cyril had spotted. A little bell rang as he pushed open the door.

The young man behind the counter—in a Fair Isle knit vest and tortoiseshell cat's-eye glasses—set down a book and stared. "My goodness. Welcome."

"Where are your graphic novels?" Cyril yawned. "Sorry. We want them and—what do you read again, Nora?"

"History."

"—oh yeah, history for you *and* Amar. And a dismal, gory fantasy for another one of us. And a funny romance with a trans girl for another. We're going to get a lot, Mr. Bookshop Man, so you might as well start a list. Charge it to your local Council office."

The bookseller pointed. "Graphic novels are behind you. I'll pick up some grimdark fantasies and rom-coms for your fellow knights. And please: Anything you want in this shop is yours, free of charge. Thank you for your service."

"You're going to be a lot more generous than you really mean to be." Cyril disappeared down the aisle.

"No, I *really* mean to." The bookseller's voice trailed. He faced Nora with a shy smile. "So, you like history. What periods and subjects?"

Why is he looking at me like that? Oh: I'm a knight. And I'm a bit bloodstained. And venom-stained.

She cleared her throat. "One of our knights likes Brann-landian history, like medieval. If there's a new book out, that would be great. And I want myths—wait, do you have books on the history of the Umbrae? And the MacAskill Orders. Going all the way back to the beginning."

The bookseller's name was Archie Cohen and he never went outside or even downstairs into his shop once it was gloaming. Nora learned that before they reached the Chil-dren & Teen section.

Archie plucked six books from the shelves for Eve and Tove, disappeared into History to get three for Amar, and came back with a stack for Nora.

"As you can see, a lot of people have written about the Umbrae and the MacAskill Orders. I wouldn't call all of these *true* history since many of them are conjecture. Except this." Archie handed her a book. "This was written by Sir Colm MacAskill. It's a collector's item."

Nora took the slim old volume and opened it carefully. The pages were ivory-colored and thick, the type crisp and clean. "This feels really valuable. How much is it worth?"

"You've got a good feel for books." Archie crossed his arms. "It's one-of-a-kind. But I want you to have it. It's my gift in thanks for all you've done."

Nora looked up. "I haven't done much. This is my first duty."

"I recognize you: the silk bow. You were the one who

gave the other knight the antidote. People saw you from the pub. The whole town's talking about you." He paused, then went on, softer: "They say you moved like lightning."

Tears welled up in Nora's eyes. "I didn't move fast enough. If I had, he'd never have been bit." A sob pushed out.

Footsteps thumped—and Cyril appeared in the aisle. "The *whole* point of coming here was so you'd feel better." He marched up. "I'm rubbish with hugs—I hate them more than spiders—but do you want one? Yes? Okay. Just don't hug me back."

Then he hugged her: a massive, tight, bony hug that crunched his glasses against her ear.

It was the sweetest, purest hug she'd ever received.

Archie slipped out of the aisle. A few moments later came the click of an electric kettle.

"Amar would be like a zombie right now if it weren't for you," Cyril told her. "We wouldn't be able to go out tonight. But he was moving fine this morning, like he'd never been bitten. That shouldn't have happened with his third bite, or with a bite *that* bad."

"How bad?"

"The worst. I know because there was a picture of a wound like his—a degree thirty—in a book we read in Level Three: the gross book, called that because I literally threw up in it twice." Cyril wrinkled his nose. "Yes, there are thirty degrees of bites. And that book had a picture of each. You can see why I did what I did to it."

A shaking laugh began deep in Nora's chest.

"No!" Cyril grimaced. "I didn't mean to make you cry harder. Look, if I hug you more, your head's going to pop off. But if that would help—"

Her laugh burst out. Cyril staggered back.

"Sorry," Nora gasped. "I was crying but now I'm laughing because you're so funny, Cyril."

"Really?" He flushed. "Everyone but Tove thinks I'm annoying."

"That's because no one but Tove has a sense of humor—wait, do you *not* mean to be funny?"

"I—I don't know. It's just the way I talk. My mum said I was an intolerable loudmouth and should be locked in a box and thrown in the sea."

Nora shook her head. "I *love* the way you talk. Never stop it, please. You make things a *lot* easier to deal with."

Cyril took a deep breath. "That's the nicest thing anyone's ever said to me. I used to think Eve said the nicest thing, which was, 'Those words could flatten an elephant.' That probably wasn't a compliment." His blush returned.

"May I interest either of you in a cup of tea?" called Archie.

"We'd guzzle thirty cups," Cyril returned, "but we have to sleep because this town is a cesspool of depravity and we need to kill all your monsters for you."

NORA'S BOOK

Five hours later, Nora woke to a hum of laughter.

Eve's and Tove's beds were empty. Cracks of light shone past the blind in the window. Someone had left a fresh ice-blue uniform at the foot of Nora's bed, the silk cloth folded on top.

Nora slowly dressed, her arms weary and her mind sluggish.

I shouldn't have gone to the bookshop. I should have slept.

But then she thought of all her new books and the one that excited her most: Sir Colm MacAskill's.

And then she thought of Cyril and how brightly he'd smiled as they left the bookshop. He'd looked so happy when they returned that Murdo had stared—then grinned.

Nora opened the bedroom door.

Murdo was sitting on the sofa in a royal-blue T-shirt with his muscular arms crossed behind his head. His legs were outstretched, boots up on the coffee table. He was focused on a tablet in his lap.

Amar was beside him with the swords and Nora's axe, examining the weapons. He looked relaxed, more like himself.

Eve, Tove, and Cyril were clustered around a book.

"Kemp!" Eve shook the book in the air. "Did you pick this up on purpose, or did the book man sneak it in the pile? It's *hideous*!" She angled out the cover.

On a black background, hot-pink swirls wafted over sparkling gold letters: *The Umbrae: Nature's Perfect Revenge.*

I like the cover, Nora thought.

"May I have my book, please?" She held out her hand.

"Wait. Let me read you something. It's super funny." Eve flipped it open. "'Gentle giants, they glided over the swamps and marshes, releasing little more than sound and odor as they went.'"

"Are they talking about *Cochlea umbrae* or bodily gas?" said Cyril.

Eve waved at him. "Quiet. This is *literature*. And there's more: 'Their songs were tender melodies. If you listened carefully, you could hear the earth's laughter.' Now here's an artist's rendering of a *Cochlea umbra*." She held open the book, revealing a glossy illustration of a dewy-eyed black snail.

"Is that a fantasy?" Amar asked.

"I think the snail's a metaphor." Tove shrugged. "I don't know for what, though."

Eve smirked. "For stupidity. Because *anyone* who thinks a *Cochlea umbra* looks like *that* has snails for brains."

Nora cleared her throat. "*Cochlea* means 'snail' in Latin. Someone must have named it that for a reason. They don't look anything like snails now, but maybe this really *was* an early form, before they became monsters. May I please have my book?"

"No, I want you to lecture me more about snails because I'm *so* interested in what you have to say."

Nora's face burned.

"Do we talk like that to a fellow knight?" Murdo lowered his arms. "Eve, give Nora her book."

"I was just trying to be funny. This book is so stupid, it's hilarious." Eve tossed the book to Nora—who caught it— and flopped back into her chair.

Blinking hard, Nora shuffled to a chair in the corner.

Tove followed. "Do you think *Cochlea umbrae* were ever *not* monsters?"

"I was just wondering about the name and why they're called that." Nora glanced up at her gratefully. "When I was little, I had to watch this scary documentary in school. I couldn't fall asleep, and Dad tried to make me feel better by telling me what the name for each Umbra really meant. I remember thinking that *cochlea* for 'snail' sounded cute.

And that picture—I think it's serious. I've got to tell Dad—I mean—"

"How are you going to tell him when he's dead?" Eve called, her head lolling back in her chair.

Cyril lowered his book. "Level Three: Happy Moment Time, a temporary imagined state to combat stress on duty. I quote from the textbook: 'Pick a happy moment from your youth and put yourself in it.' We're on duty. This is stressful. Nora's doing Happy Moment Time. Thanks for sharing, Nora."

She stared. "Did you *really* have a training chapter called 'Happy Moment Time'?"

Amar nodded. "It's a great chapter. There's breathing exercises in it too."

"Like any of it helped *you* last night." Eve stretched her arms. "Murdo, how long before we go out?"

"An hour. Amar, would you like me to step in?"

"No, I can handle it." Amar rose. "Okay, knights, this is a *big* failure. We're going out soon and we've got all this bad energy." He marched toward Eve, who covered her face.

"Go away."

"Eve, we need to talk."

"I mean it: Go away, Amar."

He knelt beside her chair. "*Do* you mean it?"

Eve was quiet. Then she lowered her hands. "Look, I was just trying to make everyone laugh. I'm sorry. But that book—you saw it, right? Pretending that Umbrae are soft

170

and cuddly when they're trying to *kill* us every night? They were *never* not monsters. They killed Lucy. And they almost killed *you*—"

Suddenly, Eve's eyes filled with tears. She leaned over and hugged Amar.

"I really, really hate it that you got bit again." Her voice cracked. "When I saw that jerk pull you down, I was ten feet away, and I couldn't—I just—I—" She broke off and buried her face in his shoulder.

Amar returned the hug. For a full minute, he stayed like that. Then—

"Sorry." Eve let him go and huddled back in her chair.

Amar stood. "Are you okay?" he asked gently.

"I'm okay if *you're* okay." Eve wiped her eyes. "*Are* you?"

For a few seconds, he was quiet. "Yes. Thanks."

Amar drifted to Cyril's chair. "Hey Cyril, thanks for bringing up Happy Moment Time like that, and modeling what you say when someone's shared a memory. You're contributing a lot to this Order, in more than just battle."

"Really? I was just talking."

"You're helping with morale. Everyone can feel it."

Cyril flushed happily. "With the bookshop and now this, my whole persona's changed."

Then Amar came to Tove, who was sitting cross-legged by Nora's chair. "Are you good?"

"I'm good, Amar." Tove gave him a thumbs-up.

He offered his fist. She gently bumped it. "Thanks for

hanging out with me this morning. I know I didn't say much, but . . ." He trailed off.

"It's never good to be alone on duty, right?"

"Right."

Amar crouched on the other side of Nora's chair.

"So, Nora: Murdo was telling me after I woke up that it really *was* a bad bite, the worst I could have got. But you froze the venom before it could go anywhere, so it acted like a scratch. My other bites sent venom to my heart. This one didn't come close, thanks to you. You're *really* good at this."

Nora's throat was thick. "I should have been quicker when I saw that man grab you."

"You were doing your job. Remember what Murdo said? Don't talk to citizens. I should have just left them." He gave a faint smile. "Sorry we made fun of your book. We get sensitive when anyone talks about the Umbrae, but that's no excuse. You have the right to read whatever you want."

"I just want to learn more about them, like where they come from and why they're here. Even a book like this might help."

"Will understanding them help you destroy them?"

"Oh, yes! In this video game I play, if you know the histories of different mobs, you get hints about their bosses, like what they're weak to. I've gone up *so* many levels doing research. I'm trying to do the same with the Umbrae."

"If that's your personal strategy, I say go for it. Especially if it involves history." Amar fingered a paper sticking out of the book. "What's that?"

"I'm not sure." Nora fished it out. *"Oh."*

It was an old clipping cut from a bulletin with a photograph of a teenage Murdo Patel.

"Wow." Amar shifted to his knees. "He's so . . . *young.*"

Tove sat up. "Is that who I think it is?"

Cyril and Eve scrambled over.

"That *is* who you think it is," said Cyril. "Check out the hair."

"Whoa," said Eve. "He's . . . um . . . yeah . . . *young.*" She winked at Tove and Nora. *"Very* young. Right?"

Nora slipped the clipping back into the book, her face burning.

Eve burst out laughing.

"Don't," said Amar.

Cyril stood, met Murdo's glance, and crouched again.

"What are you laughing at?" Murdo lowered the tablet. "Nora: Are they bothering you?"

"No, they're just—it's—" She held up the book to cover her red face.

"It's a clipping of a young knight from many years ago," Amar said coolly.

Murdo thought, then smiled and looked back at the tablet.

"That one got me fan mail."

MORE BAIT

The Order of the Hawk was in a good mood when it went outside that night—and soon was in action.

The first *Lupus umbra* burst out of the gloaming as they walked onto the road. It slammed into Nora, knocking her off her feet.

But Nora caught it with her axe as she fell. From her knees, she slashed the next one as it attempted to leap over her.

It was as if the Umbrae had been waiting for them. The silver wolves rushed upon the knights, coming from all sides.

But the Order of the Hawk was like a well-oiled machine, Murdo's muffled voice directing them. He was the bait but the brains as well.

So was Nora.

She saw familiar behavior in these foes. They were not like most dogs but they *were* like Terry: predictable in their cleverness. They would try to outsmart the knights. They feinted, jumped, and lunged to get the knights away from their target: Murdo. She'd seen it all before.

Soon Nora was attacking first, catching them as they lunged, herself feinting and dodging.

Within five minutes, the *Lupus umbrae* weren't leaping for her. Their bright red eyes watched fearfully as she darted toward them, quicker than even they.

Soon all the Umbrae were gone, slashed into lavender mist, and the Order of the Hawk was in front of the shops, its knights panting.

"I just noticed something." Cyril pushed up his glasses. "Nora doesn't like dogs."

They went to the church and waited for ten minutes.

"This is no good." Murdo marched up to the door and pounded. "We need more bait."

A minute later, the minister was standing at the bottom of the church's front step, clutching her coat at her neck.

Murdo had "suggested" she show her thanks for the night before and assist them on their final evening.

The bait of two adults drew a fresh pack of *Lupus umbrae,* enough to surround the car park where the knights had fanned out.

The minister closed her eyes.

"Go on and watch," said Murdo lightly. "It'll be good for your character."

"Ten points to whoever gets the first ten!" Amar slashed two, one after the other.

Tove slid and swung her sword to catch three.

Nora crouched, waiting, and saw the calculation in a *Lupus umbra*'s eyes as it prepared to leap over her.

She darted in and caught it, then lunged, whipped her axe back and forth—

And returned to her place, lavender mist rising from five other spots.

"Nora's killing us." Cyril pierced a *Lupus umbra* heading for the minister. "*Six*. She got *six* already."

An hour passed, then all was quiet.

"Well done, knights." Murdo turned to the minister. "I hope seeing them in action taught you something. Go in."

Wordless and shaking, the minister stumbled inside.

"To the pub!" bellowed Murdo.

There, he dragged the publican out onto the steps and blocked the door behind him.

"I'm not safe out here!" The publican—a pale-faced balding man with a sparse beard—looked around frantically.

"No, you're not. But you didn't care whether my knights were safe or not yesterday. So let's give you a taste of what *we* have to live through. Go forward." Murdo shoved him off the steps.

A *Lupus umbra* lunged for the man, knocking him down. Nora caught it seconds before its jaws would have closed on his face.

"You'll want the antidote for its spit." Nora tore into the next one. "That will leave a bad rash."

The publican choked out a sob. And stared. "How old are you?"

"Twelve." A lunge, a roll, and a leap—Nora swept three *Lupus umbrae* into mist. "How old are you?"

"I—forty-nine."

"No talking to citizens!" roared Murdo.

Wave after wave of *Lupus umbrae* came but the Order of the Hawk was ready. Lavender mist filled the air. The knights kept going, their weapons gleaming black in the light from Murdo's helmet.

Then suddenly—the Umbrae were gone.

The helmet light clicked off.

"Is it dawn already?" Murdo looked around.

The publican, who'd been curled up by the bottom step, raised a rash-covered face. "May I go inside, please?"

Murdo hauled off his goggles and mask. "Yes. Thank you for your help."

They walked back to the lodging house, still in formation, as the sun peeked through the clouds.

Inside, they checked for bites and saliva or fur. Nora had *Lupus umbra* saliva in her hair and had to be doused with the antidote, but that was all. They washed their hands, drank their breakfast protein shakes, then packed their cases and went out to the car.

People lined the road—more than a hundred. As Murdo drove past, the townsfolk saluted.

"Don't look at them," said Murdo.

In the front passenger seat, Cyril bent over the heating vents. "I'll look at this and see how long it'll take my eyelids to fry."

Nora leaned against her window.

Small children with their parents, students like Wilfred, shopkeepers—she waved at Archie—elderly residents, and businesspeople in suits. Each one had their hand to their forehead in a salute as the car passed.

Goodbye, thought Nora. *Good luck.*

She returned their salute, then settled back, took out her sleep mask, and prepared for the drive.

They drove to the coast, to a fishing village in the far north.

A woman in a suit like Daniel's met them in the yard of a trim stone house. She let them in, spoke softly to Murdo, and handed him a single printed page.

"Bad news," said Murdo after she'd left.

They were standing in the main room, a rustic space with weathered beams, white plaster walls, a warm roaring hearth, and padded wooden benches.

"The Order of the Stag just lost a knight. Hours ago. Maria-Luisa Cordova, the senior knight, had their fourth and fifth bite. They're safe at a hospital, but they won't be fighting again."

"Can Stag still go out on duty?" Nora asked.

Murdo folded the paper. "Not with four knights. And no

one has a Level Three ready to move up, not in any region. Poor Huong—she's their Legendary. This is the second time that's happened to Stag this year."

Tove marched over to Nora and hugged her. "Thank you for coming to Noye's Hill."

Amar joined them. "Thank you."

Then Eve. And then Cyril, with two fingers tight on Nora's shoulder. The five of them clung to one another in silence, eyes shut.

"It's an hour before gloaming," Murdo said gently. "Try to relax."

Cyril seized his graphic novel and curled up on a bench. Eve thumped beside him with her fantasy. Tove grabbed her rom-com and sat on the floor by Cyril's feet. Amar opened his case and took out his sword.

Murdo settled onto one of the benches with the tablet.

"Will there be a lot tonight?" Nora sat beside him with the yarn and knitting needles she'd found in the girls' room with a handwritten note:

To Nora Kemp:

Murdo told us that you like to knit. We hope this is the right kind of yarn.

—Staff, National Council Office, Wickston

"I expect a lot," replied Murdo. "This area has regular visits. We'll do a quick pass, then go to the next three villages down the coast. This is seaside with beaches, so what shall we see?"

Cyril's and Eve's eyes met.

"Aranea umbrae," they said in unison.

"Nora's first one in the wild." Tove gave her a thumbs-up.

Amar set his sword on the table. "That's what Nora dealt with before she came to Noye's Hill. She's good with them."

Nora cringed. *Ugh. Spiders.*

ANOTHER BITE

Wickston was quiet and empty when the Order of the Hawk went out. It was as if the Umbrae had heard of the knights' prowess in Ravinscrag and fled. Tidied winter gardens sat in front of nearly every home. Lights were on but the streets were bare. The knights walked for an hour, then returned to the car.

"The Umbrae don't like me here." Murdo pulled off his mask. "We should have brought that publican."

It was snowing as they drove to Innisdene, the next village. They parked just beyond the village's sign.

The Order marched down every street, past houses fully lit. In one, people crowded a window.

"Get away," muttered Eve. "I *hate* it when people watch us."

"I don't understand why we're not attracting any *Aranea umbrae*," said Murdo. "They always find me appealing." He shrugged. "Maybe they need to see the hair."

They walked on past more houses on the silent main street, then to a harbor crowded with fishing boats, and approached a school: a low brick building down a bank with a set of swings.

It looks like my old school in Jedburch.

A whirl of memories from her last day at school hit Nora: Wilfred's grin over lunch, a girl's jeering laughter about her sweater, her glance at the photos of the knights she didn't yet know in the main hall—and back to Wilfred, only this time it was Wilfred staring at the pause screen right after she'd told him she was leaving.

I need to chat with him as soon as I get back.

"Do you see something?" Murdo stepped beside her off the road and pointed his helmet light toward the swings.

"No, I was only thinking of my school and how— Is that a fox?"

Something moved under a swing: a red fox, frantically retreating—

Nora shoved Murdo back, just as an *Aranea umbra* clattered up the bank.

A claw seized her and flipped her onto the asphalt.

Nora's head thumped. For an instant, she couldn't see. But she felt that claw lift—

She whipped up her axe. Mist showered her as the *Aranea umbra* disintegrated.

"Here they come!" shouted Murdo. "Back, everyone!"

Umbrae flooded up the bank, climbing over Nora as if she were a log, clacking and rattling.

"Stop it." Pain drove through Nora's head. She tried to sit up—and collided with an *Aranea umbra,* which began to push her aside, then changed its mind and tried to pin her down.

Lavender mist everywhere. Amar seized her hand and pulled her to her feet.

"Can you walk?"

"I hit my head—"

More mist surrounded them as Amar's sword flashed in a circle and beat back the tide.

"Amar! Nora! Get over here!" Murdo bellowed.

Amar dragged Nora up the road to where the rest of the Order was standing.

"Nora, have you been bitten?" Murdo grabbed her from Amar and knelt.

"I hit my head."

"Do you have a searing, burning pain? Are you dizzy? Queasy?"

"No."

"Can you fight?"

Something moved at the lip of the bank at the edge of Murdo's light.

"Yes," said Nora, though she wanted desperately to lie down on that cold asphalt.

"Schiltron formation," said Murdo. "Quick."

The knights arranged themselves around him.

Murdo let Nora go. "Between Amar and Eve."

The Umbrae surged up before he'd finished speaking.

Nora stumbled to her place. Her head ached but she saw clearly now: a nightmare of spidery legs rattling toward her.

Eve cut down every beast that came near. Amar was faster than the *Aranea umbrae:* When they reached for him, he already had his sword thrust into their furry bodies.

Puff. Puff. Puff.

Clouds of lavender mist surrounded the knights.

Nora fought through the ache in her head, the sting in her scalp, and the sob rising in her throat.

At last, the tide of Umbrae ebbed. The final *Aranea umbrae* retreated down the bank and disappeared into the darkness.

The knights panted, hands on their knees, swords carefully pointed away from one another.

"Well done," came Murdo's muffled voice. "Amar, what do you think?"

"I'd call it a night."

They walked toward the car: Tove in the lead, Murdo with Eve and Cyril flanking him, and Amar at the end. Nora trailed behind.

"Keep up." Amar hastened to close the gap behind Murdo. "Come on, Nora!"

She plodded. But fell farther and farther back.

A crackling, rattling sound came behind her—just one.

Nora spun around.

An *Aranea umbra* was creeping near. It stopped and hunched low.

And before she could move, a claw grabbed her ankle and tripped her onto her back. Something hot pressed against her shoulder—and stung.

Then everything was mist. Amar pulled her up.

The other knights raced to them and finished off the ring of *Aranea umbrae* that had just materialized around Nora.

"Back to the car," said Murdo. "There's more coming and Nora can't fight."

He scooped her into his arms and set off at a sprint, the knights around him.

They reached the car just as the next wave came. Murdo got in first, slamming his door on an *Aranea umbra* claw. Eve fought off others in front of the middle door while Cyril climbed in, then she followed. Amar and Tove together knocked away enough to open the back door and duck inside.

Aranea umbrae crawled up over the car, scratching against the windows.

"They can't get in," said Murdo, as if reminding himself. But he shifted to reverse and drove over the Umbrae, screeching onto the main road. Soon he'd gained enough speed to lose them.

Nora curled up in the front seat, pain thumping through her shoulder.

Eve leaned forward. "Murdo, Amar says Nora got bit."

Murdo shot a glance at Nora. "You're not throwing up; that's always a symptom. Do you have a wound? Does it feel like it's burning? Intense, hot pain."

"I have a wound. It hurts."

He grimaced. "I can't stop; they're keeping up with us just off the road. Eve, climb up here and look."

Eve crawled forward between the seats. "It's okay, Kemp. Where does it hurt?"

"My shoulder." Nora twisted so Eve could see.

"Is there pus?" asked Murdo. "How much venom?"

Eve leaned close. "I don't see pus *or* venom. And it doesn't smell—you know, sour."

"Eve, take her back into your seat with Cyril. Both of you: Check to be sure."

Eve helped Nora crawl back. Whimpering, Nora lay with her head in Cyril's arms as Eve cut open her stretchy top with her sword.

"Water." Eve thrust her hand toward the seat behind.

Amar stuck a bottle of water, then a pad, a spray tube, and a small canister between the headrests. "Disinfectant and the antidote. Remember, if it's a bite, you'll see their tooth marks and then pus and excess venom right after you rinse it. Then please, let's give her the antidote." He flicked on the car light above their heads.

Bracing cold splashed Nora's shoulder, then something soft pressed the wound.

"What do you think, Amar?" said Eve. "No pus or venom."

He squeezed between the armrests until he was hanging over the seat. "Let's have more water. Sorry, Nora. We just don't want to take a chance. It's bad for your immune system if the antidote's trying to freeze venom that's not there. But if it's a bite . . ."

More cold water, then air, then the pad.

"Is it a bite?" called Murdo from the front.

"Yes and no." Amar took the disinfectant and quickly sprayed it over Nora's shoulder.

Numbing cold—and the pain faded.

"It got its teeth in her," Amar went on, "but there's no venom."

"It can't be a bite, then," said Eve. "They spew that everywhere."

"Not always," Cyril said slowly. "That book of bites we had in training—there's a page that said there's a one-in-a-thousand chance that another knight can beat the Umbrae's venom if they slash fast enough." He paused. "Amar was fast."

Amar sat back in his seat. "Tove, can you climb up with Cyril and help Nora come back here with me? Eve, tell Murdo what's going on."

Eve crawled into the front seat and Tove squeezed between the headrests to the middle.

Nora clambered back.

"You're safe, Nora. Just relax. Do you want a hug?"

Nora leaned into his arms, a sob bubbling up in her throat.

He held her silently, not speaking, just holding her until her trembling slowed.

Her shoulder was numb and the cut on her scalp stung, but Nora tried not to think of that. Instead, she focused on Eve's voice in the front, the shadows of Tove's and Cyril's heads, and Amar's arms around her.

THE FINAL DAYS

Murdo reached their lodging in Wickston just after dawn. Amar, Cyril, Tove, and Eve went to bed while Murdo examined the bite on Nora's shoulder.

"A bite wound with no venom. Incredible." He shook his head. "That's been purely hypothetical up to now. I'll let Ursula know."

He spread healing gel over her wound, bandaged it, then gave her a sleeping vial.

Nora staggered into the girls' room and collapsed in her bed. Within minutes, she was asleep.

For the first time on duty, Nora dreamed. It was a series of fragments set in the places where she'd fought the last few days. Umbrae swarmed her, but she was frozen and couldn't move fast enough to stop them.

She woke, heart pounding, to Eve's and Tove's empty beds. A clean uniform waited on a chair.

She dressed and stepped into the sitting room.

It was empty. Voices came from the dining room down the hall.

And a familiar smell.

Two pizza boxes lay open on the table. One was empty with only a greasy circle left. The other still had half a cheese pizza.

"I'm a mess," Tove said, her mouth shiny with grease, "but it's *so* worth it. Oh, look, Nora's awake! Nora, we saved some for you."

Amar slid down the bench, making room. "How's your wound?"

"I can't even feel it."

"Healing gel's *amazing*. I couldn't feel my bite the next day either. Now it's entirely gone." Amar slid two slices onto a plate and held it out to Nora. "Breakfast."

"Is it . . . normal pizza?"

"It's not the pizza we have at Noye's Hill, if that's what you mean. But we're allowed to eat this on duty." Amar set the plate in front of her.

"Have your protein shake too, though; it'll give you energy tonight." Murdo appeared behind them. He was wearing jeans, socks, and a pale blue T-shirt, and almost looked like a normal man. He grabbed a familiar canister from the counter.

Nora gulped it down—this one was flavored like miso soup—then started on the pizza.

After breakfast, Murdo checked the scrape on her scalp

and the wound on her shoulder and proclaimed them both in excellent condition. Then he led everyone into the sitting room, where he'd laid out the techno-fabric trousers he wore during battle and one of his tall techno-leather boots.

"I want you to see what an *Aranea umbra* will do to get something it wants." Murdo straightened the three-inch slash on the trousers. "That's where one grabbed me." He pointed to another slash in the boot. "It went straight through both as well as my sock. This is the latest high-tech armor Noye's Hill has come up with, and it *still* doesn't withstand them."

Then he put his foot on the table and rolled up the hem of his jeans.

A wide, shiny red rash circled his lower calf.

"Oh, Murdo," murmured Eve. "Does it hurt?"

"It burned when it touched me, but it doesn't hurt now with the healing gel. And I gave myself an antidote. Another touch could be enough to poison me, though. Be on your game tonight if you want me there tomorrow. Knights, you have an hour before we leave."

Nora spent it knitting, her fingers flying over the yarn. Then she played her fiddle for five minutes, a random string of reels. Lastly, she sat still for Tove to braid her hair.

"A fishbone with tendrils," said Tove. "Like a princess."

They packed into the car and returned to the fishing village they'd left the night before.

It began snowing big, wet flakes, which increased the farther west they drove.

"The weather's going to make this uncomfortable," Murdo said. "Let's clean up Innisdene and move on to Penmeith. Tomorrow night, we'll do a final pass in those two, Wickston, and Gansey."

In the back seat, Cyril leaned toward Nora. "*What* is that?"

Nora had carried her knitted creation into the car without anyone noticing. "It's an ugly cap I just finished for Amar. Do you think he'll like it?"

"It's hideous. He'll love it."

Tove twisted around in front of them. "Show me?"

Nora pushed the lumpy blue-and-orange cap between the headrests.

Eve burst out laughing. "It looks like vomit!"

Tove handed it to the front. "Amar, Nora's knit an ugly cap for you. Put it on."

Amar pulled on the cap and leaned between the seats so everyone could see.

Tove, Cyril, and Eve burst into giggles.

"Are those *horns*?" Cyril choked.

"Tassels," said Nora.

Amar flipped open the passenger side mirror—and fell forward with his own laughter.

"It's adorable," he called back. "And perfect. Thank you, Nora."

"Are you *really* going to wear it?" demanded Eve.

"Totally. I *do* look eight years old."

At Innisdene, they went straight to the school and waited in their schiltron formation for the *Aranea umbrae*. As the first one scuttled up the bank, an unsettling emotion filled Nora:

Pure hatred.

When it was close, she lashed out.

The Umbrae did not falter that night—except before Amar. A claw would reach, then freeze, as if the beast had just caught sight of his dangling tassels flecked with snow.

Within twenty minutes, the first wave was gone.

The second wave came halfway down the bank, but the knights were ready. They rushed forward and cut the enemy into a huge lavender cloud.

It was like that in Penmeith, the next town, when a wave of *Aranea umbrae* scuttled over the pebble beach. But they were sluggish and the knights' swords and axe soon tore them into mist. The Order spent only an hour on those streets and by the seaside before returning to the car.

"That was a strangely easy night," said Murdo as he drove back to their lodging. "I think Nora needs to knit more ugly caps."

One more week of driving and battles.

The Order of the Hawk scoured the streets of the four

little fishing villages through a frozen rain that the stretchy fabrics barely kept off. Only a few waves of *Aranea umbrae* came forth in each town. They seemed hesitant. More than once, the Order gave chase. Then it was morning, and they returned to their lodging, packed up, and went on.

To Aberdale, a town owned by an earl, with a rose-colored postbox in its center. They met an army of *Aranea umbrae* on the green.

To Mithwaith, where they caught a teenager sneaking out to see his boyfriend—and slashed the pack of *Lupus umbrae* that materialized around them.

To Deemsborough, where the River Deems rippled alongside the main road and *Cochlea umbrae* slithered out from under an eighteenth-century bridge.

Then back to the very first bothy for three nights, and the new concentration of Umbrae that had swelled in the valley.

Nora fought, drank her protein shakes, went to bed with her muscles like custard—and dreamed of being unable to fight. She woke with her heart pounding and spent an hour knitting, reading, and playing fiddle to calm down. She made caps for everyone with the skeins of yarn that had been waiting for her in Aberdale: lumpy turquoise, silky baby blue, neon blue and silver, and fuzzy azure. Eve picked the blue-and-silver cap, which had a massive pom-pom on top. Tove claimed the baby blue with its floppy ears. And Cyril chose the turquoise—with actual horns. Nora wore the fuzzy azure with her pale blue scarf tied around it, the bow in front.

Even the *Cochlea umbrae* in the valley faltered at the sight of the knights in their ugly-cute caps.

When they returned to the bothy after their last night in the valley path, a night of mostly waiting, Murdo took out the tablet and projected the map over the table.

"See anything?" Patterns emerged: blue showing their route, with purple, green, and red lines showing the other Orders'. "What do you notice about the yellow dots?"

Eve sat back with a grin.

"We're getting our numbers back!" Tove punched the air.

"We left Noye's Hill as sticks of gum but now we've all been chewed up together." Cyril paused. "Right? We've bonded properly. That's what I meant."

Amar said nothing.

"Why do the other lines have so many yellow dots while we have none?" asked Nora. "Have the other Orders not gone out yet?"

Snickering.

"I wouldn't blame the Order of the Stag for their performance, considering they just lost a knight." Murdo pointed to the purple lines, which swarmed with yellow.

Eve touched one of the green lines. "But you *can* blame Oak. They've been out for nearly a week. Look at that. What a mess."

More snickering.

194

Nora stiffened. *That's really mean. This is scary and they're doing their best.*

"They must be having trouble with their new knight," said Amar softly. "That's not funny."

The snickering stopped.

"How many active Orders are there now?" Nora counted on her fingers. "Us, Oak—is there another?"

"Boar," said Murdo. "When we left Noye's Hill, they were in the crowd. Pavith Singh Barmi, their Legendary, was the one who complimented you."

Nora held out a third finger. "Is that it? And the map—except for our line, it's all yellow."

"Don't worry about the rest." Murdo flashed a smile. "When Hawk goes out, we do *more* than our share. We'll take care of the rest of the map on other duties." He zoomed out until all of Brannland and its islands were visible. "Maybe we'll take a road trip down to Bardownie and the southern towns. Now that we've tidied the north, we might as well clean up the south."

The knights grinned.

Except for Amar.

Across the table, he was sitting quietly, gazing at the map, his jaw tight.

The image of the *Lupus umbra* attacking Amar came back to Nora. Her smile faded.

Brannland's being overrun.

And three Orders won't be enough to stop them.

195

COMING HOME

"There's this routine I do when we come home from duty: As soon as we're at Noye's Hill, I count the people in my Order. I do it twice, make sure they're all here, and see if I can tell how they're doing: like, here in their body, and here in their heads." [pause] "It helps me be here both ways too."

—Tove Sinclair, Order of the Hawk
The Noye's Hill Interviews (internal)

At the gates and then the front door, soldiers saluted the Order of the Hawk. Murdo led the way through all the doors to the room where Nora had been scanned the first time she'd come to Noye's Hill.

The room was different. Hospital beds, box-like monitors

with blinking lights, racks of vials, glowing bars of different-ent colors, and trays of syringes lined the walls. Dr. Liu was there with her gold-tipped hair and her white lab coat, and Ursula.

The director marched up to Amar. "That was an *extraordinary* duty, Amar. Your knights did well. And *you* were exceptional."

His face instantly turned cold. "Thank you."

"I know what you're thinking. But even with a third bite, you achieved astounding numbers—and fulfilled a senior knight's highest responsibility: to keep their knights safe and ensure they return home."

"We were lucky."

"An Order's success comes from more than luck, Amar. You proved yourself in this duty."

For a few seconds, they stared at each other.

Amar's icy look faded. "Thanks."

Ursula shook his hand, then went to the rest of the knights. One by one, she spoke of their successful duties: their exceptional skill and brilliant performances. Tove blushed. Eve smiled. Cyril beamed.

When Ursula came to Nora, she shook Nora's hand, but then, for a few seconds, was silent.

"I've never heard of anyone achieving your success in their first duty," Ursula said at last. "Nora, you adapted to this difficult work with ease. You made a difference for your Order. Especially Amar. We're going to see how much venom he absorbed, but it's highly unusual for someone to give the antidote in the heat of battle with such confidence. Well done."

Then she left the line of knights and approached Murdo. "You said you wished to talk as soon as you returned. My office?"

He nodded.

Ursula marched to the door. "Mei-Mei? They're yours."

As soon as Ursula and Murdo were gone, Dr. Liu gestured to a hospital bed. "Have a seat, Amar. Nora, you're next." She pointed to another bed across the room.

Nora skittered to her bed and clambered up.

Dr. Liu sauntered to Amar. "Let's see that third bite, Hawk."

Amar's face dropped back into the cold, blank look he'd worn for much of their last duty. Wordlessly, he rolled up his sleeve.

Humming, Dr. Liu peeled back the gauze and examined the wound. She took a blood sample, then stuck a light blue circle onto Amar's forehead. And another. And a third.

Medicine? Nora wondered. Amar's hard look had turned into a helpless one. *Wait. Are those* smiley *stickers?*

Within seconds, Dr. Liu had covered Amar's face.

"That looks better. You *should* be smiling with numbers like yours: You have a two hundred and forty-three percent success rate. Unbelievable. Now keep those on for a few seconds so I can check your immunity."

The stickers were already changing color: from sky blue to bright azure.

Dr. Liu strapped a cuff onto Amar's arm. "Your stickers say your immunity is still good. And I can see why: Your blood test shows high levels of completely obliterated venom that didn't make it anywhere near your heart. Never seen *that* before."

Amar raised his chin. "Thanks to Nora."

"Yeah, I heard. You must be super fast, Hawk." In three steps, Dr. Liu was at Nora's bed, her fist ready for a bump. "Roll up your sleeve for me?"

Trembling, Nora watched the needle prick, and then the cuff tighten around her bare arm.

"See if you can relax." Dr. Liu pressed a smiley sticker on her forehead. "How was your first duty?"

"Scary," Nora whispered. "But my Order's wonderful."

"Speaking of that, let's see this bite-with-no-venom."

Dr. Liu picked off the gauze and held a magnifier over the wound.

"Ooo, totally healed. You won't even have a scar." She held up a vial of blood. "And check this out: Not a trace of venom." She grinned. "Look at that bright blue sticker. Full immunity. Officially, you're at zero bites, Nora Kemp. Hey Amar: How do you keep being so amazing every time you go out?"

Dr. Liu did a thorough examination of each knight, then

sent them into a huge bathroom near the entry room with five shower stalls and towels over the doors.

"This is the best part of coming home." Amar, his face now sticker-free, put his hand on a stall. "Washing everything away. And doing it in *consistently* hot water."

Nora stood under the driving hot water for a long time. So much of what she'd just seen made her feel good. Ursula, Director of the National Council, had come down to see them. She cared about her knights. So did Dr. Liu. They'd both made Amar feel better.

Because we mean a lot to them.

Nora frowned.

Because they need us.

Because Brannland is being overrun.

Nora thrust her face into the tingling water.

When she finished, she found a clean royal-blue uniform under the towel on her stall door—with a handwritten note:

Welcome home, Nora! Congratulations on a <u>marvelous</u> first duty. I knew you could do it. We on staff are all very, <u>very</u> proud of you.

—Daniel Fenton

I guess he's seen our numbers.

Nora couldn't help but smile. She dressed and came out.

Tove was alone outside the stalls. "Everyone was going to wait, but I told them to go up. There's a fancy tea. Want me to give you a quick four-strand?"

No one was in the hall when they emerged: the same hall where Nora had first walked with Daniel and Shaun—years ago, it felt.

Tove led the way up the Hawks' spiral staircase to a room near the top. Inside, the other knights and Murdo were waiting around a table covered with a lavish spread.

Tiny frosted pastries, little sandwiches, and full-size scones crowded a three-tier silver stand. A cake with whipped cream and raspberries sat off to the side. Steam curled from the spout of a huge teapot.

Nora and Tove slid into the two open seats.

"First, your tea." Murdo lifted the teapot and served everyone. "Now dig in."

Amar seized a currant scone and smeared it with strawberry jam.

Tove grabbed four little pastries from the tier.

Eve took a cheese scone and three little sandwiches.

Cyril cut into the sponge cake and slid a huge slice onto his plate.

This is . . . bizarre. We come back from destroying monsters for two weeks straight with no hot showers, no real downtime, and terrifying battles—to a formal afternoon tea?

"What's training like today?" Nora asked.

"There isn't any. This is our one day—or night, I should say—of total rest." Amar held out a plate. "Have a scone."

"Wait." Tove plucked a tiny almond-covered pastry from the top tier and slid it onto the plate. "This is the best one."

"And this." Eve added a little sandwich. "That's cream cheese and olive with hot chilies. Trust me, it's incredible."

They were all smiling at her, but something bleak flickered behind their expressions.

Nora took the plate. "Is everyone all right?"

"It's hard to come home," Murdo said. "If you don't feel it now, you will in an hour."

Amar nodded.

Tove's jaw tightened.

Eve closed her eyes.

Cyril stared at the table.

"Don't think of that now. Eat as much as you like. Going on duty is draining."

Nora sipped her tea, savoring it. "What does everyone do on the first day back?"

"We sit in our common room and read the books we picked up in our book run." Amar grinned. "*All* day."

That sounds like a dream.

Nora added butter and jam to her plate, then pointed to the cake by Cyril's elbow. "Will you cut me a piece of that? The same size as yours, please."

THE NIGHTMARE PAGE

"It seems increasingly unlikely that the Umbrae will ever return to their historical forms. It is hard sometimes to come to terms with what that means for the future of Brannland."

—*The Umbrae: Nature's Perfect Revenge*

Two piles of books from the bookshop run, each stacked as tall as her bed, waited on the floor of Nora's room.

"We put our new books in the library after the first day," Amar said as he followed her in, "since there's not room for them here. But if there's one you want to keep by your bed, that's fine."

"May I keep two?" Nora hesitated. "And I have that one from the library I'm reading. May I keep that here as well?"

"We're not supposed to have personal possessions in our rooms, or clutter." A smile tugged at his lips. "I stick books under my bed."

"How many do you have there?"

He glanced at the door. "Twelve."

They joined the other knights in the common room and curled up on the sofas with their books, Nora beside Cyril, who muttered quietly to himself as he read.

It was like a school vacation when she was little and had sat with Owen on the chairs by the fire, each with their books, relishing the soft quiet that came with studied concentration.

Nora had chosen *The Umbrae: Nature's Perfect Revenge*. It was short and heavily illustrated, and the early pictures of the Umbrae were beautiful: shadowy *Cochlea umbrae* rippling over a river like blue satin ribbons, sparkling *Lupus umbrae* blending in with the snow atop mountains, *Aranea umbrae* with delicate twig-like bodies poised among the sheep on hillsides. She'd never thought of shadow beasts as lovely.

They grew less lovely as the chapters went on, gaining aspects of their current forms—slime, teeth, menace—until the final illustrations, which were terrifyingly real.

"Does anyone want snacks?" Amar went to the door and came back with two baskets that had been waiting outside.

Grapes, strawberries, and cheese and crackers with ice-cold bottles of sparkling water. Amar distributed the food and everyone sat munching.

This is weirdly . . . normal.

"What's everyone's book like?" Amar asked.

"So far, most of the characters in mine have died and turned into zombies, except the heroine, who's been ripping them apart." Eve grinned. "It's fabulous."

Cyril waved his book. "Mine's about Vikings invading a bug-infested town that uses bugs in its defenses. It's the grossest thing I've ever read and I love it."

"Mine's sweet and powerful," said Tove. "The protagonist's trying to run her family's bakery and everything's going wrong."

"What are you reading, Nora?" asked Amar.

"Mine's about the Umbrae." She hesitated. "It says they used to be gentle and shy. Like three hundred years ago."

"Is it *that* book?" Eve made a face. "I wouldn't believe anything *it* says."

"I know. I wouldn't. Except . . . it feels real."

"It doesn't *look* real."

Nora traced her finger over the cover. "This library book I was reading said the worst Umbrae were found near mines. This book goes into that even more. It says that mining destroyed their habitat—especially *Cochlea umbrae,* because it polluted their water."

"I've read that too." Amar reached out. "May I? Trade books for a minute?"

He's going to think this has too many pictures for someone my age. But Nora handed it over.

Everyone went back to reading. Nora glanced at Amar. He was focusing on her book, examining the pictures, reading the text. When he was done, he set the book down, his face thoughtful.

"Okay, tell us." Eve lowered her novel. "Is it as bad as it looks?"

"It's actually quite good. It's hypothetical in the beginning about the Umbrae because no one knows what they were like, and it makes that clear. But the rest of it's factual."

"Who's the author?" Tove asked.

Amar examined the cover, then flipped the book open. "That's funny. It's by Lakshmi Tulloch. She was one of the early scientists on MacAskill's team. I didn't know any of them wrote books."

"Is it short enough to read to us?" asked Tove.

"I think so."

In his strong, even voice, Amar read aloud, showing the pictures as he went.

No one smiled. The parts that had seemed ridiculous when Eve had read them on duty now seemed serious and even sinister in Amar's reading.

By the end, everyone's face was grave.

"I never read anything like that in training," said Eve slowly. "What do you think that book's meant to do?"

"Warn citizens not to be stupid?" But even Cyril's voice was quiet.

Tove frowned. "It's weird that one of the early scientists

wrote it, and not the people who write the bulletins. I never knew scientists wrote this kind of thing."

"What were the early scientists like?" Nora asked.

"Young and wildly imaginative." Amar sat back. "People don't remember that MacAskill was only thirty when he invented his Iron and came up with the Orders. They were all geniuses."

"They were weirdos," said Cyril. "Before they made the Orders, they tried out freaky kid-like weapons for grown-ups: liquid Iron squirt guns, weighted nets, exploding kites. But if you're a grown-up and you're facing an enemy that turns into a shadow and back again in less than a second, you don't have a chance. Even with liquid Iron squirt guns."

"I don't know about anyone but MacAskill," admitted Eve, "and I don't know much except his picture was everywhere and he created all the training games we played." She paused. "Do you remember the invasion game? You had to climb over all sorts of obstacles—like branches and rocks—to get the flag, and then it took forever to untie it while the other team was going for you."

"My dad played a game like that with me," said Nora. "We called it Rough Terrain."

Everyone stared.

"You're kidding," said Eve. "That's what *we* called it."

"Really? Maybe Dad knew a knight." And then she remembered the former knight she'd met by the pool. *Nadia Bakari. She said she'd known Dad.*

"That must be it." Amar flipped again through *The Umbrae: Nature's Perfect Revenge.* He stopped at the illustration over the back end pages. "Does anyone remember the unit in Level Three that covered bait-posts? Cyril, you were in training most recently. Do you remember something that looked like this?"

He held up the book.

The illustration showed layers of soil, then stone, and a series of sinister black roots threading through them, all the way across Brannland and under the sea to the Upper Islands.

Nora flinched. She remembered a similar picture from the website she'd looked at with Wilfred.

"That's a rooted bait-post." Cyril cringed. "Will you close that?"

Amar shut the book. "That's what it looked like to me too."

"What's a bait-post?" Nora asked. "You mentioned them before."

"Bait-posts were a *big* mistake. When MacAskill invented his Iron to repel Umbrae, he also invented MacAskill Ore, which *attracts* Umbrae. That's what bait-posts are made of. You won't read about them except in Level Three because they're so terrifying."

"Why would anyone build something with MacAskill Ore?" Nora hugged herself.

"MacAskill thought that if they planted bait-posts in different spots over Brannland, it'd draw *all* the Umbrae and they'd be easy to annihilate. So he planted them and set up Orders of knights around each one. And then he made a new discovery: His Ore didn't just *attract* the Umbrae; it more than doubled their spores at dawn. Eight knights died before he figured that out."

Eve rolled her eyes. "Talk about the importance of knowing your substances *before* putting them in the field."

"Totally," said Amar. "But don't worry, Nora; MacAskill himself went around and dug up those five bait-posts. They're in secure storage here at Noye's Hill."

Here? Nora shuddered.

Tove rested her chin on her hands. "I remember that page in training. It had a little box that said bait-posts root if you leave them in the ground for more than a day. MacAskill had trouble digging them up because they'd rooted so deep."

Cyril curled up on his sofa.

"He hypothesized that if you leave them for longer, the roots will spread—that was the caption for that picture." Tove shifted.

"Would you *stop* talking about it?" Cyril burrowed his face into a cushion.

Amar slid the book aside. "Okay, everyone, let's do some circular breathing. In for one, two, three, four. Hold it one, two, three, four."

Amar led three rounds of breathing. When he was done, Cyril sat up, but still didn't look at anyone.

"Should we put in an order for ice cream?" Amar asked gently.

Nora had never felt closer to her Order than on that afternoon in their common room. They had massive ice cream sundaes, took turns reading Cyril's book, ate a huge dinner of pasta with garlic bread that was delivered to their door, then read until they were sleepy.

Before they went to bed, everyone bumped fists.

"Thanks for an incredible duty, knights," Amar said. "See you in about six hours for our 'morning' run. Nora, we'll be back to off-duty time in a couple of days."

As soon as she closed her door, Nora picked up her game player from her fiddle case and logged in. It was before dawn, close to what had been bedtime when they'd been on duty, so Wilfred wasn't on. She sent him a quick chat to let him know she was back, then put it away and went to bed.

As she pulled down the blanket, a scrap of paper caught her eye. It was tucked under the sheet with a few scribbled words:

Talk when you get back?

—Nadia Bakari

THE SECRET OF OWEN KEMP

Nora lay in bed until she was sure that everyone else was asleep, then crept into the dark common room, into the dimly lit hall, and down the stairs.

She was jumpy, but with anticipation as much as with nerves. Nadia Bakari had known Owen Kemp. And they'd been friends: He'd played his fiddle for her. Nora didn't know much about her father's past except he'd run away from an abusive family. She'd never asked questions, and he'd never shared more. This would be her chance to learn about her father's history—a happy one with his friend. She realized as she went on, her heart beating faster and faster, how much she needed to know that her father had been happy.

At last, Nora reached the room with the pool and the laboratory door.

"Hey there, Hawk."

Dr. Liu—without her lab coat, in her gold-colored shirt with the wyvern tattoo vivid against her skin—was standing behind her.

Nora froze. "I was going to the pool—"

"It's okay. Nadia asked me to meet you. Come on with me."

Dr. Liu led Nora up the stairs a flight and stopped at the landing. She leaned close to a retinal scanner.

A click. A crack. A hidden door opened.

Nora followed her through.

It was an empty black hallway with close walls. Another door lay ahead.

Suddenly, Nora felt sick.

I should have told Amar. I shouldn't be here without my Order—

The door opened.

Nadia Bakari stood inside, in a trim black sweater and jeans.

"I'm sorry I had to sneak you in." Her smile was tired. "But I wanted to talk with you as soon as you returned." She gestured at the room. "Come in. It's just Mei-Mei and me, and it's four a.m., so no one's going to hear us."

Nora slipped past her into a room much like her Order's common room, only there were two sofas, gold and black, and a little coffee table between them with clawed dragon feet.

Dr. Liu closed the door and gently kissed Nadia Bakari's cheek.

"Courage, Wyvern," Dr. Liu murmured. Then, to Nora: "Want some chamomile tea?"

I shouldn't be here.

But Nora said yes, and, when Nadia Bakari motioned toward one of the sofas, she sat, her heart pounding. "Thank you for speaking with me, Dr. Bakari."

"Call me Nadia." The scientist sank onto the sofa across from her. "I'm sorry I dropped that bit of information about your father and left, but I couldn't tell you more before you went on duty; I didn't want to scare you."

"I don't think it would have scared me to learn more about Dad. When did you meet him?"

Dr. Liu returned with the tea in three black mugs. She handed them around, then settled on the sofa beside Nadia.

"I need to say this before anything else." Nadia clasped her mug. "Your dad was the bravest boy I knew. He and I were the best of friends. For years."

"For years?" Nora echoed. "Did you know him when he was still living at home?"

Nadia took a photo from the pocket of her sweater. "Do you recognize this boy?"

It was a picture like the ones on the wall at school: a knight, unsmiling.

Nora shook her head. "Is that another of Dad's friends? I never met him."

"This is Jack Goudie. You won't see this picture on display or in any books. He disappeared. He'd gone through training to become a knight, then ran off during his first duty after his first battle."

Nora studied the picture. There was no sign of fear in that boy's face; in fact, he looked excited, barely able to tamp down a smile.

"Why did he run off? Did he get bit?"

"Twice. When we came inside, he was frantic. Our Legendary sent us all to bed and sat alone with him. I thought she'd calm him down and tell him that two bites didn't matter. It'd be better his next time out. He was still a fine knight. But once she went to sleep, he walked out of the bothy."

"He probably thought he'd failed." Nora thought of Amar. "You didn't find him after? Maybe he just needed to be alone for a bit."

"No one found him. The Council sent soldiers to comb the area. No luck. I never heard about him again. Then one day, I was examining the newest bite victims—I research how venom affects citizens—and there was Jack Goudie, all grown up. Except his death certificate said he was Owen Kemp."

Nora shook her head. "Dad must have had—what's it called?—a doppelganger. Someone who looks like you."

"We have Jack Goudie's blood on file from his immunity test, just as we have yours. Owen Kemp's matched Jack's. That's your dad in the picture, Nora."

Everything slowed around her.

Owen had said that his childhood had been dark and miserable.

He'd spent his teen years in hiding. He'd told her no more than that.

And she'd never seen him truly angry, except at her test, at Daniel Fenton.

The proud young face stared up at her.

"It never occurred to me that you were Jack's daughter," Dr. Liu said wistfully. "I mean, I didn't know him as a Kemp."

"I knew from the death records that he'd left a wife and daughter, but I had no idea you were a knight, here, until I heard you play his music." Nadia sighed. "That reel . . . I heard it all through training; it was his favorite thing to play. But he stopped playing when he came to Noye's Hill."

"Yeah," said Dr. Liu, "I never heard it."

"Can you blame him?" Nadia murmured. "We were *awful* to him."

Nora stiffened. "Awful? Wasn't he in your Order?"

Dr. Liu leaned forward. "Annabelle, our senior knight, had been hoping for an all-girl Order. She was very good at hiding things and our Legendary, Jenny Tsukada, never noticed. And then that first battle . . . he got two bites because Annabelle didn't let us stop, even though we were *all* worn out. Then on the drive, she sat in the back just with Jack—right behind Nadia and me—and told him *he* was why our numbers would be low."

Nora looked at Nadia. "If he was your best friend, why didn't you tell her to stop?"

215

"I wasn't a good friend. I was young. Foolish. I felt giddy around all those girls. And Jack . . . he didn't belong. We made sure he felt that. In many small, cruel ways." Her voice faded.

Nora set her mug on the coffee table. "I want to go."

Dr. Liu grabbed Nora's mug and pressed it back into her hands. "No, not like this. You have no idea what it was like when we realized he was gone. First, Nadia and I felt so bad, we threw up. And Jenny—she got the truth about Annabelle and chewed out everyone like you'd never believe. Then Sir Colm—he flew in to the bothy by helicopter a few hours before gloaming and made us all drive to our last battleground. It was by some mines and he went down into them alone to see if Jack was hiding there. When he came out, he looked like he'd seen a ghost: literally shaking."

"He cut Annabelle from the Order that very night and sent her from Noye's Hill in disgrace." Nadia's eyes were haunted. "Then he put the rest of us on probation. And he made his Rules: Knights had to be loyal to their Order and to the people in their Order alone."

"The MacAskill Rules?" Nora's throat was dry. "MacAskill was alive then?"

"He was in his eighties," said Dr. Liu. "Died a couple of years later."

"Sir Colm and your dad were good, good friends." Nadia sat back. "That's why he was so angry. They spent a lot of time talking in Sir Colm's office, just the two of them."

"Yeah, Sir Colm scooped up Jack during library time his first day. The rest of us were *so* jealous."

Nora closed her eyes. Once, during their month alone in the Upper Islands, Owen Kemp had railed against Colm MacAskill. He'd called him a monster, a liar, a thief. And then he'd wept.

A hand touched her arm. "Are you all right?"

Nora opened her eyes. Nadia Bakari was kneeling beside her at the end of the sofa.

Nora nodded and slowly drank her tea.

"Can I tell you something?" Nadia's voice broke. "When I heard you say that you were Owen Kemp's daughter, I felt peace for the first time. Because it meant my friend hadn't been alone. He'd been in love. He'd had a life, a family. I wanted to ask you about that. Was he happy?"

Nora straightened. "He was *very* happy. We lived on a farm in an old stone house—and he loved that house, and our sheep and Mum and me. And his fiddle—I have it now, but it was his first, and he played it every day. He'd traveled all over Brannland learning fiddle when he was young."

"You're good with the fiddle. Like Jack." Nadia returned to her sofa, slid the photo back into her pocket, and picked up her tea. "So. Tell me about *your* first duty. Mei-Mei said you were brilliant but I want to hear it in your own words."

"I guess . . . I did okay."

"*That's* the understatement of the century. You were incredible." Dr. Liu rocked forward. "You're a perfect Hawk.

I liked you the moment I met you—you're the sweetest kid who's ever walked through that door—and I'm *so* tickled you're a mean fighter too."

"Coming here at twelve, no training. Is that pure talent or what?" Nadia faltered. "I guess Jack thought it'd be bad for you."

"Sorry, Jack," said Dr. Liu. "But she's a natural."

Nadia smiled faintly. "Jack would be furious if he knew we were keeping his brilliant girl up from her bed. You've got a full day of training tomorrow."

It hurt Nora to hear them talk about Owen like that—as Jack, as someone she'd never known.

Both Wyverns walked Nora to the door by the stairs. Before she started back to her room, they promised that they'd always be there for her if she needed them.

The Hawk common room was still dark. All the bedroom doors were shut except hers. Nora crept in, closed her door, and climbed into bed.

Thoughts whirled in her mind:

Of her father, who'd been a knight, yet kept it secret, even from Deena.

Who'd been trained. Who'd been in that world of intense friendship and purpose since he was seven.

Who'd been bitten twice because of his senior knight.

Who'd been bullied.

And no one had known.

Nora curled up tight in her bed and let herself cry.

NORA'S SECRET

A new bout of training began the next day—with twenty laps.

Nora didn't know how to tell her Order what she'd learned. It hurt too much to say it, yet she couldn't stop thinking about her dad. But she knew she shouldn't keep secrets.

I wonder if people bullied Dad on this track.

In ten minutes, Nora doubled over gasping.

"Can I—have—a rest?"

"No! Keep up with this interval! You need to work on your endurance." Amar jogged by.

I should tell him.

Tove grabbed her hand and pulled her along a few feet. "Shuffle."

"There'll be a yummy protein shake for you when you're done," said Cyril as he shot past.

Tove would understand. And Cyril.

"Water." Eve thrust a bottle into her hand and pounded by.

On his next lap, Amar took the bottle. "Not until you start running again. Sorry."

Nora launched into a shuffle.

"That's pitiful." Amar handed the water back. "Okay, this is another walking interval. Have a drink."

Nora gulped it down, then passed it back to Amar and plunged on.

I need to tell someone. But I'm almost crying again. . . . I'll do it after breakfast.

But she couldn't. She promised herself she'd speak after the weight room, then lunch, then library time. At the start of each new activity, she imagined what she'd tell them— *Dad was a knight, and he ran away. Because he was bullied—* but when it was time, the words lodged in her throat.

What if they'd say that Jack should have taken it?

What if they called him a coward for running away?

After library time, the Order went to the target room on a floor Nora had never seen. The space was smaller than the bedrooms and all white.

"You'll like this." Amar handed her a hard foam paddle. "Strike the red dot when it shows up on the wall. Don't worry about smashing it into smithereens; it won't fly apart in any cool way. The goal is just to hit it."

"And not hit me." Tove took a second paddle from Amar. "I'm going to be in there with you."

Amar closed the door behind them and leaned over the window with Eve and Cyril. "Ready?"

A bright red dot, the size of a cherry, appeared on the white wall.

Nora slapped it with her paddle.

Another appeared near her feet, then another above her head.

She ducked and got the lower one while Tove thumped the higher.

"I'll go high, you go low." Tove whacked the next.

I'll go high and you go low, Nora.

Owen's voice. He'd winked, then raised his fiddle to his chin as she raised hers.

A pang filled Nora's stomach—and the words came out. "Tove? I learned something last night about my dad."

Red dots covered the wall near the ground. Nora dropped to her knees and slammed them.

"Did you go out somewhere? I thought I heard your door open."

More dots, more slamming.

"I went to see Nadia Bakari—a scientist from the laboratory. She'd known my dad and left me a note. My dad . . . he'd been a knight, Tove. A Wyvern in her Order."

"Really?" Tove slapped a series of dots on the ceiling. "He never told you? And he didn't want you to be trained?"

"He—wasn't a knight for long; he ran away after his first battle. He was bit twice." Nora attacked the dots on the wall, her throat thick. And then she said the worst part. "He left because his Order bullied him. And it sounds like they let him get bit on purpose." Tears rushed down her cheeks.

Tove lowered the paddle. "Amar, stop the targets."

The door opened a crack. Amar stuck his head in. "What's wrong?"

"Nora just said something you all need to hear. Nora? Can you tell them?"

The door opened all the way.

Nora took a deep, trembling breath. And then, her eyes on the floor, she told them. By the end, she could barely speak.

Tove's arm, which had been around her shoulders the whole time, tightened. "It's okay, Nora. You're here with us."

Wordlessly, Eve joined the hug and pressed her cheek against Nora's.

Cyril raised his hand. "I say let's chain those two scientists to the gates at gloaming—on the *outside.*"

"We're not going to chain anyone outside," Amar said, "but this is bad. Nora: I'm so sorry. Your dad didn't deserve that. I can't believe his Legendary let that happen." A pause. "Or that his senior knight *actively* tried to destroy their Order."

"I wish your dad had told someone," Tove murmured. "Like Colm MacAskill in one of their meetings."

"I bet those meetings are one of the reasons they bullied

him," Eve said. "And he didn't tell anyone because he was trying to be . . . good, and not mess things up."

Amar nodded. "It sounds like Nora's dad didn't have anyone he could trust."

Nora struggled to speak. "I—I wish I could do something for Dad. I know I can't make it better, but . . ." Her voice broke.

Amar slipped his arm around her too. "Okay, knights. We're going to get the full story, and put all this on record so everyone knows what happened. Let's make this an official part of the history of the MacAskill Orders and get your dad's picture back on the walls. How does that sound, Nora? Good?" Then his voice turned cold. "But let's start by finding out why Jack Goudie's Legendary didn't notice anything."

JENNY TSUKADA

Amar led them through the empty halls to a stairwell at the far end of the fortress: the Wyvern tower where their Legendary still lived.

It was just like Hawk's stairway. They passed the door to the Wyvern common room, the Wyvern library, the tearoom—all locked—until they reached a black door at the very top.

"She must be a scary Wyvern if they're keeping her up here alone." Cyril began bouncing.

"We're scary too." Amar knocked.

Ten seconds passed.

Amar knocked again.

"We should barge in," said Eve.

Tove shook her head. "I don't think you barge in on Legendaries."

"Especially since she might be sleeping with her sword

by her side and would hack us to death." Cyril bounced harder. "I wish we'd brought our swords. Then we could hack *her* to death—"

The door opened, revealing a trim elderly woman in a black uniform with a gold patch and a golden wyvern pin.

"What are Hawks doing at my door, talking about hacking someone with their swords?" Her voice was like a dull knife: soft, but still dangerous.

"Pardon us," Amar said, his voice below freezing. "We have a question. We understand you were a Legendary when Sir Colm MacAskill was alive. Could you tell us about the knight he befriended—"

"I'm not here to answer your questions. If you were one of *my* knights, you'd be training for your next duty right now."

Amar's eyes glittered. "I need this question answered, as it pertains to one of *my* knights. It also pertains to a certain Wyvern who didn't understand that the emotional health of an Order is one of a senior knight's *top* responsibilities. That's something I take very seriously."

A long pause. Then—"I will give you five minutes."

They followed her into a chamber hung with billowy black-and-gold cloth. The rug was black too, with a gold pattern of a wyvern just like the pin.

Jenny Tsukada gestured to a cluster of cushy chairs and settled into one of them. "What 'friendship' do you want to know about? Sir Colm talked to all the knights."

Nora slid into the chair closest to the Legendary. "This

knight was different. He and Sir Colm were good friends. But he ran away after his first battle—"

"None of my knights ran away." Jenny Tsukada picked up a glass of water from a nearby table.

Amar and Nora exchanged glances.

"Not Jack Goudie?" Nora held her breath.

The Legendary shook her head. "I've never heard that name."

Amar took another chair. Tove and Cyril settled on its arms. Eve leaned against Nora's.

"I wonder if Ursula has," Amar said.

"No, she *hasn't*. Because if a knight *had* run away, it'd be a disgrace, enough to bring down an Order. If a knight *had* run away during Sir Colm MacAskill's time, Sir Colm would have made sure that every record of that knight would have been erased."

"Except his blood sample," said Nora. "From when he was tested when he was seven."

"Did you come here to start trouble?" Jenny snapped. "It's time for you to go—"

"Why did you let your Order bully my dad?" Nora blurted.

The harsh mask on the old woman's face instantly dissolved. "Jack's your father?"

"Yes. But he never told me he'd been a knight. And he's dead now. So he can't tell me anything."

The Legendary closed her eyes. For ten long seconds, she didn't move. When she opened her eyes, they were wet.

"I didn't know how they'd treated him until he'd gone." Her voice was much softer. "They concealed it. He said nothing. And then he had his first battle, and ran away. But that was because of what he'd smelled that night, not his Order."

Amar shook his head. "He ran away because his senior knight—"

"I don't think so. Even with her vile behavior, I don't think he'd have given up everything if there hadn't been that smell." Jenny hesitated. "He said it was like rot. They were by the mines and the Umbrae were worse there than anywhere I'd seen. I'd thought Jack meant the smell of his bites—he had two. But after the rest had gone to bed, Jack told me he'd smelled a rooted bait-post: a foul, barnyard smell. He remembered reading about that odor in training."

Cyril bolted up.

"It's okay, Cyril," Amar said gently. "It couldn't have been a bait-post. They're all here in storage." He glanced at Jenny Tsukada. "Yes?"

"Yes. When you're a Legendary and have your full tour of Noye's Hill, they'll show you where." She cleared her throat. "I went down to count them when we returned. There are only five, and every one was still in its case."

Cyril sank back onto the arm of Amar's chair.

"But I didn't know it then, in the bothy." Jenny's eyes fixed on Nora. "What if Jack was right? I listened to him. And when he asked me to ring Sir Colm, I did."

Sir Colm MacAskill had been very quiet. It had been

early in the morning and Jenny had assumed she'd woken him. She'd apologized, but said it was an emergency. Was there any chance that a bait-post had been left by the mines?

"He accused me of trying to start a panic. He said that if I mentioned Jack's fears to anyone, the Orders would collapse. I'd destroy Brannland. He'd send me to prison." Jenny shook her head. "That didn't scare me. I'd count the bait-posts when we got back and find the truth. But to threaten a Legendary—I was shocked. And when he asked to speak to Jack, I handed over the phone. If I could change *one* thing about that duty, I'd have told him no. I'd have hung up. I'd have worked with Jack to calm him down—"

Jenny Tsukada broke off and took a trembling sip of her water.

"He shouted at Jack," she went on. "At *my* knight. I could hear every word, he was so loud. He told Jack he was a liar and said if Jack told anyone, he'd go behind bars for life. When Jack handed me the phone, Sir Colm had three words: 'Are we understood?' I said yes. I said yes and hung up and told Jack we needed to sleep to be ready for the field at gloaming. I'd never felt so helpless." Her face was bleak. "Jack was wrong about it being a bait-post. But he'd smelled something. I don't know what, but Jack Goudie was no liar."

"Thank you for saying that," Nora whispered.

Jenny clasped Nora's hand. "I have regretted that phone call all my life. And Jack—I've thought of him and his wretched Order each time we bring in a new knight." Her cheek twitched. "There's no record of him but his blood sample. Sir Colm made it look as if he'd been disqualified in training and burned all his files. He threatened my Order to keep it secret. Not even Ursula knows the truth. And I think—I fear if we tell anyone, it *will* destroy the Orders. How could young people believe in this work if they knew what Colm MacAskill had done to a knight?" Her voice trailed. "Though sometimes, I think we should tell the whole world."

They sat in silence for five minutes, maybe more, Cyril bouncing on the arm of Amar's chair.

Nora was lost in all the new things she'd learned. It was almost enough to send her back to the swamp of despair that had engulfed her when Owen had died. But the wrinkled, strong hand that held hers kept her in the present.

Except for one thought:

Dad said he smelled a bait-post. And Jenny said he wasn't a liar.

"Tell me about Jack," Jenny Tsukada said abruptly. "What was he like as a father? Was he happy?"

"Yes," said Nora.

I need to always remember that.

WARRIORS
OF THE
FROZEN BOG

CHATBOX

PLAYERS LOGGED IN:

TechnoLad—High Paladin (213 minutes)

sheepGrl9—Grand Necromancer <(1 minutes)

sheepGrl9: wilfred?

. . .

TechnoLad: nora!!!!!!!!!!!!!!!!!!!!!!!!!!! sorry was just fighting. i just ran toki's bog dungeon 17x & died only 5x!!

sheepGrl9: POG!! i would have died way more

TechnoLad: omg i am so stupid/insensitive. you are alive, that=so good. wasn't thinking, which is weird b/c i've been thinking abt u every day & so worried. that=why i ran toki's bog dungeon 17x. u are back!!!!!!! are u ok?

sheepGrl9: yes. i almost got hurt but senior knight did amazing move & saved me

TechnoLad: POG!

sheepGrl9: so true

TechnoLad: what was it like?

sheepGrl9: . . .

sheepGrl9: kinda weird

TechnoLad: did u do a lot of fighting?

sheepGrl9: tons

TechnoLad: what were the monsters like?

sheepGrl9: . . .

sheepGrl9: kinda weird

sheepGrl9: so u=high paladin now. u leveled up!

TechnoLad: . . .

TechnoLad: yes

sheepGrl9: dungeons or quests?

TechnoLad: . . .

TechnoLad: everything

sheepGrl9: do u like having Slash IV?

TechnoLad: nora, u were gone for 2 weeks. every night i thought u might be dead

sheepGrl9: . . .

sheepGrl9: i dont want 2 talk abt it

TechnoLad: . . .

sheepGrl9: so what is going on in jedburch? how is mum?

TechnoLad: she=fine. horace gave more pressies

sheepGrl9: who? oh mum's caseworker. does he bring pressie every visit?

TechnoLad: yes. pressie1=poetry book, burned. pressie2=nice mug, smashed.

sheepGrl9: oh mum

TechnoLad: pressie3=temari ball=ball w/tons of thread making patterns

sheepGrl9: did she hurt it?

TechnoLad: pressie3=on table=safe! pressie4=origami butterfly=also safe on table!

sheepGrl9: is she getting used to him?

TechnoLad: yes. horace=really nice

sheepGrl9: i am happy 4 mum x10000

TechnoLad: no other news. home=boring lol. soooooooo want 2 play warriors???? have new strategy 4 new paladin spell=Command Knight=tough knight who smashes things. we can do Hidden Forest & u can resurrect knight if dies!!!

sheepGrl9: . . .

sheepGrl9: wilfred i just came back from fighting irl

TechnoLad: . . .

TechnoLad: i knew that. just thought u might like 2 play.

sheepGrl9: i dont want 2 fight now

TechnoLad: . . .

TechnoLad: ok

sheepGrl9: wilfred can u do me big help w/mum? need u 2 ask question 4 me. question= why did dad say i could go in mum's last convo w/him before he died?

TechnoLad: that=weird question

sheepGrl9: she'll know what i mean

TechnoLad: i don't know what u mean

sheepGrl9: it=okay. she'll know

TechnoLad: ??? that question=2 weird from me. u should ask her.

sheepGrl9: i cant from here. they wont let me.

TechnoLad: . . .

TechnoLad: are u trying 2 find sneaky way 2 come back home?

sheepGrl9: WHAT???? NO!!!!!

TechnoLad: OK OK STOP SHOUTING AT ME

sheepGrl9: . . .

TechnoLad: . . .

sheepGrl9: . . .

TechnoLad: so . . . is fighting as knight like playing warriors?

sheepGrl9: it=*nothing* like playing warriors it=*real life*

TechnoLad: duh i know i meant . . . forget it

sheepGrl9: wilfred warriors=fun. being knight=*so* important

TechnoLad: i said forget it

sheepGrl9: . . .

TechnoLad: . . .

sheepGrl9: will u ask mum my question for me?

TechnoLad: u need 2 find way 2 reach her yrself

sheepGrl9: ?? i told u i cant!! why cant u do this for me??

TechnoLad: why cant u do it? arent u=*so* important=*real*
knight=can boss people around?

sheepGrl9: ?? i dont boss anyone

TechnoLad: lol read the chat

sheepGrl9: . . .

sheepGrl9: i just asked u important question 2 help me w/
something big b/c i need answer 2 help me here

TechnoLad: see

sheepGrl9: ???

TechnoLad: boss boss

sheepGrl9: . . .

sheepGrl9: wilfred i=knight & . . .

TechnoLad: really??? i did not know u=knight. WOW!!!!!!!!!!!!!!

sheepGrl9: . . .

sheepGrl9: i thought u=my best friend

TechnoLad: i thought so 2 but u wont tell me anything abt
being knight. you=keeping secrets. does that=best friend???

TECHNOLAD LOGGED OFF.

SHEEPGRL9 LOGGED OFF.

THE ORDER OF THE OAK

The next four days were a blur: of laps, weights, the target room—and a heaviness that came each night when Nora saw the game player in her fiddle case.

I could have died. I don't want to talk about it. And he just wants to know everything.

For the first time, she was beginning to understand why knights weren't allowed contact with their former lives.

She never turned on the game player. Instead, she focused on her fellow knights. When she couldn't sleep, she slogged through MacAskill's book in search of clues about what Jack Goudie might have smelled. The great scientist described his Iron, his concept of the Orders, and his philosophy of the Umbrae with sentences that lasted half a page. There was nothing about bait-posts or smells.

Her Order was strangely kind, as if to prove that Hawk would never be like Wyvern.

Yet as they ran in silence—Nora struggling, as usual—there was tension on their faces: Eve's was fierce, Cyril's frustrated, Amar's deeply clouded, and even Tove's was sour.

They'd talked only once about what they'd learned from Jenny Tsukada. It was MacAskill's shouting at Jack, at calling him a liar, that haunted them most. And because it made them feel so horrible, they agreed to tell no one.

On the tenth lap of their fifth day back, Murdo marched onto the track, his face grave. The knights gathered around him.

"The Order of the Oak's coming back today," he said. "They lost one."

Nora held her breath. *Not Shaun. Not on his first duty.*

"Isaac Schwartz," Murdo said. "He had his fourth bite—an *Aranea umbra.* Before his Order could get him to the car and give him the antidote, the Umbrae dragged him away. The knights panicked. Sophie's report—it's terrible. I won't tell you more."

No one moved.

"Don't walk in the main hall downstairs," Murdo said at last. "No one knows when they'll arrive." He started toward the door. "I have to go. Ursula wants to speak with the Legendaries."

"Who's left to go on duty now?" Eve asked as soon as Murdo was gone.

Amar winced. "Just Boar and us."

They finished their laps, then went through the rest of the day's training. The knights barely spoke. In the library, all was silent.

I'll never be able to jam with Isaac. They'll never hear him sing again. He must have been so scared . . .

Amar set down his book. "Nora? Do you want to talk? You haven't turned a page since we got here."

"I just—I keep thinking about Isaac. And Oak." Nora clutched her book. "And how they must be feeling right now."

Tove slid her book onto the floor. "Losing a knight is the worst feeling."

"Your whole body hurts," Cyril agreed. "Like you've swallowed a bucket of Iron shavings."

Eve hugged her book. "You're totally alone. I mean, you're not alone with the rest of your Order, but . . . you're alone here at Noye's Hill. It's like no one else cares, no one gets it."

Wilfred could never understand what this is like.

Amar's face turned thoughtful. "It's four in the afternoon, right? So it's the morning for knights on duty. And I bet Oak's back." He stood. "Let's go see them."

No one questioned him. Everyone followed: down Hawk's stairs, to another stairway and up, to the landing of Oak's common room.

Amar knocked gently. "Averill?"

The door opened a crack. Averill's face—weary, with reddened eyes—peered out.

"Hey, Amar."

"Can we come in?"

"Sure." She shuffled back and opened the door all the way.

Kazu, Bronwyn, and Shaun were huddled together on the same jade-green sofa. Their faces were hopeless and bleak.

Nora ran to them. "Shaun, do you like hugs? May I hug you, please?"

Shaun staggered to his feet. He was bonier than even Cyril, and his hug was tight and trembling.

Amar held out his hand to Averill.

"Could I have a hug?"

"Of course." Amar folded her into an embrace. "It wasn't your fault, Averill."

Soon the Order of the Hawk was arrayed on the sofas with the Order of the Oak, Shaun squeezed beside Nora.

They talked:

Of Isaac's twisted songs and Lucy's sweet and pointless stories.

Of how the absences made them all feel like they were drowning.

Of how they sometimes thought they heard Isaac's and Lucy's voices in the silence.

Of how time had seemed to stop in the battle when they knew their knight was gone.

"I've never seen so many *Aranea umbrae*," Averill said at last. "It's like they were rising from the ground, from the grass or something."

Nora stiffened. "Did you just say they came from under-ground? It sounds like what people have said about bait-posts."

Averill exchanged a look with Kazu. "Hawks, I'm going to tell you something, but you've *got* to keep this secret. Do you promise?"

Amar looked at his knights. "Are we agreed?"

Everyone nodded.

Averill took a deep breath. "We had a bait-post. Sophie set it."

Horror flashed over Amar's face. "*What?* Why?"

"She was watching your numbers when you were out and said we'd be able to compete if we fought with one." Averill ran a shaking hand over her bun. "I must have read about bait-posts in training, but I didn't remember they'd been outlawed—or why."

Nora sat very still. *Dad smelled a bait-post in the field.* "Where did Sophie get it?"

"She said she brought it from here. I thought it'd been approved. But she told us on the way home not to mention it." Averill shifted. "We were actually doing quite well at first, but . . . they kept coming. I wish one of us had paid more attention to that chapter in training. Shaun transferred before he'd got to it in the book. If I'd had any idea, I'd have rung someone. I'd have refused to let my knights out."

"You should tell someone now," Amar said. "Tell Ursula. This can't be a secret."

Averill cringed. "Sophie would kill me."

"You almost died out there, Averill. She almost *did* kill you. And Isaac . . ." Amar broke off and offered his hand. "I'll go with you to talk to her."

Averill looked at her knights.

Bronwyn and Kazu nodded.

"What do you think, Shaun? If I tell Ursula, Sophie won't be our Legendary anymore."

Shaun flinched. "I don't trust her."

Bronwyn wiped her nose. "Isaac would be all, 'That's the word of the day.' Go on, Averill. I don't trust her either now."

"Do it," said Kazu.

Amar was still holding out his hand.

Averill slipped her hand in his. "Okay. Let's . . . let's do it now."

34

A NEW DUTY

"Bait-posts were engineered to attract the Umbrae and restrict them to one spot, the goal being easy eradication. When a bait-post rooted, all Umbrae in the surrounding area were expected to gather above the roots."

Did anyone think about how roots spread? All over the place. One of those scientists should have studied botany.

—Level Three, Chapter 50: "Final Note: Bait-Posts"
Becoming a Knight (National Council training text)

Nora put down her book. They were reading after dinner in the library, their chairs pushed together. Nora had tried to get back into MacAskill's tome but couldn't focus. Even though she hadn't seen him since her second day at Noye's Hill, the fortress felt empty without Isaac.

I never got to hear him sing.

"What are you thinking about, Kemp?" Eve's voice was gentle.

"Isaac."

Amar closed his book. "I'm glad we're thinking of him. We should do something in his honor—and Lucy's. I'll talk with Murdo."

The day before, he'd returned from the meeting with Ursula with no news, just that the director had thanked him and Averill for coming. He'd been quiet all day.

"Maybe we can get together with Oak tonight." Amar folded his hands. "The first days after are the worst. Let's be there for them. Okay, knights?"

"That's sweet of you," Tove said. "Let's do it."

Eve pointed at Amar. "Who is that? I don't recognize him. Our former senior knight had all the MacAskill Rules inked on his arm. This new one's broken two Rules and counting."

"For good reason. Agreed?"

Eve grinned. "Agreed."

They settled back in a friendly silence.

Then Nora sat up. "Where did Oak go on duty? Was it to the west?"

"Good memory," said Amar. "Yes, since you chose north, they got west."

Jedburch is in the west. "Can I see the map?"

Amar pushed the button under the table. The hologram appeared.

Clusters of yellow dots scattered across Brannland, more numerous than before.

And more than ever on the green line for Oak.

Not in Jedburch. Nora breathed. But then she frowned.

"I know that place. That's near Buffleton Mines, the biggest mine in the Shires."

Amar zoomed in the map. "Look at that yellow spot. That's got to be four or five hundred."

"How is there that many?" Tove frowned.

"Well, a bait-post attracts about fifty per night," Amar said.

"But Averill said Sophie planted it before gloaming, so it's been there just one night." Tove met his eyes.

"It's the mines." Nora put her finger on the floating image. "Buffleton's a ruin now, but it was a big groundwater polluter in its day."

Amar pushed the button and the map disappeared. "I guess that's it." But his face remained troubled.

The Order of the Hawk stayed in their common room with their books before dinner. Nora curled up beside Cyril and together they read his copy of *The Goblin's Wish*.

It was almost dinnertime when Murdo came to the door.

"Knights, we need to talk." He sank onto the sofa beside Nora. "There's a problem with Oak's unfinished duty—a *big* problem. Ursula has asked if the Order of the Hawk could solve it. Before I answer, I have a question: Is Nora ready to go out on duty without a fortnight break?"

"Yes," said Amar. "Her endurance has gone up in running, she's lifting well in the weight room, and she hasn't missed once in the target room."

"What do you think, Nora? Are you ready to go out without two weeks of rest?"

"Yes."

"Good. Amar, Ursula said you and Averill told her about Sophie's bait-post. Sophie left it on Oak's last battleground. The Umbrae have been doubling around it every night since. Hawk's next duty is to destroy the post."

"You mean dig it up?" asked Amar.

"No, she wants us to destroy it for good. It takes three strikes of a special MacAskill Iron hammer to deactivate it permanently."

"So our job is to hit it three times?" Eve asked. "Why didn't Sophie do it?"

"It only works when the post is active: *after* the gloaming. So you have to treat it as if it were an Umbra. With the Umbrae it's attracted swarming you." Murdo leaned forward. "You are the only knights who've dealt with massive numbers in the field. You're the only ones Ursula trusts with this. So let me ask you this: Is Nora ready to fight over five hundred Umbrae at once?"

"Yes," said Amar, Eve, and Tove simultaneously.

"You haven't seen her in the target room, have you?" added Cyril.

Murdo faced Nora. "Do you agree?"

"I've beaten over five hundred in the target room."

He studied her, then smiled. "Thank you for saying that. Knights, we'll have one day to prepare our bodies for the shift, so you're not getting much sleep. Find a way to relax. I'm going to spend a few hours with Ursula and learn what I need to know about bait-posts."

Nora watched Murdo leave, then hugged herself.

"Wow," said Eve. "This is big. Our numbers will be incredible, but . . ." She trailed off.

"It's not something we can't handle." Amar put his elbows on his knees. "I wish we had a few more days, though."

"I wish Sophie had risked her life to stop it," said Tove.

Amar nodded. "It's been there more than a day. That's why the numbers are so massive: It's totally rooted. That's why Ursula is sending us out tomorrow: We can't afford to let it root any more."

Eve grimaced. "They're going to swarm us constantly. There won't be a moment to breathe."

"We'll have plenty of time to breathe." Amar raised his head. "And we'll destroy them. Don't worry, knights: We always do."

WARRIORS
OF THE
FROZEN BOG

PLAYERS LOGGED IN:

TechnoLad—High Paladin (59 minutes)

sheepGrl9—Grand Necromancer <(1 minutes)

sheepGrl9: wilfred?

. . .

sheepGrl9: wilfred are u there? i need 2 tell u something.

. . .

TechnoLad: ok. am safe. what is it

sheepGrl9: i'm going out soon

TechnoLad: have fun?? not sure what u want me to say

sheepGrl9: u dont have 2 say anything. i just wanted 2 say
goodbye

TechnoLad: okay byeeeeeee

sheepGrl9: please tell mum i love her

TechnoLad: sure will

sheepGrl9: . . .

sheepGrl9: i just wanted u 2 know that i=grateful 4 knowing u &= sorry we are not friends here but we were irl & i wanted 2 say goodbye as if irl

TechnoLad: what are u talking abt? did u seriously just start chat 2 say goodbye?

sheepGrl9: . . .

sheepGrl9: love u wilfred. goodbye

TechnoLad: wait dont logoff. are u giving up game 2 follow knight rules or something?

sheepGrl9: . . .

sheepGrl9: i am going on duty tomorrow & will not be able 2 say goodbye later so am saying it now

TechnoLad: . . .

TechnoLad: nora u are freaking me out a little. why are u saying this?

sheepGrl9: . . .

sheepGrl9: i might not be back if things go badly. have 2 go now. goodbye wilfred love u

SHEEPGRL9 LOGGED OFF.

TechnoLad: nora?

. . .

TechnoLad: omg

UNEXPECTED COMPANY

"We'll go in right before the gloaming, plant ourselves round the post in a schiltron formation, and I'll smash it as soon as it's active. It won't bring out any more *Aranea umbrae,* but you'll have to defeat what it's already produced. Which will be hundreds. So my suggestion is this: Defeat enough to make a path to the car." Murdo took a deep breath. "We've done this before."

Amar nodded. "It helps that we're always fighting a massive number."

"And we blast Nora with tons of targets when we practice," added Tove.

"We're used to it," said Eve cheerfully.

Cyril said nothing.

"Dealing with a bait-post is extraordinarily dangerous," Murdo went on. "For all of you—and for me especially. We have to move like clockwork and not make a single mistake. No other Order has our skill or precision."

Murdo leaned over and pushed the button under the table. The holographic map appeared, spattered with colored lines and clusters of yellow dots.

One area was pure yellow.

Buffleton Mines, thought Nora.

Murdo put his finger on the spot. "That's where we're going. Our base will be here, a Council bothy—"

"That's on the way to Braeburgh Castle," Nora interrupted, then caught herself. "Sorry."

"Do you know this area?"

"I know that castle *and* the mines. I live over . . ." She searched the map and found Jedburch. ". . . here. *Lived* here."

"What's it like near the mines? The bait-post is about five miles in from them."

"Quiet. A lot of meadows and little roads. And no one for miles."

"If Sophie had to put the post down somewhere, that's a good place for it." Murdo crossed his arms. "But there's nothing around. No clinic. That'll make it hard for us if anyone gets bit."

It was night for the rest of Noye's Hill, but duty time for the Order of the Hawk. They spent it reading, running, and walking up and down the hall. At dawn, they ate their final meal, showered quickly, and dressed in their ice-blue on-duty uniforms. In the bathroom, Nora braided her own wet hair.

They met in the common room, where their cases and weapons were waiting for them. Murdo was there as well.

"I put your ugly caps in your cases," he told them. "Be sure to wear them."

With their cases in their arms, the Order of the Hawk marched down the hall. It was empty this time. And deadly quiet.

Only Ursula and Sophie were at the end. Ursula wore a simple black turtleneck. Sophie wore her uniform. It no longer had its jade-green patch.

"Good luck, Hawks. Be sure you come home." Ursula frowned at Sophie. "Remember your promise."

"*What* promise?" Murdo said coldly.

Sophie raised her chin. "I'm coming with you."

"To do what? Sit in the car and watch us fight? Ursula, this is against every rule—"

"I know, Murdo, but *this*—your going out to clean up another Order's disaster—is *also* against every rule. I want her in the car to drive. This will be the toughest battle of your lives, knights. Having one person whose sole responsibility is to bring you to safety could be the difference between life and death." Ursula glared at Sophie. "You will not interact with his knights. You will drive them to safety when they are ready. That is your only job. Do it."

Sophie's jaw tightened. "I will."

"Fine," snapped Murdo. "Sit in the back."

They went outside into the cold. The morning sun glared down at them, the sky a cloud-stamped sea of blue.

Murdo climbed into the driver's seat, Amar into the passenger seat. Tove and Eve opened the doors to the middle seats.

"Hop in, Cyril," said Tove. "Let's share."

"Same with you, Kemp," said Eve.

Nora climbed into the middle seat, scooting over until she and Cyril were shoulder to shoulder. Tove and Eve fished out the bags from the doors in the back, then climbed in beside them.

"Your sleeping things." Eve handed Nora a bag.

The back door closed: Sophie had slid in.

Eve leaned over Nora toward Cyril and Tove. "I don't like her being here," she mouthed.

"She scares me more than the Umbrae," Tove whispered.

"Same." Cyril pushed up his glasses. "Them we can stab."

The four slipped on their eye masks.

"Come give us a hug, Kemp," said Eve. "I like hugs."

Nora curled up against the older girl and felt her arm close around her.

"You okay?" Eve's voice was soft.

"I think so. What about you?"

"I'll be fine. We'll all be fine."

A rush of love filled Nora—for Eve, for Tove and Cyril,

for Amar and Murdo in the front. This was her family. She'd never felt it more.

Soon, with Eve's gentle breathing in her ear, Nora fell asleep.

When she woke four hours later, Nora and Cyril were alone in the seat. He was just waking up too.

"Where *is* everyone?" Nora yawned. "Should we get out?"

They were parked in front of a white-painted stone bothy with a red door and a tin roof. Snow-covered meadows surrounded them, stretching on for miles. The sun was low in the steel-gray sky.

"Are the cases still here?" Cyril twisted around.

Sophie Moncrief was sitting in the back seat behind Nora, her eyes on her hands.

"Them we can stab," mouthed Cyril. He climbed out.

Nora opened her door but glanced back one more time. Sophie's face was bleak.

She lost Isaac because of what she'd tried. She must feel horrible.

"Sophie? Are you all right?"

Sophie raised her eyes. "No." And then, softer still: "I might have been if Ursula had put you in my Order."

Nora stumbled out of the car and slammed the door. Her heart was suddenly pounding. She followed Cyril into the bothy, guilt washing over her—until Amar met her eyes.

No, thought Nora. *I belong here. I save people here.* This *is* my Order.

Tove patted the cushion next to her on the bench. "Come sit with me, Nora."

Grateful, Nora hastened to her side.

"I'm going to fix your hair. How about a double four-strand?"

"Sophie didn't bother you?" Murdo strode in from a side room, a case in his arms. "I didn't want to leave you alone with her, but I also didn't want to wake you."

"I've never been instantly petrified on waking up," Cyril announced. "She's like Medusa."

"Then don't look at her again. She'll be in the front when we go out."

"Driving?" asked Amar.

"Not on the way. *I'll* drive. She'll take over for the ride back." Murdo set the case on the table. "Here's your last meal before battle, knights. Each one of these shakes has extra energy and muscle strengthening—my own combination—so you'll be at the top of your game."

He gave each canister a good shake and handed them around, then picked up his own. Everyone drank. It was a blended masoor dal soup with turmeric and cumin: delicious.

Murdo checked his watch. "We have twenty minutes before we leave. Amar, let's prep."

Eve and Tove sat with their hands linked, eyes closed,

breathing slowly. Cyril bounced from foot to foot. Nora had forgotten to pack her fiddle. She tapped a jig on her knee and watched Amar and Murdo remove the wax from the axe and swords. When they were done, everyone picked up their weapon and waited by the door while Murdo double-checked the contents of his case.

"Our most important tool." He tucked a gleaming black hammer into his belt. "Oh, your ugly caps. Don't forget. It's cold out there and they'll come in handy."

Everyone went to their cases and grabbed their caps.

"Ready, knights?" Murdo took a deep breath. "Let's go clean up this mess."

THE BATTLE OF THE POST

They drove in silence through the waning day, down one narrow road, then another. The meadows stretched blank and white around them for miles.

To Nora, this landscape was home.

She thought of Deena at the table as she signed the paper, of Daniel smiling at the door, of Wilfred waving as his father picked her up at her house on their last Saturday together.

She was in the middle seat with Cyril and Amar. In the back, Eve and Tove sat by the windows.

In the front sat Sophie.

"I know I'm not supposed to speak, but may I tell you where to go?" she'd asked when they first got into the car.

"Only that." Murdo didn't look at her.

But Sophie gazed at him with a strange expression: pained affection, like a very old friendship that had gone wrong.

They'd been driving for almost an hour when Sophie pointed.

"There's the turn to the mines. The battleground's just past them."

Murdo drove off the road onto the path in the snow made by Sophie's tire tracks. After twenty minutes, the mines appeared: an old stone building, low and close to the ground. A bright orange fabric fence surrounded it, flapping in the wind. The car shot past.

Sophie was silent for a few minutes more. Then—

"It's in half a mile."

"Did you park next to it?"

"Of course. I *always* park right next to wherever they're fighting." Her lips pressed—then her face crumpled into tears.

Murdo slowed. "Sophie." He put his hand on hers. "It's all right."

"It's *not* all right. I thought my knights were good enough. I'd seen them do well, and the post—I had *no* idea it would attract so many. I thought—Averill and Isaac, they were as fast as *your* knights in the target room—"

"That's enough." Murdo stopped the car. Before the knights had even opened the doors, he was out and marching up toward the post.

Her axe in hand, Nora sprinted to catch up with him.

"I can beat five hundred in real life too," she panted. "Just watch me."

Murdo laughed. "Let's do it."

The others soon joined them and they marched together, five knights with their ridiculous caps and their Legendary in his sleek black uniform.

They came to the post.

It was a MacAskill Iron fence post riddled with black mold. A stench like rotting meat wafted from it.

"We have five minutes before gloaming." Murdo set down his case and prepared himself.

The stretchy jacket with its pockets bulging with antidotes. Gloves reaching over his biceps. The mask. The goggles. The helmet with the light.

And the hammer.

Murdo knelt by the post and tapped it with that tool.

A chill shot down Nora's spine.

"Three blows," Murdo said, his voice muffled. "They don't have to be hard. Just three on top. I'll strike them as soon as gloaming starts. Be ready, though: The Umbrae will burst out of the ground. So keep close to me and don't hesitate in your fighting."

Murdo straightened.

"Schiltron formation. Amar, you behind me. Tove, in front. Nora, here, by Tove. Eve, here, next to Amar. Cyril, between Nora and Amar."

They encircled Murdo in that order and waited.

"Almost time," murmured Murdo. "Get ready, knights."

A long minute passed.

"Ready," breathed Murdo. "The gloaming is . . . *now.*"

As he spoke, the light on his helmet flicked on. In the same second, he brought down the hammer. Sparks showered from the post.

The next second, the ground before them churned—and a mass of *Aranea umbrae* burst from the snow.

And in the next, they swarmed the knights: legs snatching, furry bodies hissing, lavender mist rising as the swords and axe met them.

Another bang. More sparks.

Nora's axe sliced through five *Aranea umbrae,* then five more.

Murdo lifted the hammer for his final blow—

Cyril shouted.

Nora pivoted, axe flying, and cut the *Aranea umbra* crawling over his head.

And the one that had just reached Murdo.

Which had just thrust its furry body against his kneeling leg.

Murdo did not scream. But he grunted. And dropped the hammer.

"He's been bit!" shrieked Nora, whirling her axe around her.

"Cover me!" Tove darted back, dropped her sword, and ripped open the sleeves over Murdo's convulsing body. She tore out the antidotes. With both hands, she plunged them once, then twice, into Murdo's thigh.

Nora's axe wove in the air, slashing every *Aranea umbra* that launched at her, constantly moving to avoid their claws.

"The hammer," groaned Murdo.

Tove grabbed the hammer, dropped it, found it, and slammed it on the post one last time.

A shower of sparks.

But the *Aranea umbrae* still swarmed.

"We need to get him to the car!" shouted Amar. "Tove, lift him on your back—leave your sword—and carry him down. We'll surround you. Knights! Schiltron formation round Tove!"

The knights closed in, weapons flashing.

"Forward!" roared Amar.

It was like fighting the sea. Waves of *Aranea umbrae* crashed over them, trying to reach Murdo.

The Order of the Hawk kept them back—just barely—as they crossed the field.

Murdo convulsed again. His whole body shuddered.

We're too slow, Nora thought. *The venom's racing through him.*

"Amar, can you cover me?" Nora called. "I'm going to draw some away!"

Without waiting for his response, she plunged to the side, into a mass of *Aranea umbrae,* slashing nonstop, until they were crowding her, furry bodies and legs blocking her vision, jostling her between them—

And puffing into mist.

A blow took down ten. Through the lavender mist, Nora saw the knights approach the car, surrounded by Umbrae.

"Come and get me, you big ugly spiders!" Nora shouted. "Yeah, *you!*"

It was enough to distract them, enough for Sophie to throw open the door and for Tove to shove in Murdo's body while Eve, Cyril, and Amar cut down the Umbrae that tried to crawl over them.

The door shut.

"He's in!" called Amar. "Everyone, get in! Nora! Come!"

She ripped her axe through the mob, mist rising, fresh hairy bodies rushing through it. "They'll come after you if I do! You get in!"

The huge black car backed up, squealing, and sped off over the snow.

I'm alone. But I can do this. Mash them into little bits— like the target room—and then I'll walk home and ring the Council from there. Won't Mum be surprised!

Then she noticed movement eight or nine yards from her on the snow: a flashing sword.

More than one: three swords.

"I need my sword!" hollered Tove.

Amar, Eve, and Cyril were in a triangle around Tove, fighting the mass of *Aranea umbrae* descending on them.

For an instant, Nora felt sick.

They waited for me.

ALONE

"Get back!" Amar bellowed. "We need to get Tove's sword! Nora, over here! Now!"

Nora whirled her weapon and fought her way to the knights.

"I can't do anything without my sword!" Tove was almost crying.

"Can we run up to the post? What do you think?" Amar wove his sword in a figure eight, puffing *Aranea umbrae* into lavender mist.

"Let's go!" howled Eve.

Nora threw herself into the mob. She made a mist so thick, she couldn't see.

At last, they reached the post—where Murdo's helmet was still lighting the scene. Tove grabbed her sword. With a roar, she cut a whole line of Umbrae.

"Schiltron formation round the post!" shouted Amar. "Don't get distracted!"

They took their positions.

"It's strange!" cried Eve. "It's *easier* because there are so many! They can't grab us!"

"They're nothing but a hairy wall to cut down!" Cyril laughed.

Then an *Aranea umbra* latched onto his ankle and jerked him forward—

Nora had it—and the one behind it, the one about to jump, and the one on the side—in one swing, then seized Cyril's hand and helped him up.

"Don't pretend it's easy," Amar panted. "And don't stop moving." He ducked, and cut upward, slicing through the Umbra leaping onto him.

They fought, never pausing, their senses alert, their energy pulsing through them for a full hour—

The flow of beasts ebbed: from a sea to a river.

The fewer numbers meant they had room to grab.

Nora plunged into a beast that had latched its legs onto Eve's and thrown her back against Tove, who fell. Two *Aranea umbrae* tried to lower their furry mandibles onto them, but Nora's axe rattled through them and they puffed into mist.

She didn't stop moving. And then—

An *Aranea umbra* faltered in front of her.

Amar slashed it. "They're starting to behave normally."

Aranea umbrae—without the lure of a Legendary.

No one had ever seen anything like it in the field.

They faltered often and were easy targets. Many seemed to be staring at the knights' ugly caps. Soon they backed away. A scatter of giant wicker spiders crawled off over the snow.

The five knights leaned over, panting hard.

"Is it done? Is it dawn?" Eve gasped.

"Not even close." Then Amar put his hand to his chest. "I can't breathe."

He sank to his knees.

"Have you been bit?" Nora fumbled beside him.

"No, I—just need to rest. That—was too much."

"Nora! By your ankle!" called Tove.

An *Aranea umbra* claw was creeping close.

"Get *out* of here." Nora leaned forward and slashed it.

"I'm sorry, but I need to lie down." Amar collapsed on the snow.

Tove stumbled over to him. "Is there water?"

"I think there's some in Murdo's case." Eve knelt and pulled out a bottle. "Yes! And an antidote!"

"That's one of the ones I used. That's its shell." Tove choked out a sob. "Murdo."

"He's going to be all right. Thank goodness you're so tall and strong; no one else could have carried him." Eve patted Tove's shoulder as she stepped around the post to Amar. "Amar? Wake up. I've got water."

Cyril huddled next to Tove. "Is Murdo going to die?"

"It felt like he was dying." Tove began to cry softly. "I can't believe he got bit."

"I can't believe Sophie left," whimpered Cyril. "She wants to get rid of us."

Eve propped Amar with her arm and held the bottle to his lips. "She left to take Murdo to the hospital so he'll live. She knows we're the best and can handle this." Her gaze flicked around, fierce. "And we *are* the best. And we *can* handle this. And they'll send a car in the morning."

The night was long. Without Murdo it felt dire.

The *Aranea umbrae* came, sometimes in a wave of fifty, sometimes just three. Twice, Cyril's sword dropped from his sweaty hand, but each time the *Aranea umbra* reaching for him faltered at the sight of the wet-eyed boy in his cap with its lumpy horns.

They were all tired, weak, and trembling after the onslaught.

Amar wobbled. Eve tripped. Tove missed. Everyone needed someone else to save them.

Except Nora.

Her muscles were limp, as if they'd been pulled to their limit and then let go. Yet each time an *Aranea umbra* neared, she was ready, axe swinging. Muscle memory, terror, and all

the bosses she'd defeated in Warriors of the Frozen Bog—
that combination kept her going.

As her body did its job, her mind ran an endless track:

Murdo's going to be all right. Sophie took him to the hospital.

Then a horrible thought came to her: The nearest hospital
was in Cairnmouth, a good two hours out.

Could Murdo last for two hours? Or would he die from
the venom first?

38

A WEE BIT

Hours passed. The knights took turns and fought in pairs while the others rested. But at last, the dark sky lightened.

"Almost dawn," said Eve.

The next second, the light flicked off. An *Aranea umbra* only a foot away puffed into pearl-gray mist. Little puffs rose across the meadow as far as they could see.

Nora frowned. *They're turning into spores. And each spore is going to be two or three new Umbrae.*

"Okay." Amar struggled to his feet. "The Council's going to be sending a car. We'll be picked up in an hour or less."

"Let's meet it on the road." Eve shuddered. "I don't want to stay here."

Tove grabbed the hammer and packed up Murdo's case. She carried it under her arm as they hobbled back to where the car had been and followed the tire tracks in the snow over the meadow.

"This is pathetic," Cyril grumbled. "We're in the middle of nowhere."

"I think this is a road," Tove said.

"It's not." Amar's brow furrowed. "She drove on the meadow. We need to get to the main road, and soon, if we want the car to find us."

Eve threw out her arms. "It's a wide-open meadow. We'll see them. They'll see us."

They marched on. Amar and Eve led, Tove and Cyril followed, and Nora, as usual, dragged behind.

Now that the fighting was over, she could barely move her legs.

"Keep up, Nora!" snapped Amar. "Don't leave us again."

Nora stopped. "I never left you."

"*We* were about to get in the car. *You* were ten yards away."

"I said go without me."

"Yes, and we ignored that because it was a *massively* ignorant thing to say." He whirled to face her, glaring. "An Order does *not* abandon one of its knights. Look, I know you weren't trained, but did you just not realize that by running off—and destroying our schiltron formation—you put us all in incredible danger?"

"I—"

"Did that even occur to you?" His voice rose. "*I* told you to get in the car. But *you* didn't listen. Okay, so you don't follow commands, but maybe you can try *this* one: Keep. Up."

Nora stared. It was as if a new person had entered Amar's skin.

"Amar?" Tove put a hand on his back. "I don't think we would've made it to the car if she hadn't drawn them off."

Amar pivoted toward her. "What are you supposed to do in a situation like that when everyone's life is threatened?"

"Obey our senior knight. But Amar, there was *no* way—"

"How do *you* know that?" Amar's shout echoed over the meadow. He whirled back to Nora. "You're going to have a conversation with Ursula when we get back to Noye's Hill. Or not, if we *die* out here at the next gloaming thanks to you!"

"*Amar,*" murmured Eve. "Calm down."

"Let's get to the road." He started walking again.

"No." Trembling, Nora tucked her axe under her arm. "I'm sorry, but I need to rest. I've been fighting all night and . . . I'm a wee bit tired."

Amar opened his mouth—

Cyril's laugh filled the meadow.

"Did you hear what you said?" He stumbled toward Nora. "We've been mashing them to bits all night, it's a miracle none of us got ripped apart like taffy, and now you say you're a *wee bit* tired."

Cyril stopped a foot away from her, his laughter hysterical.

"A wee bit." Tove held up her fingers in a pinch.

"Because," gasped Cyril, "it's not like Nora didn't just save Murdo's life!"

"And ours!" Tove put her hand on her stomach, her own

laughter convulsing. "It's not like they all left *us* to swarm *her!*"

"They thought she'd be easy prey, all alone." Eve wiped her face. "Stupid monsters. Since when has *Kemp* been easy prey?"

"But she ran off." Amar's voice was tense. "They could have bitten her again and again. They could have taken her away like Isaac and there was *nothing* we could have done."

"I was keeping them away from you and Murdo," Nora said. "Was that not a good move to make?"

Amar marched over, his face tight, and caught her in a hug. He was shaking. It took Nora a few seconds to realize he was crying.

"I'm sorry," he choked out.

Soon all the knights were crying—in a warm knot of sweaty, weepy hugs around Nora. Even Cyril.

When their sobs quieted, Amar cleared his throat. "Nora: I'm so sorry. That was a ridiculous outburst. We were in a terrible and unprecedented situation and you did what you had to. I was worried when you ran off like that." He took a deep breath. "You're my family. You're all I have. I was sure we were going to lose you."

"I just got going," Nora said. "I'm sorry I didn't come when you told me, but I thought I'd be leading too many back to you. And I knew I could handle them where I was."

A ghostly smile. "It's good you didn't listen: I don't think any of us could have got in the car."

With his hand in Nora's, Amar started onto the path again.

BUFFLETON MINES

Built: 1745   Height of Production: 1812
Status: Ruined

Buffleton Mines was the first mine to be built in the Shires. It is widely considered to be the most successful—as well as the most destructive—of the mines in Brannland. (See Chart vii for pollution levels.) On 5 May 1920 at 2 am, supports in the western shaft collapsed, igniting explosives in a chain reaction. Over 300 miners died. Buffleton Mines has been abandoned ever since.

—*A History of Brannland: Industry & Umbrae*

The Order of the Hawk continued walking at Nora's pace. After an hour, a crooked stone building appeared in the distance.

"That's Buffleton Mines." Nora wrinkled her nose. "Do you smell something?"

"Let's walk into the field and get away from it," said Amar. "Nora, how far is the road?"

"Fifteen miles or so?" Something was pulling at her mind. "Wait—that smell. The bait-post smelled a little like it. But not this bad."

Everyone froze.

"No," whispered Eve. "I'm too tired."

"There isn't another bait-post." Amar's voice was firm.

Cyril's chin shot up. "I just remembered something. It's the only thing I remember about bait-posts from training because they gave me nightmares and I tried to put them out of mind, but . . . they get horrifically stinky when they root."

"There isn't another bait-post," Amar repeated. "Remember? There were only five. And they're all at Noye's Hill, except that one we just destroyed."

"Twenty years ago, my dad said he smelled a bait-post by some mines." Nora pointed with her axe at the entrance. "If that's the one he smelled, it's *really* rooted."

"No one would have put a bait-post in abandoned mines." Amar's voice was just as certain as before.

Cyril took a deep breath. "I hated the Level Three book because of that bait-post page. I called it the disaster-nightmare page because there was that map of how the roots would spread all over Brannland—and under the sea because it wouldn't be enough of a disaster without the islands getting their share. I couldn't sleep for a week. But

I'll never forget what the page said at the bottom: 'A deeply rooted bait-post smells like rotting goat.'" He paused. "Are we smelling rotting goat?"

"This is what foot rot smells like," said Nora. "In sheep. One of our flocks had it."

Amar stiffened. "No."   .

They all turned to the mines.

The bright orange fabric encircling the building hung limp. Beyond it, broken metal rails were embedded in the cobblestones and the snow-flecked grass. The rails disappeared into the crumbling stone building.

"I want to see," said Nora. "If my dad was right and it *is* a rooted bait-post, Ursula needs to know."

"It won't hurt to look." Tove squinted at the sky. "It's not close to gloaming."

Amar sighed. "We can look."

Tiny chunks of ice bobbed in the high, dead grass. Clouds swallowed the sun, shadowing the meadow. It was almost as dark as gloaming by the time they reached the fence.

Nora climbed over the orange fabric. A pair of broken double doors hung open at the front of the building. The rails in the ground disappeared into the dark past the doors.

It smelled even worse.

Something's down there. And if it's a bait-post and we leave it, it's going to more than double the Umbrae every night. With no one here to stop them.

Nora turned to Tove. "May I have the hammer?"

Tove fished it out of Murdo's case.

"Is there a flashlight?"

"There's Murdo's helmet. He had it set to turn on with the gloaming, but you can switch it to normal." Tove handed it to Nora, her eyes damp. "It fell off him when I picked him up." She wiped her nose. "Are you going to look in the mines?"

Nora turned the helmet light on and, taking off her ugly blue cap, set the helmet in its place. "Just for a quick peek."

THE PATH

The rails went down from the entry of the mines into a very deep pit. Cyril dropped a chunk of cobble, and waited.

Three seconds, then a splash.

"This is a truly bad idea." Amar touched her shoulder. "Nora, there's no way down."

"There has to be if someone put a bait-post here." Nora leaned over. "Look: The rails have ties in between, like train tracks. But they're close together, like a ladder." She swung a leg over and tested one. "And they're solid."

"I don't like this." But then Amar sighed. "Here, stand up straight. You'll need your hands free, but you'll want your axe."

With his sword, he carefully sliced off the bottom of his stretchy top and used the piece to tie Nora's axe around her waist. Then he cut off another layer and tied his sword to his own waist.

"Oh! Are you coming with me?"

"There's no way I'm sending you down there alone." Amar looked around. "Will the rest of you stay up here?"

Eve frowned. "What if you need help? What if you get stuck?"

"Then head for the road and when the car comes, have someone get us out."

"What if the Umbrae come for you while you're down there?" Eve's mouth trembled.

"That's why we have our weapons." Amar offered a faint smile.

Cyril raised his hand. "I'll be the mongoose. Isn't that how they used to send messages for some war? And by that, I mean I'll climb up and down with messages between you and Eve and Tove."

"That would be great, Cyril," Amar said. "Okay, Nora, let's start."

Nora reached for the first rung with her foot. She climbed down, Amar just above her, and went on slowly, rung after rung. In less than a minute, everything was dark except for her helmet's beam. The smell was even stronger.

That smell—like foot rot mixed with mud and wet wool—was oddly familiar, a smell from home.

Suddenly, a shadowy opening appeared on the left.

"Here's a passage," Nora called up. "The smell coming out is even worse."

"Great," said Amar.

"Can we go into it?"

"Sure."

Carefully, Nora crawled in, then shone her light toward Amar as he followed.

"Cyril?" Amar peered up. "We're in a tiny passage now."

There was a scrape. Cyril appeared in the light. "That looks tight. Be careful it doesn't squeeze you into toothpaste. I'll go tell the others." He scrambled back up before they could answer.

"It's not *that* tight." Amar squinted. "Can you shine that in the other direction, please?"

On her hands and knees, her axe dragging, Nora crawled on. Chunks of stone littered the passage. Her head felt foggy. In her mind, she ran through the march from "The Castle in the Sky" to keep calm.

And all at once, she remembered her father's voice as he played that march: *The message here is "Just ahead," Nora. Just ahead. Think of that when you're in a tough place, all right?*

After a minute, the passage opened up with room to stand.

"I think this is the right direction," Nora said.

Amar pinched his nose. "I think you're right: I'm about to be sick."

Something scraped behind them, and Cyril appeared again. "Are you going on? By the way, it smells like—"

"Please don't say what it smells like," said Amar.

"I'll tell Eve and Tove what it smells like." Cyril disappeared into the darkness.

"I hope he doesn't keep doing that." Amar gestured onward.

The path was narrow. The stench grew heavy. They clambered on—and then the passage opened up.

Nora cleared her throat. "You get used to the smell if you're treating sheep rot."

Amar covered his nose and mouth. "I don't think I would."

They were about to go on when a thump came from behind.

"Where are you?" It was Cyril.

"We're in a wider passage," Amar called back. "You don't have to keep coming after us, you know."

A pause.

Then scraping.

Amar sighed. "Is he going to check every five minutes? I really don't like him scrambling in the dark."

The scraping grew louder.

"What's he doing?" Amar twisted around. "It sounds like he's pulling a load."

A few seconds later, Cyril appeared in the light.

Followed by Tove.

"What are *you* doing here? Tove, did you leave Eve all alone at the top?"

"No," came Eve's voice from behind her.

"We didn't like the idea of you searching for a bait-post by yourselves," Tove said apologetically. "We *are* an Order. We should be together."

"And if you find it, you'll have a whole mess of Umbrae to deal with," Eve added. "There's no chance you'd make it out alive if it were just the two of you. There's a chance if it's all of us."

Amar shook his head. "We're going to be out of here way before gloaming. We're just looking for the bait-post. If we find it, we'll tell Ursula and let *her* take care of it."

"You know who she'd send to 'take care of it,' right?" Eve's voice was hushed.

Amar winced. "Okay. So we find it and destroy it. We'll need to wait until gloaming, but we'll do it then, just like the one aboveground. Who has the hammer?"

"I do." Nora tapped the tight knot she'd made to hold it in her top.

"So one of us strikes it three times at gloaming and the rest of us fight. Agreed?"

"Yes," said Tove.

"Yes," said Eve.

"Totally," said Cyril. "That's going to be a record: smashing two putrid posts in two days."

"I still don't know how this could be a bait-post, unless Jenny counted wrong." Amar sighed. "But onward."

Nora led the way.

If it's just like the bait-post aboveground, it won't be so bad. *They can't come through stone. Wait, they can. So they'll be rushing at us from all directions.*

Nora's stomach twisted.

We shouldn't have come down here. We should have kept walking and waited for the car. Now no one will know where we are—and what if someone gets bit? We don't have any antidotes. What if it's Amar or Eve? It'd be their fourth—

"Nora: Stop thinking whatever you're thinking," said Amar. "You've grown way too quiet."

"Sorry." Nora looked over her shoulder. "It'll be strange to see it: a fence post in the middle of these mines—"

Her next step came down on nothing.

Amar grabbed her arm and hauled her back just as she began to fall—

But the sudden motion sent Murdo's helmet tumbling off her head: into the dark below.

WHAT WAITS BELOW

"No!" Nora scrambled to her feet.

"Hold on." Amar's arm was tight around her.

"But we can't find the bait-post without a light." A sob broke Nora's words. "I'm so *stupid!*"

"No, you're not. We're winding our way through an abandoned mine tunnel and the floor just ended. It's not your fault."

"The floor ended?" Cyril squeezed up beside them. "Where's Nora?"

"Here. She's a little freaked out."

Cyril patted the side of her face. "It's okay. At least you didn't fall and squash yourself."

"Is there nowhere to go now?" Eve asked softly.

Cyril dropped to his knees and crawled past Nora. "Let the mongoose see what's below."

"Cyril, that's a really bad idea—" Amar began.

"Whoa!" Cyril's cry rang out in a space much bigger than their tunnel. "And no, it's not a pile of skeletons. I wish."

Nora crawled beside Cyril.

The helmet had landed on a platform thirty feet below. It was shining on chunks of gleaming black metal. The smell was sickening.

"That's MacAskill Iron," breathed Nora.

"Someone's packed MacAskill Iron down there?" Tove joined them on the edge. "Why would anyone do that?"

"To protect the people who planted the first bait-posts." Amar was quiet. "That was something they always did."

"So . . . does that mean there's a bait-post down there that's *been* down there since MacAskill's team planted them?" Eve faltered.

"Since 1947."

Tove helped Nora stand up. "How do we get down there?"

"If we had a rope, we could make a noose around that boulder and let ourselves down—" Amar stopped. "Wait, I know: our leggings. The fabric's incredibly strong and it should be long enough if we can tie it leg to leg. Who can tie knots?"

Nora bit her lip. She couldn't imagine the other knights would agree to crawl down in their underwear.

There was a rustle to her left.

"Here are my leggings," said Tove.

"Give me a sec—mine," added Eve.

"I tie fabulous knots." Cyril hopped. "Here's mine. Give me yours, Tove." He grunted. "Okay, tied. Nora?"

Do I really have to?

Nora slid off her boots, peeled off her leggings, and put them into Cyril's hand. A blast of icy cold hit her bare skin.

"And here's mine." Amar stepped close to them.

Cyril made short work of their leggings and soon had a rope tied securely around the boulder. He flung the other end over the edge and shimmied down.

"It holds!" he called from below. "And it's just long enough! There's a drop of about four feet."

"I'll go next." Tove climbed over. A few seconds later: "Ha! That's barely a drop for me. Nora? You come next and I'll catch you."

"I . . . I'm not good at climbing."

"It's okay." Eve gently pushed her toward the rope. "Remember: Tove's there."

Nora grabbed it and slid over.

Tove will catch me. I hope.

The first foot was slippery and she almost lost her grip. But Cyril's knots provided solid holds. Soon she was climbing well. As she reached the end, a pair of large hands grabbed her waist.

"Gotcha," said Tove. "Are you cold? You're really shaking."

A thump behind her. "I'm seriously going to throw up from this smell," said Eve.

"I bet it's here." Cyril picked up the helmet and handed

it to Nora, his sword bumping against his skinny bare leg. "Check out all that MacAskill Iron."

Amar thumped to the ground. "Do you see it, Nora?"

Nora shone her light around the platform. Hammered sheets of sparkling black Iron covered the walls. A glistening stain of dripping water ran down the middle.

"It *should* be here with all this Iron."

Tove joined her. "Where's that damp coming from?"

Nora stepped closer. It wasn't water but a thick, long piece of something plant-like, wet and sticky, that disappeared into the stone above and below. None of it touched the Iron.

Nora leaned forward—and received a pungent nose-full. "I think this is the bait-post. And . . . I think it's grown."

THE ROOT

All the knights gathered as Nora shone her light onto the gleaming damp. It wasn't like the bait-post in the field. It was more like an actual root reaching into the stone, top and bottom.

For the first minute, no one spoke.

Then—

"I don't think the hammer's going to do much," said Eve.

"There's got to be a way to destroy it, though." Amar rubbed his neck.

Another long pause.

"Do you think they'll come out while we're here?" Tove asked, hesitant.

"We have to assume they will." Amar picked up a loose stone and dropped it over the edge.

A splash.

"And I know what we'll be seeing: *Cochlea umbrae*." He joined Nora in front of the root again.

Eve followed. "How do we destroy it? Was there anything in your histories, Amar?"

He shook his head. "We have to figure this out on our own."

"Three blows." Cyril clapped three times. "One, two, three juicy blows with something that'll react with MacAskill Ore—" He broke off. "I hope it doesn't explode all over us."

"That didn't happen with the bait-post aboveground, so that's not going to happen here." Amar sounded a little too certain. "What do you think, everyone? How should we chop it?"

"With this." Nora held up her axe in its holder. "*This* is made to chop."

"Three times, then." Amar gave a short laugh. "I bet you could do it in your sleep, Nora. So we'll arrange ourselves around you."

"And we'll know it's the gloaming when Murdo's helmet switches on." Eve stopped. "But that means we're going to have to move the setting. And be in absolute darkness until then."

"I don't mind absolute darkness," said Cyril.

"But we don't know how long we have," Eve moaned. "They're going to burst out of that pool behind us, and if we're not ready—" She broke off. "I'm *so* tired."

"Get some rest." Amar sat on the ground by the root and hugged his bare brown legs. "Wow, it's cold."

Eve joined him and leaned her head on his shoulder. "I'm freezing."

Tove sat and put her arm around Eve. "I'll keep you warm."

Cyril went to Tove's other side—"I want some of that warmth"—leaving Nora standing alone.

In my underwear. With a hard hat on my head. Of course, they're all wearing ugly caps . . .

Amar patted the ground beside him. "Here, Nora. And give me Murdo's helmet."

Nora handed him the helmet and curled up beside him.

"I'm going to switch it now. Ready everyone? One, two, three."

Darkness filled the cavern.

Nora felt Amar set the helmet back on her head.

"I set it to give us two minutes before the gloaming," came his voice. "So we can be ready."

Eve groaned. "We fought all night. And Murdo—he might be dead. And now we're going to fight again with no rest, no protein shake, and we all might die—"

"It's okay, Eve," Amar said gently. "Let's do some breathing. Ready? Breathe in for one, two, three, four."

Everyone was quiet as Amar took them through five rounds of breathing. When he was done, Nora no longer trembled.

"We're going to be fine," Amar said. "We're just going to defend Nora as she chops down that thing."

"Like Jack and the Beanstalk," added Nora.

"Jack and the what?" Cyril asked.

"The Beanstalk."

"Was this something in that illustrated Umbrae book?" Amar's voice was perfectly serious.

They don't know Jack and the Beanstalk? Do they know any stories that aren't about the Umbrae?

"It's . . . from my video game."

As the knights waited, they told stories.

Of the mountain path where they'd fought during Cyril's first duty, where the moonlight had sparkled like diamonds on the damp.

Of the forest during Eve's first duty where they'd heard owls.

Of Tove's first duty, in Bardownie—only she and Amar had been in the Order then, along with three much older knights—and how the National Museum of Brannland had shone like a lit-up ship in the middle of a street.

Of the valley path and the driving sleet and Nora's brilliant fighting during her first duty.

"Do you always do a schiltron formation?" asked Nora. "Are you trained to do any others?"

"No one's trained to do formations." Amar stretched his

arms. "The schiltron formation is *our* thing. It's based on something from medieval wars. It's not historically accurate, but we like the word: schiltron."

"A courage word," Tove murmured.

"That's right." Eve raised her head. "It was Tove's idea: Come up with a word that would snap us to attention."

"And turn us into murderous clockwork," said Cyril.

"So we'd feel strong and think of nothing else when we heard it. And then Amar came up with the formation." Tove leaned into the group. "Thanks, Amar."

They were just settling into companionable silence again when Murdo's helmet clicked.

A searing, bright light burst over the platform.

And over the motionless pool before them.

DESTRUCTION

Amar scrambled to his feet. "It's two minutes to gloaming. Get ready for them to swarm out of the water."

He helped Nora up; then, with his sword, cut the strap that held her axe.

"Okay, Nora. Don't touch the root. Just chop it. Everyone else: schiltron formation round Nora. Give her room to swing."

Nora stood in front of the root, Cyril by her left arm, Eve her left shoulder, Tove at her right, and Amar directly behind her. The root glistened in the light, oozing slime.

"One minute." Amar began to count.

That was the longest minute Nora had ever lived. Worry after worry shuttled through her mind.

What if the spores get in my hair and turn into Umbrae on top of me?

What if chopping doesn't destroy it?

What if this isn't a bait-post but something worse?

Nora's breath came so fast that she nearly blacked out.

"Thirty seconds."

Behind her, Eve was slowly breathing in and out.

"Twenty."

Please make this work.

"Ten."

Cyril inhaled.

"Five."

Tove murmured something.

"Four. Three. Two. One. Gloaming."

A slimy roar came from below—and the *Cochlea umbrae* were upon them.

"Swing your axe!" Amar swept down the first huge wet shape that lunged for them.

Nora grasped the shaft with both hands and swung.

Thump.

The blade tore into the oozing stem. Nora yanked it out, then swung again.

"Cyril, by your foot!" shrieked Eve.

Thump.

The axe plunged in even deeper.

"Watch out!" cried Tove.

One more.

Nora hauled out her axe, then swung as hard as she could.

The axe burrowed deep into the root—and disappeared.

"No! It's taken my axe!"

Nora whirled around.

The *Cochlea umbrae* were rushing from all sides.

"Nora, we need your help!" shouted Amar.

She whirled back to the root.

Where her axe had disappeared, the slimy, wet stem was turning into mist. Not lavender mist like the Umbrae, but brown mist that reeked of rot.

Open veins branched up the root, covering it in a lacy weave. The place where Nora's axe had been was suddenly gone: burned away, bare against the stone.

"It took my axe, but I think I killed it!"

"Keep focused, knights!" cried Amar.

The death mist—she could think of it as nothing else—raced up and down the root. And where the lacy web had been, the root shriveled, until, in ten seconds, it was gone and the wall was bare.

Nora stepped close and looked up. A hole in the stone was clearing rapidly. Pebbles fell into her face. She set her hand on the wall for balance.

Something moved under her palm.

A crack.

It widened, spreading, covering the rock face with tiny lines.

"Everyone?" said Nora. "I think we should climb out now—"

But her final words were swallowed in the rush of stone as the platform beneath them—and the overhang above—simultaneously broke apart.

SURVIVAL

The ground disappeared beneath Nora's feet, and she fell—into a wet nest of thrashing *Cochlea umbrae*.

She screamed as she sank underwater—then a massive slimy tail shoved her against stone.

A hand seized her wrist.

Amar slashed the *Cochlea umbra* and pulled her up onto a landing. He positioned himself in front of Nora, the light from the helmet—miraculously still on her head—illuminating the scene beyond him: a huge pool filled with writhing *Cochlea umbrae* and falling stones.

Tove climbed onto the platform, pulling Cyril, whose forehead gushed blood. Both still had their swords.

"Where's Eve?" shouted Amar.

Another rush of stone.

Nora tensed.

"Eve!" Amar called again. "Where are you?"

Tove's arm tightened around Cyril, who was slumped against her, his sword dangling from his hand.

"Eve!" Amar's voice was desperate.

A wet shape crawled out of the pool at the far edge of the platform: Eve, still with her sword. Her massive braid had come undone and her micro braids dripped around her face.

Amar ran to her and pulled her away from the water. "Can you walk? Are you all right?"

"Oh, I'm just peachy." A hollow smile.

"Let's get back." Amar drew Nora and Eve away from the water to the far end of the shallow cave behind them.

Tove carried Cyril in and gently set him down.

"They're not coming for us." Eve swept back her micro braids. "They're distracted by the falling ceiling."

Every few seconds, a new rush of stone thundered down. But each time, the *Cochlea umbrae* swarmed up again. It went on for almost a full minute.

Then it stopped.

All was silent.

Amar let out a breath and glanced back. "Cyril? How badly are you hurt?"

Nothing.

Then—

"My glasses are bent and it feels like a ton of stone crushed in half my head, so now I'm going to be lopsided and Tove will have to beat up anyone who makes fun of me."

"He's okay." Tove wiped the blood off Cyril's face with her sleeve.

With the tip of his sword, Amar trimmed off one of his own sleeves, then stretched the makeshift bandage around Cyril's head.

As Amar straightened, a *Cochlea umbra* slithered up toward the cave.

Eve slashed it. "Amar, I can't fight anymore."

Amar took a deep breath. "I know. None of us can." He cleared his throat. "Let's try this: Put down your swords to overlap. Let's make a barrier and sit inside."

Quickly, the knights arranged their four swords. There wasn't much space, but everyone sat back to back, their legs pulled up, with Nora in the middle.

"I'm sorry," Nora whispered.

Amar twisted to face her. "Why? You destroyed that thing. Nora, that's *amazing*."

"I heard you thumping." Cyril patted her shoulder. "It was disgusting and horrifically violent. I *loved* every second."

"I think I wrecked Buffleton Mines."

"Kemp, that's actually a *good* thing." Eve rubbed Nora's other shoulder.

A boom sounded across the pit: more crashing stone.

Tove frowned. "Amar? How are we going to get out of here?"

"We're going to wait until Nora's helmet says it's dawn and then climb out." Amar exhaled. "At least we're safe."

"I wouldn't call being stuck in collapsed mines with hundreds of swarming *Cochlea umbrae* 'safe.'" Cyril shrugged. "But whatever."

"No more gloomy thoughts, knights," ordered Amar. "We've got at least six hours before dawn."

"What should we do?" asked Eve.

Amar thought. "How about Happy Moment Time? The book said it's supposed to ensure 'emotional survival in periods of immense stress.' And it's supposed to help even more if we say them aloud." He looked around. "What do you think? Do you want to do that? I'll share mine."

Eve nodded.

"I'd love to hear yours," Tove said. "And I'll share."

"Same," called Cyril.

Amar stretched his legs over the swords—then quickly pulled them up again. "Let's see MacAskill Iron do its job."

A *Cochlea umbra* had slithered up the bank.

Every knight's eyes followed it to the ring of swords—

Where it paused.

Then it retreated back into the water.

Everyone breathed.

"Should I go first? Yes?" Amar folded his arms around his bare legs, back straight. "So, it's late. My ammi and mum have spent the whole day cooking. I'm sitting at the end of our table with all my aunties and uncles and a *huge* mound of food: saffron rice, bhindi korma, malai kofta, and about six other dishes. We're celebrating because I'm leaving tomorrow for training."

From her place in the middle, Nora could see his wistful profile.

"I've always dreamed of being a knight and becoming a Legendary. But I can't eat. I go to bed without supper. As I'm lying there, hearing everyone's voices through the wall, I have this horrible feeling that I'm about to go through training, become a knight . . . and fail."

Amar rested his chin on his knees.

"Then my ammi and mum come in. They've been cooking all day and they've *got* to be tired. But they sit on my bed and start telling stories of when I was little. I don't remember those stories now. But I remember thinking that night that even if I failed, I'd at least try. And I'd have my own stories to share."

For a few seconds, everyone was quiet.

Then Tove reached over and hugged him. "Ever since you became our senior knight, Amar, I've felt safe."

Cyril nodded vigorously. "My normal state of rest would be a basket of vomiting panic if it weren't for you."

"You haven't failed," said Eve softly. "Ever. And you never will."

"You're the best senior knight I could ever imagine." Nora leaned against him.

"Thanks, everyone." Amar gave a faint smile. "Tove, do you want to go next?"

"Give me a sec to get comfortable." She began to stretch her legs over the swords—but stopped, and rolled her shoulders instead. "Mine takes place in the morning, two hours before I'm supposed to leave for training. I wake up to Uncle Merlin singing in the kitchen. He's making pancakes—that's what I wanted for my last breakfast at home. But when I sit up, there's Dad—right at my desk."

Tove stopped and fiddled with her earpiece.

"Hang on. This is waterproof, but it just made a weird noise." A pause. "Okay. So Dad . . . when he gets angry, the whole building knows. But Uncle Merlin—he's Mum's brother—he stands up to Dad. Mum's scared to. And I know something's happened: Dad's face is all red. When I sit up, he jumps like he was hiding. And just stares at me. I wish I could stand up to him. But I can't. So I get out of bed and go downstairs.

"There's a chair missing and a dent in the wall. Mum's eyes are all red, so . . . yeah, I know what happened. And it's hard because I'm leaving for training in a few hours but she has to stay. I barely taste Uncle Merlin's pancakes. I'm suddenly feeling guilty about being able to leave. And I make this wish—that Mum's going to be all right."

Tove's eyes were wet.

"When I go upstairs to get dressed, I don't see Dad. Not in my bedroom. Not in Mum and Dad's room. And not downstairs. As we're waiting for the Council to pick me up, I ask where Dad is. 'He's gone,' Uncle Merlin says.

"And you know what? I can breathe. So can Mum. I picture Mum and Uncle Merlin in our flat, just the two of them, like that's the way it'll be when I'm gone. *He's* gone. Forever. My wish has come true." Tove's mouth twisted. "Is that a weird Happy Moment?"

"No," said Cyril. "That's not weird at all." He rested his chin on Tove's shoulder.

"No," whispered Nora.

Tove stared at the water. "Who wants to go next?"

"I will." Eve straightened. "Mine's like yours, Tove: It's got sad parts, but a happy ending." She bowed her head. "It's the night before I'm supposed to go for training. Two in the morning. I've woken up, and I'm crying, because I'm already homesick. Daddy comes in and asks what would make me feel better. I say akara with pap. Now, there's no way *anyone's* going to make me akara with pap in the middle of the night. But we're talking about *Daddy* . . . so he takes me to the kitchen. He heats the oil and grinds the beans and chops the onion and starts frying the akara. He's making pap with honey when Mum comes in."

Eve breathed in hard through her nose.

"Mum's been lecturing me about training since my test. Like *she* knows anything about it. And when she sees me with Daddy with the akara frying . . . she loses it."

Eve's mouth trembled. "Right there, Mum and Daddy

have their worst fight. Back and forth, and it's all about how Daddy treats me. Like I'm a *baby,* Mum says. Then she notices the akara are all burned. Before she can start shouting, Daddy scoops me up, takes me to my room, and hugs me. I feel like *I've* just been burned, but I'm getting the biggest hug in the whole wide world. I tell myself I'll *never* forget it. And I never have." A laugh. "See? Not happy until the end."

Tove wrapped an arm around Eve's shoulders.

"I'll ask the kitchen to make us akara with pap when we get back," Amar said. "Thank you for sharing, Eve. Who wants to go next?"

Cyril spoke—rapidly.

"Here's mine: It's the happiest day of my life. I'm on the doorstep of the Council Office, Tallydale. It's taken me all day to walk here. I'm wet, tired, and covered with thistle and nettle, but I'm here."

He took a breath.

"But it's five minutes to gloaming. Everyone's gone home. I'm crying my eyes out—and the door opens. There's a woman with a name tag that says 'Preeda.' I tell her I was tested that morning and need to start training tomorrow and can I please come in."

Another breath.

"*Any* moment, my mum's going to roar up behind me. *Any* moment, she's going to grab me. But Preeda lets me in and locks the door and tells me she can get me to training tomorrow. She takes me to this massive chair and gives me ice cream on a stick and goes off to arrange things."

A quick breath.

"I don't eat; I melt. The ice cream melts. Preeda has to scrape me *and* the ice cream out of that chair when she comes back, but she doesn't mind. And then I realize for the first time that no one's going to hit me ever again—or slap me, or kick me, or choke me, not even once, so I'm safe, I'm really safe—" Cyril broke off.

Tove twisted until she was facing him. "You *are* safe. We'll never let *anyone* touch you. You know that, right?"

He nodded, breathing hard.

"If anyone tries to mess with you, Cyril, they're going to have to mess with *me* first," said Eve.

Nora set two fingers on his shoulder.

Cyril put two trembling fingers on top of hers.

"That's a powerful Happy Moment, Cyril," said Amar softly. "Thank you for trusting us with it."

Everyone was quiet.

"What about you, Nora?" asked Amar at last. "Do you have a Happy Moment you want to share? How about your memory of the day you left?"

"That's . . . not very happy." Nora cringed. "My mum got *so* mad because I didn't tell her until the night before. I couldn't wait to get out of the house. I didn't even finish my tea."

"You didn't tell her until the night before you left?" Eve leaned close.

"Nora only learned the night before she left." Tove nodded encouragingly.

"I—um—Daniel told me two nights before."

"How did you keep that a secret for two whole days?" Amar sounded genuinely curious.

"It was easy, actually: I barely saw Mum. I went to my friend Wilfred's house first thing on Saturday and spent the night—"

"But you told *him* right away." Amar raised his eyebrows. "Yes?"

Nora squirmed. "After . . . five hours. And a bit."

Eve burst out laughing.

"Miscreant," Cyril said. "Were you always that bad?"

"No! I was never bad, I just—look, it was hard to tell Wilfred that I wouldn't see him at school on Monday, and my mum—if you *knew* her, you'd understand!"

"Sorry." Tears of laughter streaked Eve's face. "I understand. With my mum? I *really* do. But *we* knew a day and a half before you came. What is it with your family and secrets?"

"No more teasing," Amar said sternly. "Nora didn't have anyone at home she could tell that news. And that must have been hard. A big part of my Happy Moment was sharing the anticipation with my ammi and mum. Nora: I'm sorry it was hard to tell your mum about this. That must have made you feel so alone."

Cyril's bony arm snaked around her shoulders.

Tove's arm followed.

"I wasn't laughing at you. You know that, right?" Eve leaned back until her head touched Nora's.

"I hope you know that you can tell *us* anything." Amar found her hand. "You're not alone here. You never will be."

"Yes," said Nora. She closed her eyes and snuggled into the secure, damp huddle of her Order. "I know."

THE TROUBLE WITH CLIMBING

The night was long. For hours, *Cochlea umbrae* rushed upon the Order of the Hawk. But each time, the Umbrae backed away from the ring of swords. When the lamp clicked off, the sound of Umbrae puffing into mist filled the cave.

Amar took the helmet and switched on the light. "Now we climb. Do you mind if I wear this, Nora? I'll go first."

He stretched, picked up his sword, and tied it to his waist. He was shivering, his legs and one arm bare, yet grinning.

The knights gathered their swords, tied them to their stretchy tops, and followed Amar as he began the climb up the cave.

Nora was tired and cold—more than she had ever been—but the other knights were upbeat. And that made her feel better.

Amar led the way up the massive pile of stones above

the cave, followed by Eve, then Cyril, Nora, and Tove at the rear.

For close to an hour, there was no sound but the rattle and scrape of their climbing. Then—the drip-drip-drip of water.

"Look!" Amar shined the helmet light straight up. "We've found the rails again—the ones we climbed down."

Everyone pushed and squeezed until they were crowded together on the same stone.

"We are *so* lucky to have found them," breathed Eve.

"That's great engineering." Tove pointed. "Those rails were made to stand up to collapsing mines. So they stayed put, even with massive chunks of stone missing."

"Be careful on those missing parts," warned Amar. "The ties might be weak. Okay, everyone. Ready to go on?"

When it was her turn, Nora grabbed a wooden tie and hauled herself up.

"Good job, Nora," said Tove from behind.

Nora looked over her shoulder. "Do you want to go ahead of me?"

"No, it's okay. Keep at your own pace."

My own pace is going to be nothing soon.

Nora pulled herself to the next rung.

After five minutes, she'd dropped far behind and could barely see Amar's light.

"How are you doing, Nora?" called Tove.

"I'm sorry." Tears crept into Nora's voice. "I'm so tired—"

"It's all right." Tove scrambled up beside her. "This isn't a race." She patted Nora's arm.

"I can't do this."

"No problem. Climb on my back and hold on. I'll give you a ride."

Gratefully, Nora clasped her hands together around Tove's shoulders and clamped her knees on Tove's waist.

"Here we go." Tove cheerfully launched up the rails.

Her pace was twice as fast as Nora's. Within minutes, Cyril appeared ahead of them. He was puffing hard, and glanced down.

"You fight like a vengeful demon and you've just destroyed the biggest bait-post in the world, so *what* is this?"

Nora tried to answer, but had no breath. She shook her head.

"What's going on?" Eve shouted down.

"Nora's really tired," Tove said.

"Is Nora way down there?" called Amar. "Does she need help?"

"I've got her." Tove sped up and brushed the heel of Cyril's boot. "And she's keeping me nice and warm."

"No fair! I'm freezing. *I* want to give Nora a ride." Cyril slowed. "Here, Nora, climb on me."

"She'll pull you down; you haven't got the arm muscles for this."

"Oh, yeah? Let's wrestle when we get to the top. You'd better watch out, Tove: Small can be mighty."

The chatter continued: airy, silly, happy. Nora closed her eyes and held on.

Then—"Here we are!"

Amar's voice from above.

Nora blinked. There was light ahead. It grew brighter and wider as the knights climbed on—faster now, no longer talking—

They reached the surface.

Nora scrambled off Tove's back, past the doors, and out onto the frozen cobblestones.

Three huge, black off-road vehicles—like Murdo's—were waiting. Six soldiers in Council berets and camouflage stood before them in the snow.

Amar marched forward with a confidence that made it seem as if he were wearing a Legendary's black uniform—and not just his underwear and half a top.

"Good morning," he announced in his commanding voice. "We're the Order of the Hawk. We need a ride to the nearest hospital. One of our knights has a head injury."

All the soldiers saluted. One of them marched to Cyril, knelt, and wrapped a fresh bandage around his wound. Two others marched to a vehicle and opened the back doors.

The knights piled into the middle seats together.

"Amar? Nora's really shaking." Tove hugged her.

Eve fished out a bag from the door and ripped it open. She tucked the blanket around Nora but shook her head at the sleep vials. "We need more than this."

Amar leaned forward to the soldiers in the front. "We need hydration immediately—"

"Yes, sir." The soldier in the passenger seat reached down, then handed back a thermal cooler. "These were ready for you, sir. Healing and hydration."

The cooler held five canisters, each with a name scrawled on top. Tove cracked open Nora's, then her own.

Nora knew she should wait for everyone, but she was desperately thirsty, and drank. The warm liquid rushed down, soothing her throat and her body.

All the knights drank. Then Eve and Amar reached back for the other blankets. Soon everyone was covered.

"Is Murdo Patel alive?" Amar asked the soldiers as the car picked up speed.

Nora's heart seemed to stop.

"Yes, sir. He's very worried about you." The soldier in the passenger seat twisted to face them, her eyes troubled. "We've been searching for you for the last thirty-three hours, and we only just noticed that case by the mines. If you hadn't left it there, we'd be miles away by now."

Nora leaned back and shut her eyes, and, for what felt like the first time in days, let herself sleep.

URSULA'S SECRET

"To become a Legendary is the greatest honor a knight can hope for. It's something we all dream of. And while luck and skill clearly play into it, the composition of one's Order is the ultimate deciding factor. None of us could be this on our own."

—Murdo Patel, Legendary, Order of the Hawk
The Noye's Hill Interviews (internal)

The next thirteen hours passed in a blur: of driving, hospital doors opening, and being carried through; of the cool mist of the antidote bar and the warmth of a bath; then straps on Nora's arms, the prick of a needle, and the softness of a pillow.

She woke in a hospital bed in a room filled with light. Eve

and Tove were sitting on beds on either side of her, Amar and Cyril on beds across the room. Dr. Liu stood talking by Amar, and someone else was leaning against the wall.

Murdo.

He looked weak and sick, yet in seconds was at Nora's bed, his arms around her.

"Everyone! Nora's awake!" Tove joined him.

"Don't crowd her!" scolded Eve. "Kemp needs to breathe."

"I think she can breathe through water and sludge, probably oil, because she's a superhero and they've all got powers like that." Cyril's face, with a small bandage above his glasses, appeared over Tove's shoulder.

Amar settled on the end of Nora's bed and gently squeezed her foot.

"You." Murdo let her go. "We are *so* lucky to have you."

Nora coughed. Her throat was splintery and dry. "I almost got us all killed."

"Give her room." Dr. Liu marched up and shooed the knights away. "How are you feeling, Hawk? *Don't* move your arm."

There was a needle in her arm and a tube hanging from a bag above her head. Something sparkled on that bag: a glittery sticker of a bright blue hawk.

"Am I sick?"

"Dehydrated. Like a potato chip." Dr. Liu pressed a small white knob to Nora's forehead. "Good. Fever's about gone. You were in rough shape when you came in."

Amar squeezed Nora's foot again. "You need to let us know next time you feel like that."

"I hope there's not a next time—I mean, when we're stuck in a pit filled with *Cochlea umbrae*."

"There won't be," Amar said. "And if there is, we'll take better care of you."

The Order gathered around Nora's bed: Tove and Cyril on one side, Murdo on the other, and Eve and Amar at her feet.

"Amar told me what happened." Murdo clasped Nora's hand. "I don't know what to say. All of you were exceptionally brave. But you, Nora, to do this on your *second* duty . . ."

Dr. Liu slipped out of the room.

"She was incredible," Amar said softly.

The knights spoke quietly of what it had been like: the chaotic battle by the first bait-post, the realization that they had to go into the mines, the climb down the precarious rope of leggings, and how cold and tense it had been as they'd waited for the gloaming underground.

Nora sipped her water and listened. Even with the grim talk, being there with her Order in a warm, bright room was like a dream. She had a strange feeling that if she closed her eyes, she'd wake up in her bed in Jedburch on Monday morning.

The door clicked. Dr. Liu had returned—with Ursula.

"Mei-Mei tells me you might be ready to talk."

Murdo rose and gave Ursula his place.

The director's eyes were shadowed and red, as if she

hadn't slept for days. But her voice was firm. "I need to hear what you found in those mines, Nora. You were the closest to the bait-post. In as much detail as you can remember, please: What did it look like?"

Nora thought back to the cavern and the root. "Like . . . a gooey stem. Or a bit of wood that's been underwater for a long time. Except the roots were reaching up *and* down into the rock, on both ends. I think I chopped its middle."

"Rooted from both ends," Ursula repeated. "What did it feel like when you chopped?"

"Like super-sticky toffee. It gulped in my axe the third time. But then the whole thing—it turned to mist, a really nasty mist that smelled like—like something dead that's baking in the sun." She hesitated. "*Was* that a bait-post?"

"Yes. In the worst possible form you could have found it."

Amar raised his head. "Where did it come from? I thought we had all five bait-posts at Noye's Hill before Sophie took one."

Ursula glanced at the door. "What I say next must not leave this room. Understood, knights?"

Nods all around.

"Yes, Amar, we *did* have five bait-posts at Noye's Hill. But Colm MacAskill made six: One for each Order. We don't share that information in training."

Cyril slid to the edge of Nora's bed. Tove patted his hand.

"Okay." Amar frowned. "But why didn't he dig up the sixth with the other five?"

"Because he was afraid." Ursula's lips pressed together. "Because he'd lost eight knights in his recovery of the others, which he'd planted in easier locations. The sixth was too ambitious. Too dangerous in the mines. He could not risk the knights, and he could not take it out alone. So he left it, and eradicated all evidence to hide what he'd done."

"How could he do that? And didn't people know?" Amar broke off, his face suddenly hard. "*You* knew there was an active bait-post in the mines. *You* sent us out to it—"

"*I* sent you to the bait-post in the meadow, *not* the one in the mines." Ursula's eyes were suddenly fierce. "I'd *never* send you there. And no, people did *not* know about the sixth post. Details around bait-posts were top secret then—and now."

"May I ask how long you've known that there was a bait-post from 1947 planted in Buffleton Mines—rooting all over Brannland?" Amar's voice was like ice.

"I had no idea—until I became director and found Sir Colm's confidential papers locked in a safe in my office. The director before me had built a virtual model of how a bait-post would evolve—a theoretical exercise, I'd thought, until I learned the truth." Ursula clasped her hands. "I established a team to create a tool that would destroy a bait-post. We developed the hammer, but it didn't work reliably on models of an advanced post." She took a deep breath. "We had not tried a tool with the proportions of Nora's axe. If her body had been like every other knight's and the axe had been fitted for anyone else . . ."

Ursula took off her glasses and pressed her palms against her eyes.

"We would have died," whispered Tove.

"But Nora's axe was perfect," Amar said. "Because *Nora* is perfect. So the post is gone." He looked around. "Because we fought brilliantly. All of us together. That was a big part of it, knights."

Ursula replaced her glasses. "It's no less than a miracle that the post is gone—and that all of you survived."

Her eyes wet, she rose and gestured Murdo back to his spot.

"It is too soon to tell for certain what an impact your last duty will have on the Umbrae. But I've already seen a decrease near Buffleton Mines. My theory is that the majority was emerging from the roots nationwide. If I am correct, the population should be much easier to control now. It will take years to be rid of them entirely, but there should be an end in sight."

The room was silent. Then:

"Thank you for trusting us." Amar stood and shook her hand. "We will, of course, keep this information confidential."

"Thank you. It is crucial that morale in the Orders remains high—and that *your* morale remains highest, as Hawk will be leading the efforts to come."

Ursula started toward the door.

"Ursula?" Murdo rose. "Before you go: I made a request

after our last duty that's relevant to my Order's morale. Have you reconsidered it in light of what's happened?"

She paused mid-step. "I have. In light of what's happened, I'll gladly grant it." Her gaze flicked to Amar. "You officially have two bites, Amar: Venom that is obliterated before it reaches the heart doesn't count. You're on track to becoming your Order's Legendary when you turn eighteen."

Amar's mouth dropped open.

Ursula continued to the door. "Thank you, knights. You'll have a proper break now."

She glanced over her shoulder as she turned the knob.

"And please: Try not to think about bait-posts."

Dr. Liu followed her into the hall.

Amar closed his mouth. "Can she just change the Rules like that?"

"Yes." Murdo squeezed Amar's shoulder. "The Order of the Hawk needs you in that role, and she knows it." He grinned. "I'll be sorry to retire in three years, but I'll be far more honored than sorry when I see *you* take my place."

Amar stood very still, as if he didn't quite believe what Murdo had just said. Then Murdo's arms closed firmly around him.

"Amar!" Tove dashed over and hugged him from behind. "You're going to be a Legendary!"

"Fine! Leave me alone in the three-bite club." Laughing, Eve joined the embrace.

Cyril started clapping. "This is the *third*-happiest day of my life!"

We have so *much to do. But there's an end in sight*. Nora wiped her eyes, careful of the bag that tethered her to her bed. *And Amar will get what he's always wanted*.

"Amar! You have to hug Nora!" Tove squirmed free of the huddle. "She wants to hug you too but she's not allowed to move."

Amar let go and staggered to Nora's bed.

"Congratulations," she told him. "You'll be leading us as we finish this, you know."

Gently, he slipped his arms around her and buried his face against her hair. "Thank you," he whispered. "This is *all* because of you."

Nora reached up with her free arm and hugged her senior knight as tightly as she could.

MACASKILL'S BOOK

"So Sophie's gone." Amar straightened Nora's pillow. "There's been no trace of her since she took Murdo to the hospital."

"I'm glad." Eve crossed her arms tightly. "I wish I'd never met her."

Amar and Nora exchanged a look.

If Sophie hadn't planted the bait-post to bring up Oak's numbers . . . if she hadn't abandoned the Order of the Hawk to handle the onslaught alone . . . if the hospital in

Cairnmouth hadn't been so far away . . . they would have never found the rooted bait-post, never destroyed what had needed to be destroyed.

"That moment—when Sophie saw Murdo and decided to leave us—that was one of those 'pivotal moments' in history," Amar had told her earlier. He'd gone up that morning to Nora's new room in the medical wing at Noye's Hill to talk with her alone. Because they *had* to talk history: both of them. What they had just experienced was too horrible to think about as anything else.

Nora had thought a great deal about history in that room. The battle with the bait-posts had nearly broken her. The Order of the Hawk was going to skip at least two duties to give her time to recover.

"All right, Hawks." Dr. Liu appeared in the doorway. "Time to let *this* Hawk rest. Go off and train."

"It's like a black hole, training without Nora," grumbled Cyril. He touched her shoulder with two fingers. "Get better soon, or I'm going to be a wobbly mess of sobs and despair."

"That's poetic." Eve leaned down and hugged Nora. "I miss you, Kemp."

Tove gave her the next hug. "You're going to be just fine. You're looking better already."

Then Amar. "I'll be up later to read to you. North Brannland folktales?"

Nora nodded.

"Get out, Hawks," Dr. Liu said brightly.

317

Muttering about the injustice of being bossed around by a Wyvern, the four trickled out of the room.

Dr. Liu shut the door, refilled Nora's water, and tucked her in. "Want to sleep or read?"

"Read, please."

Dr. Liu handed her the book from her bedside table, then went to the chair in the corner with a tablet.

Nora fingered the book—Sir Colm MacAskill's one-of-a-kind volume of memories and reflections—but did not open it. Just before her Order had come to visit, she'd read something that needed to sit in her mind a little longer.

"Want to sleep after all? I can take that for you."

Nora shook her head. "It's weird that Colm MacAskill didn't know how to destroy a bait-post and just dug them up."

"Yeah, that only puts them to sleep. Like a horror movie."

"He says in his book they were hard to dig."

"I bet they were, with the roots everywhere."

Nora hesitated. "He also says it wasn't worth it, and he wishes he'd left them all."

Dr. Liu blinked. "He wrote *that* in his book?"

"He tells everything. I think he wanted people to know. This was his confession." Nora sat up. "For Dad. I only noticed yesterday that he dedicated this book to 'Jack.'"

"Whoa." Dr. Liu set down her tablet. "Is it an apology or something?"

"I think so." Nora ran her finger across the top. "The

beginning's a lot of details, like he's trying to explain why he did what he did. And the end's about his mistakes. He says he's made the Umbrae ten times worse and the destruction of humankind will be his fault—but he'd have gladly left all the bait-posts if he could have saved those nine lives."

"How'd he get nine? Eight knights—"

"And my dad."

Dr. Liu jumped up and held out her hand. "Give me that book. That is *not* appropriate reading material for Jack's daughter."

Nora shook her head. "Dad can't read it, so I need to."

Dr. Liu sank back into her chair. "I wish your dad hadn't run off. But you know something? That was brave for a kid who'd spent his whole childhood in training." Her face was wistful. "Do you think your dad would have forgiven Sir Colm for what he said on the phone if he'd read that book?"

In her mind, Nora saw her father from their time in hiding: bent over his hands, Colm MacAskill's name on his lips, his shoulders shaking with sobs.

"I don't know." She slid her book onto the table. "I want to rest now."

Dr. Liu tapped the tablet. "Should I put on your dad's music?"

"Yes. Thank you."

Nora turned onto her side and closed her eyes.

The music was a present from Daniel Fenton, who'd somehow found a recording from when Owen Kemp was a young man playing in pubs and church basements in the Upper Islands.

A few seconds later, the rising, whirling sound of a single fiddle filled the room. The recording was old and filled with static, but the playing was crisp and strong—and distinctly Owen's.

EPILOGUE

Amar held out a bottle. "Do you want some strawberry water?"

"She can have mine if she needs it," said Cyril from the back seat. "I know I drank first, but it's not like her head's going to fall off."

"Are you hungry, Kemp? Here: salty crunchy things." Eve thrust a little paper bag between the seats.

"Don't overwhelm her, knights," said Murdo. Then: "Nora, *do* you need anything?"

"No, I'm fine, thanks." Nora rested her chin on her hand. Her sleeve reflected in the window: her fuzzy blue sweater. She was wearing her beloved sweater and the jeans she'd first worn to Noye's Hill over a month ago.

It felt strange—even wrong—not to be in uniform. The other knights were also out of uniform—Amar in an azure-blue button-down shirt, Tove in sky-blue silk, Eve in a trim navy sweater, and Cyril in blue-and-black tartan—and had told her the new clothes felt strange. They had worn only their uniforms since they were seven.

But uniforms would have felt even stranger where they were going: to see their families, who were waiting at a neutral location. The journey had been Nora's request and Ursula's gift to the Order of the Hawk.

Except for Cyril, who'd told his Order that he'd be glad to see anyone else's mum as long as no one invited his.

Nora twisted in her seat. Behind her, Cyril smiled brightly.

"Do you want my water? I barely spit in it."

The car slowed as it came to a roundabout, then lurched forward.

"Ah! Look!" Tove pointed at a road sign. "Bardownie's in a few miles! We haven't cleaned up Bardownie in years."

Murdo cut off an even larger vehicle. "I forgot how much I hate city traffic."

It took them twenty-five minutes to reach City Centre, and ten more minutes to reach Bardownie Castle. But once they passed through the first National Council–guarded checkpoint, there was no traffic, no people but National Council guards, and nothing but the gatehouse ahead.

"Look at that." Amar sighed happily. "Historic stone."

Murdo stopped at the checkpoint at the gatehouse, then drove through—

"Is that a gift shop?" Cyril stabbed his finger at the window. "It's *open*! They're never open when we're on duty!"

—over the bumpy cobbles, past a view of the city—

"If we have time, I'd love to nip up to Mighty Molly." Amar leaned past Nora. "See? The cannon. It was a wedding present to King Lachlan the Third in 1517. I've read all about it."

—and parked.

"We have three minutes." Murdo unbuckled his seat belt.

Everyone climbed out and gathered around Murdo— Amar and Tove at his sides, Eve, Nora, and Cyril behind. They raced up the cobblestones, past a cliff topped with an ancient stone chapel, then up through a passage into a courtyard.

"It's really cold," said Tove.

"Well, no uniforms." Eve hugged herself.

"It'll be better when we're inside," Murdo assured them.

"I'm as cold as a corpse in the mountains—but check out that tower." Cyril pointed.

"That's where they keep the crown jewels." Amar's breath steamed in front of him. "And ceremonial swords. I can tell you about each one if we have time to visit."

"Ooo, swords?" Eve drifted toward the entrance.

"Not now, Eve. We'll have a tour later if you're all up for it." Murdo marched toward the tearoom and opened the door. "Ready, knights?"

Are we ready? Nora was trembling. As were Amar, Tove, and Eve, their smiles fading as soon as they stepped in. Cyril alone looked happy.

None of them have seen their families in years.

And all we'll do is have lunch with them, then go back to Noye's Hill.

But that's good. No time to talk too much and feel bad about anything. We just get to see them. It'll be a happy memory . . . I hope.

A small group was clustered at the other end of the reception room: two women in purple and butterscotch hijabs, a man with locs like Dr. Ogundimu, a blonde white woman and a very tall bald white man, and Deena.

With Wilfred.

Who met Nora's eyes with a shaky smile.

"Look at our Tove," the blonde woman murmured.

The tall bald man beamed. "*Look* at you, love."

"Mum . . . Uncle Merlin," whispered Tove.

The woman in the butterscotch hijab gave a quick, rapid wave.

Amar bit his lip, then laughed. "Hello, Ammi. Fancy seeing you here."

"There's my dad." With tears in her eyes, Eve waved fiercely at the man with the locs, who waved fiercely back. "*Daddy.*"

"I don't recognize anyone, and I *love* it," Cyril announced. "I'll just glom randomly onto other people's families."

Murdo marched past the Order of the Hawk and stood in front of the families. Like his knights, he was wearing normal clothes—a royal-blue sweater and black trousers.

Unlike his knights, he looked thin and weak from his bite, yet he exuded authority before the citizens.

"Thank you for coming," Murdo said. "This is a highly unusual gathering, but my knights have done extraordinary work and this was their request."

The families and knights all shifted, but no one moved forward. Then:

"Thanks for letting us see them," Deena croaked. "This really *is* a gift."

And she took a step toward Nora.

All of Nora's awkwardness dissolved. She rushed for Wilfred and Deena, and beamed at the other mums, dad, and uncle as she felt her mum's and her best friend's arms close around her.

Her plan would work. It *would* be a Happy Moment, one to remember in future battles—a special, new Happy Moment for them all.

ACKNOWLEDGMENTS

In many parts of our lives, having a team like the Order of the Hawk is necessary for success. That was true about this book, which would have faltered early on without the incredible people in its Order.

I start with thanks to the two most crucial people in my life. First, Benjamin, whose readings of this book helped me capture the right tone, and whose brilliant creation— Warriors of the Frozen Bog (including its lore, geography, classes, progression system, equipment, builds, mobs, and quests)—added another crucial layer. Equal thanks to Michael, whose reading and comments helped me emphasize what really mattered in this book (Wilfred owes you). Thank you also for listening to my frequent ramblings about plot twists and character psychology. Every author deserves people like the two of you in their lives.

This is my most ambitious book to date, and I dared to write it in this way thanks to the encouragement of my editor, Rosie Ahmed. She was with me from a very early draft and played a major role in the story's evolution. Thank you, Rosie, for all our conversations and for gently pushing me to go so far with the plot and characters. Many thanks as well to my agent, Adriann Ranta Zurhellen, and Marin Takikawa, for their early insightful advice.

I'm grateful for the magnificent art that Vivienne To created for my cover. Thank you for making the Order of the Hawk and the Umbrae come to such vivid life. (And thanks to Mrs. Brann's and Mrs. Snell's 2020–2021 classes for advising me on artists. Don't you love the result?) Thanks to Travis Hasenour too for creating the gorgeous map!

Thank you so much to Sylvia Bi for the brilliant page design, Danielle Ceccolini for the beautiful cover design, Regina Castillo for heroic copyediting, and my wonderful publicist, Vanessa DeJesús; and to Tabitha Dulla, Lauri Hornik, Nancy Mercado, Lily Malcom, Jennifer Klonsky, and all others at Dial Books for Young Readers and Penguin Young Readers who joined me on this journey.

I'm humbled and grateful to Autumn Reynolds for reading this book and sharing her thoughtful expert advice. Also to Amber Salik: Your perception and expert advice helped me get this right (I hope). And so many thanks to Alexa Donne, whose own expert advice gave me what I needed to make important parts ring true.

Here's a big round of hugs for the street team that helped me launch this book: amazing teachers and librarians who strive to match kids with the right books, parents devoted to fostering their children's love of reading, a blogger who champions #kidlit, and dear fellow authors devoted to their readers: Jenny Adelman, Sandi Brann, Aaron Cleavely, Basil E. Frankweiler, Kristie Hayward, Jennifer Guyor Jowett, Peter Kretzman and Dylan Mitchell (proofreaders extraordinaire), Kathie MacIsaac, Laura Mossa, Jennifer Merrifield, Amy B. Mucha, Nancy Nadig, Rebecca Reynolds, Josh Roberts, Shari Sawyers, Jessica of justanotherteenreading.blogspot.com, and Gibran Graham of the Briar Patch Bookshop. Many thanks as well to Stephanie Heinz and Rachel Conrad at Print: A Bookstore; Kenny Brechner at Devaney, Doak & Garrett Booksellers; and star librarians Jill O'Connor and Mary Lehmer, all generous champions of my work. Special thanks to the authors in the Electric Eighteens, who have been with me throughout this journey. Your ongoing support and camaraderie means so much!

Finally, thank you to all the teachers, librarians, booksellers, and readers I've met since my debut back in 2018—but most of all to my young readers: You, my friends, are extraordinary. Thank you for being you. And thank you for picking up this story. I hope it was a friend to you when you needed it.